A Suspicious Breed

A Low Country Dog Walker Mystery

Jackie Layton

BEYOND THE PAGE
PUBLISHING

A Suspicious Breed
Jackie Layton
Copyright © 2024 by Jackie Layton
Cover design and illustration by Dar Albert, Wicked Smart Designs
Beyond the Page Books
are published by
Beyond the Page Publishing
www.beyondthepagepub.com

ISBN: 978-1-960511-49-2

Praise for the Books of Jackie Layton

"Kept me guessing till the end. Andi Grace is an excellent amateur sleuth . . . and *Caught and Collared* is an engrossing and enjoyable cozy mystery."
—*The Book Decoder*, Best Books of 2022

"Andi Grace is adorable, resilient, and has a doggedly curious need to solve a murder. A pleasure to read."
—C. Hope Clark, award-winning author of *Edisto Tidings*

"Completely charming—and exactly what a cozy mystery should be. Amateur sleuth (and dog whisperer) Andi Grace Scott is wonderfully endearing, and her devotion to her pooches—and to justice—will have you rooting for her from the absolutely irresistible page one. Bow *wow*—What a terrific debut!"
—Hank Phillippi Ryan, nationally best-selling and award-winning author of *The Murder List*

"I promptly fell head over heels for this cast of characters, and the dogs burrowed quickly into my heart. The plot of *Bite the Dust* was intriguing and complex, with plenty of surprising twists and turns. What impressed me the most, though, was the warm tone of the author's writing voice . . . you just want to snuggle in and keep reading."
—MeezCarrie

Books by Jackie Layton

Low Country Dog Walker Mysteries

Bite the Dust
Dog-Gone Dead
Bag of Bones
Caught and Collared
A Killer Unleashed
A Suspicious Breed

I dedicate this book to my husband, Tim. He encourages me on a daily basis. I appreciate and love him so much.

I also want to thank my family for their support. They buy and read my books and cheer me on. Thanks also to Dawn Dowdle, my wonderful agent, and thanks to Bill Harris, my amazing editor.

I don't remember a time when there wasn't a dog in my life. I'd like to dedicate this to Andy, Barney, Cindy, Blackie, Tinker, Maddie, Chloe, Chewy, Luna and especially Heinz. Heinz has been my constant companion while writing A Low Country Dog Walker Mystery Series. We had to tell him goodbye last year, but he'll always be in our hearts and memories. Sometimes he laid by my feet, and other times he nudged me to move around. He was also a good sport posing with my books. There'll never be another Heinz Layton.

Chapter One

ZARINA MILLS SNAPPED PICTURES OF HANNAH CUMMINS holding her dog in front of the main house at Kennady Bed-and-Breakfast, with the farm in the background. Gus had been a stray runt before one of my friends rescued him a while back. After taking care of the little dog, I'd convinced Hannah to adopt him. The farm was the perfect place for Hannah's political rally tonight, and she'd chosen to do her photo shoot here to save time. Instead of a sprint, her run for state representative had been a hurdle race. It was October now, and the election was only a few weeks away.

Zarina pointed to the wraparound porch. "Let's head there. I'd like you to sit in a rocker with Gus in your arms. The dog makes you seem more approachable. You know, like you're a real person."

Hannah was tall and slender, like her father. She was beautiful like her mother, and she was a good combination of both of their personalities. Hannah smiled at the young Black woman holding the camera. "You're a breath of fresh air, Zarina. I wish you'd been taking pictures for the entire campaign."

Marvin Graves had been Hannah's photographer before today. He was famous in these parts for getting the best shots. Too bad he fought anger issues. Hannah had confided in me how scared she was of Marvin, and it'd been my suggestion for her to give Zarina a shot.

Zarina's dark eyes sparkled. "Thanks. I appreciate you giving me the chance."

"Thirsty?" I followed the two to the porch and pulled cold water bottles from a cooler on the porch. I'd normally be working with the animals at Stay and Play or walking other dogs, but I was in charge of Gus today. After the photo shoot, I'd whisk him away to the air-conditioned barn to play.

When I'd inherited this property, I'd converted the farm's big barn into a place for dogs and cats. We offered day care, extended stay, grooming, and dog training lessons. Pretty much if a customer requested a service, I did my best to meet their needs. In the future, I also wanted to start a dog shelter. One of my favorite hobbies was to match animals to people. Hannah and Gus were one of my success stories.

Hannah poured some water into a cupped hand for Gus to lap up. "Thanks. We won't be much longer." Her phone played a percussion tune, and she glanced at it. "Oh, dear. It's Daddy. Andi Grace, can you hold Gus a minute?"

"Sure." I took the sweet boy and cuddled him to my chest.

Hannah walked to the other end of the porch and talked to her father.

I smiled at Zarina. "Are you any closer to getting a home in Heyward Beach?"

"As my momma would say, I'm working on a nest egg. I only plan to rent at first, but in case I don't get enough bookings I'll be more comfortable with some savings to fall back on."

"How is business?" If anyone understood the uncertainties of running your own business, it was me. I'd become a dog walker for the flexibility it allowed, and because I loved dogs.

"It's growing, and I'm excited about your wedding. If today goes good with Hannah, I'll hopefully get more work from her. I discovered word-of-mouth advertising is better than social media. Although, that helps too."

"I hear ya." I nodded. "After the wedding, I'm going to focus on building a dog shelter. I've started investigating what permits are needed, but let's focus on you. How can we use your skills to benefit both of us?"

She tapped her chin. "With a dog shelter, you'll be finding homes for dogs, won't you?"

"That's the goal." Gus wiggled in my arms, and I lowered him to the porch floor.

"If you're a nonprofit, I'd be willing to take pictures of the animals so you can try to find them good families for free."

"I'll pay you, but in the beginning there won't be much. I also need to look into grants. It's a steep learning curve."

Zarina stared at Gus. "It's an admirable thing you're doing. Lots of people would just go online and set up a fundraiser. The problem to a quick fix like that is there's no accountability. You know what I mean?"

"Yeah, but is there a specific instance you're referring to? Do you know someone who took advantage of innocent people?" I always wanted to be transparent, and it'd be even more important if I ran a nonprofit.

"Smooth-talking shysters are all around. If you're not careful, they'll take advantage and steal your money before you know what happened."

Her dark tone made me shiver. "Did someone take advantage of you?"

She shook her head. "Not me."

Still on the phone, Hannah headed our way. "Let me think a minute, and I'll call you back. Bye, Daddy."

"Is something wrong?" I met her gaze.

"Daddy said that Doc Hewitt wants to meet and discuss a social media fundraiser. He's worried it could be fraud." She reached for Gus and cuddled him close.

My heart beat faster. "If Doc's involved with a fundraiser, it might be connected to the surgeries he's been performing. Why discuss it with you?"

Hannah shrugged. "I'm not sure. If I don't get elected, there's not much I can do to help him."

Zarina snorted. "I just told Andi Grace you can't be too careful with online fundraisers. It could be a fraudulent scheme."

Money. We all needed it to achieve our goals, but was it the root to all evil? Our local veterinarian was known for his calm demeanor and clear thinking. "I can't imagine Doc would get tangled up in anything shady. I'll give him a call."

"Thanks, Andi Grace." Hannah handed the dog to me. "Zarina, let's try to wrap this up. I need a few minutes to collect myself."

"I've got a lot of good shots already. You rest until your supporters get here."

I said, "You both should rest. It could be a late night. Zarina, go into the main house. Juliet can fix you a snack, and you can even relax in the sunroom. Or walk around the grounds. You two make yourself at home, and I'll take care of Gus."

"That sounds good," Zarina said. "By the way, do you know the history of this house? It was supposedly part of the Underground Railroad, with lots of secret hiding places tucked away behind walls and other places."

"I've always found that fascinating, and it makes me appreciate the place even more."

Zarina smiled, then picked up her camera bag and entered the house with Hannah.

On my way to the barn, I called Doc Hewitt's personal number. I'd worked for him as a veterinary technician before I started walking dogs, and we were friends.

"Andi Grace, is everything okay?" he grumbled. His voice lacked its usual warmth.

"I'm at the farm with Hannah. What's going on with you?" Gus wiggled, and I let him down to walk beside me.

"Hold on, let me go to my office where nobody can hear." A dog yipped in the background, and muted voices could be heard. A door clicked shut. "I'm worried. You've met the new vet student, Caleb Fisher."

"Yeah, he's got shaggy dark hair and a goatee?" Doc Hewitt's clinic had become a popular place for students to do their rotations before graduating.

Gus scurried away, but I scooped him up.

"That's the one. I'm not sure if you're aware, but he's interested in helping poor people have the best care for their pets. He's talked me into performing some surgeries at a reduced price. Caleb's also involved with someone who raises money for pet owners. There's some way to get strangers to donate on the internet, er, social media."

"Sounds good so far." I kept my tone light, hoping to settle Doc down.

"Not necessarily." He huffed.

I arrived at the Stay and Play barn and handed Gus to Belle Zane, one of my employees. "What seems to be the problem, Doc?"

"At first, I thought it was just me not being comfortable with Facebook and all that. Caleb kept assuring me it was legal and others do it all the time. He even showed me examples, like a woman in Columbia who needed to pay for cancer treatments."

I walked into my office and sat in the chair. "You're starting to make me nervous. There are legitimate people helping others with GoFundMe and various crowdfunding sites, but there are plenty of internet scammers too."

"I want to help the dogs, but I'm beginning to think there's something fishy going on."

"Have you met Caleb's friend?"

"No. Caleb makes all the arrangements."

Okay, that was a tad weird. "Interesting, but why are you stressing out about it today?"

He sighed. "I was supposed to remove a tumor on a mutt this morning. Caleb discussed finances with the organizer—"

"Do you know the name of his contact or the organization?"

"No, but I talked to the dog's owner. His name is John Graystone, and his dog is Scout. The man lives upstate, and he seems legit."

"Who pays you for your expenses?" I switched to speaker mode so I could take notes without getting a crick in my neck.

"The bookkeeper should know." He sighed again.

"Is Gloria Voigt still working for you?"

"Yeah." His reply was flat.

Doc's distress tugged at my heart. "What did this Mr. Graystone say?"

"John first noticed a spot on the mutt's side. It was the size of a golf ball, and it's grown to the size of a softball. His regular vet told him it'd be thousands of dollars to care for Scout. John was afraid he'd have to put his dog down to prevent him from suffering. That's when he was approached about a charity who could help pay for Scout's bills."

"They approached him? How'd they know about Scout?"

"Social media. John posted on Facebook that he dreaded saying goodbye to his best friend. That's when this other person reached out and offered to raise money for the surgery."

I added this to my notes. "Why you? There are lots of veterinarians between here and the other side of South Carolina."

"Because I'm a softie and willing to perform the surgery cheaper than anyone else."

"You are a softie." I laughed. "I interrupted you earlier. Why today?"

"Scout never got brought in. We called John Graystone, and he told us people from the fundraiser picked up the dog and were supposed to bring him to me. Hold on, someone's at the door." He didn't mute his phone. "Come in. Caleb, what can I do for you?"

I didn't hear the intern's response.

"Andi Grace, I've got to go. Talk to you soon."

"Just a second. Can I speak to Gloria about the money from the funding people?"

"Sure. I'll tell her to expect your call." He hung up.

Scout was missing, and the poor pooch needed surgery. Doc was worried about the legitimacy of the fundraising organization. I called Doc's clinic and asked to speak to Gloria. It didn't take long for her to answer.

"Hi, Gloria. This is Andi Grace Scott. Did Doc Hewitt tell you I'd be calling?" I reached for a Coke from the mini fridge.

"He sure did, hon. How can I help you?"

I could picture her in my mind sticking a pencil behind her ear and messing up her curly bun. "Tell me about this charity who paid Doc for surgeries."

"Operation Tail-wagger. Their motto is something about wanting to help people get treatment for their dogs so they'll feel good enough to wag their tails again."

"Clever. So you bill them after the surgery?"

"No, it's not like that. They say they're a full-service charity, and they even provide transportation for the dogs. And then they pay on the spot when the surgery is done, and they get the dog back to its owner."

"How did they pay you?"

"Cash."

I choked on the bubbles in my Coke.

"Take your time, hon." Gloria hummed.

After catching my breath, I said, "Cash? Did that make you suspicious?"

"It sure enough did, but Doc said the main thing was to provide help for the dogs, and at least it wouldn't bounce at the bank."

Hmm. "It wasn't counterfeit, was it?"

"I don't think so. I kept meticulous records so we'd have a legitimate paper trail."

"That sounds smart. Did you always work with the same person?"

"Interesting question. The first time it was a small man who showed up with a chihuahua. Another time it was a woman, and there was an old lady once, and a college kid wearing a ballcap another time. I felt like there was something off with each person."

"Like what?"

"This is going to sound crazy, and in fact Zach told me to get my eyes checked."

Most people called my favorite veterinarian Doc, but Gloria was one of the few to address him by his given name. "You can trust me. What was it?"

"All of the people seemed to be similar. Nearly the same size and skin tone. It was like a woman who was wearing different disguises. I put a lot of thought into it. No way it could've been a man because the face was too smooth."

My mind raced. "Okay. Let's say it's a woman. She always paid you in cash, and she wore disguises. That would make you think something hinky was going on."

"See, I told you."

"Too bad it doesn't answer the question of what happened to Scout." I scrolled to Facebook on my phone. "Let me try to reach out to the person who commented on John Graystone's post."

"Don't waste your time. I did the same thing. The person blocked me."

Drat. "Do you know the last time the dog was seen? How do we begin to find the dog?"

"Caleb is talking to Zach right now. Maybe he'll have some good news."

"I hope so. In the meantime, I'll explore social media. Maybe something will jump out. If you think of anything else, let me know."

"Sure thing. This is tearing Zach up."

"I'm so sorry. Stay in touch." I ended the call and began my search for Operation Tail-wagger. The search engine pulled up thousands of options in less than a second, and I scrolled. Most of the sites contained testimonies of how dogs were saved thanks to the charity. One by one, I opened the links and began compiling information into a new document.

There were plenty of pet photos but only a few of the dog owners. After thirty minutes, a mutt's picture jumped out at me. A beagle named Piper, and he needed a tumor removed. My heart beat faster. I saved the photo then compared it to pictures I'd saved earlier. There Piper was again, except he was named Spot. I looked at the two photos next to each other. They wore different collars, but they looked exactly the same. Spot was featured as needing eight thousand dollars for thyroid surgery.

What was going on? Doc had performed dog surgeries, and he'd been paid. Was the organization raising money for some legitimate surgeries and faking other fundraisers?

"Andi Grace, do you have a minute?" Belle appeared at my office door.

"Yeah, come in. What's up?"

The young girl was a full-time employee and a singer and songwriter. Her dad was country music star Lincoln Zane, so the music thing probably ran in her genes. Her thick dark hair was pulled into a ponytail, and her blue eyes gazed into mine. "The Moonbeams are performing after the rally tonight. Would it be possible for me to knock off a little early? If not, I'll totally understand."

I pulled up the schedule on my phone and sighed. "If you will walk the shepherds belonging to Phyllis Mays, you can leave now."

She sat up straighter. "I know Captain and Pumpkin. They're much better behaved now that they've taken some obedience classes, and I'd be happy to check on them."

I passed the family's house keys to her. "Have fun."

"Thanks, Andi Grace." She jogged out of my office.

After saving my document on Operation Tail-wagger, I moseyed over to the dog play area. Yoyo, a black Lab, ran around the fenced-in area. I visited with my German shepherd and Marc's golden retriever before rounding up Yoyo. I placed a harness on the dog then told Melanie Bradshaw, my groomer, we were going for a walk. It'd help Yoyo burn off some energy, and maybe I could find Zarina and ask about the shyster she referred to earlier.

Chapter Two

Guests, news crews, and podcasters roamed the grounds of Kennady Bed-and-Breakfast. Skylar Marshall was the most noticeable newsperson, and more than one morning anchor from Charleston milled around.

Yoyo and I circled the outside of the big house and found Zarina taking photos of the river. "Hey, Zarina." I waved.

She turned and smiled. "I'll come to you."

"Sit, Yoyo." I gave him a treat after he obeyed.

"You're really good with dogs. It's nice that you found your calling."

"It wasn't my first dream, but I love dogs and it's been a good fit. I thought you might be resting."

"The day is too beautiful not to take pictures. Some of the trees near the river are beginning to turn colors. One day I'd love to go up north and photograph the beautiful foliage."

"Marc and I are heading to Maine for our honeymoon."

"Nice. I imagine it'll be beautiful." She bent down and snapped a picture of Yoyo.

"Yes, at least we hope so. Earlier, you mentioned shysters. I'm beginning to think you're right about the surgeries Doc's been performing. Have you been the victim of fraud?"

Zarina looked at the ground. "No, but my brother's life was destroyed by a scam. A girl from his high school claimed to have cancer. She needed money for her treatments, or so she said."

Yoyo grew restless. "Do you mind if we sit under the oak tree?"

"Sure."

We walked to a nearby shady area and sat in Adirondack chairs. There was a bowl of water on the ground, and Yoyo lapped it dry. After he finished, he lay at my feet and closed his eyes.

I turned my attention to Zarina. "What happened to your brother?"

"It goes back to the woman." She sighed. "Her story was she got lung cancer. She used all of her money on the surgery, her insurance company dropped her, and she needed to raise money for chemotherapy. She played on everyone's heartstrings. Then if that wasn't enough, she found a way to steal more money from those who donated with debit cards. My brother was a softie and believed her story. She took all of his money. He lost his home, and his wife left him. Before you ask, there wasn't anything romantic, but Zeke wanted to help a friend."

"Oh, Zarina. I'm so sorry."

"Me, too. Zeke left town in disgrace, and we haven't heard from him in around five years." She stared at something in the distance.

"That's terrible." I reached over and squeezed her hand.

"When I heard about the surgeries Doc was performing for that charity, I got an uneasy feeling."

"Did you say anything?"

She shook her head. "No, I should have, but my ex-husband has been popping up and calling me saying he wants more time with our daughter. Maybe even a reconciliation. He also mentioned coming here tonight. He said I wasn't going back to Charleston until we'd hashed this out."

What kind of man was Zarina's old love? A good man who wanted time with his daughter? Or just a guy trying to get in her head? It wasn't my business. "I haven't seen Sarah in a while. Is she one year old now?"

"Yes, and she's the best baby. J.T. had a bad temper. It's the reason we broke up, and I've been scared to leave her alone with him. He says he's a new man, but how can I trust him with my baby? Anyhow, he's probably the reason I didn't say anything about the charity working with the dogs. It's weighing on me. I used to love him. Maybe I still do. Trusting him is my problem."

"I understand. Trust takes time. Listen, don't be too hard on yourself about the surgeries. Sometimes you can only deal with one problem at a time."

"Uh-oh. Here comes trouble." Zarina clenched her fists.

Marvin Graves crossed the grass and stopped in front of Zarina. "Did you think I wouldn't find out that you stole my gig?" He wasn't a big man, but his anger made him formidable.

Zarina stood and clutched her camera to her chest. "I didn't steal any clients from you."

Yoyo growled and stood, baring his teeth.

"Easy now." I rubbed my hand along the Lab's side and rose to my feet. "Marvin, you're upsetting the dog."

"Is that one of the dogs needing surgery?" He pulled a phone from his jeans and took a picture.

"Stop that. This is one of my clients, and you can't take his picture. You need to delete that photo now."

"It's a free world, and I can take pictures of anything I want." He turned from me to Zarina and pointed at her. "Don't get in my way, missy."

"Marvin, lay off her." I huffed. "I'm going to call the sheriff if you don't leave us alone."

His gaze zoomed in on Zarina.

She lifted her chin. "I plan to be here tonight photographing the rally and the concert. So, maybe, er, you should stay out of my way."

"Not likely. I've been doing this longer than you've been alive. Don't intend to quit." He sneered then walked away like he didn't have a care in the world.

I slid my arm around her shoulders. "Are you okay?"

"Yeah, but maybe I will go inside and rest for a bit."

I watched her walk toward the main house. My stomach swirled. Trouble was brewing. I didn't know if it was from the possible dog scam or from Marvin Graves, but something bad was going to happen. It seemed like a good time to call my brother-in-law, Deputy David Wayne. I tapped his number into my phone and resumed walking Yoyo.

David answered, "Everything okay? Is it Lacey Jane?" My pregnant sister was due to give birth any day.

I laughed. "Why do you think I'd only call you if there's trouble?"

"Think about it."

"You make a valid point. As far as I know Lacey Jane is fine."

He sighed. "Good. What's up?"

"I'm worried about tonight's rally for Hannah Cummins. I feel like something bad's going to happen."

"Running for state representative is a big deal, and we'll have plenty of deputies around."

"Okay." I couldn't ask for more, but I'd definitely be on high alert in case something went sideways. "Thanks, David."

"Hmph. I feel like you're letting me off way too easy. Can you give me a few bullet points of what's got you concerned?"

"You know those surgeries Doc's been doing? He thinks it might be a scam, and he was hoping Hannah could stop the organization. Marvin Graves is riled up that Zarina Mills took photos for Hannah earlier today. Skylar Marshall and some other reporters are already nosing around, and there's a concert tonight, as in here at the farm, after Hannah's speech." What had I left out?

"Are there any dead bodies?"

I shivered. "No. Everyone's alive."

"I'll mention your concerns to the sheriff. I gotta run." The call ended.

For now, I'd have to be satisfied. It didn't mean I wouldn't keep my eyes open for trouble though.

• • •

By six thirty I was dressed and ready for the night's events. I'd changed clothes in Juliet's bedroom and headed to the backyard of the main house, where a jazz quartet played on the stage.

Marvin argued with his son Theo near the Old Kitchen. Theo Graves was one of Nate's employees, and they'd spruced up the grounds for this event and my wedding. To be clear, it was Nate and Juliet's wedding too.

I veered away from the argument and texted Marc. *Are you on the way?*

His reply was immediate. *Just finished a meeting with Lincoln and headed to the farm now.*

Skylar Marshall and other reporters questioned guests and Hannah's family about the election for state representative.

Where was Zarina? I ambled through the people and headed into the house.

Juliet looked up from a tray of cheesy grit fritters with a bowl of hot pepper jelly in the middle. "How's it going out there?"

My stomach growled just imagining how delicious they'd be. "The crowd is growing. Have you seen Zarina?"

"Yeah, she changed into black slacks and a top and went outside at least thirty minutes ago. Why?"

"I didn't see her, but I'll keep looking. How are you?"

"Fine. We'll serve after Hannah's speech, and four waitstaff should arrive anytime. So, I'm better than fine. I'm good, and I'm about to marry your brother. Let's move right up to fantastic." Sparkling eyes, big smile, and rosy cheeks. Yes, she radiated happiness.

"Okay, great." I couldn't be happier that my best friend and brother were getting married. "I'll keep looking for Zarina. See you later." A sense of unease settled over me. It wasn't like Zarina to not be photographing the action. Back outside I searched the perimeter for the slim Black woman, dressed in black and taking pictures.

A glint in the grass caught my attention.

I hurried to investigate. It was a camera.

Zarina's camera.

Stage lights reflected off the lens.

Where in the world was Zarina?

With the trees casting shadows as the sun lowered, I snatched up the camera with my scarf and took off across the grass. With the utmost care, I looked at the crowd through the viewfinder. My heart raced, but I took my time in hopes of finding my photographer friend.

Oh, no. There in the distance.

I blinked, hoping my eyes were playing tricks on my brain. I looked again.

Zarina's body was slumped in an Adirondack chair where we'd spoken earlier. I hurried and knelt beside her. I placed the tips of my fingers on the inside of her wrist and pressed lightly. Her skin was warm, but there was no pulse. Just in case, I tried the other wrist. Nothing.

I collapsed into the other chair and called Sheriff Wade Stone.

"Andi Grace, I'm at Hannah's political rally. What's up?"

"Oh, Wade." My breath was thready, and my hands shook. "I found another body. Zarina Mills is dead."

Chapter Three

In less than three minutes, Wade joined me. He also checked for vitals before calling for backup. The next hour was a blur.

Marc held my hand when Wade questioned me in my office at the barn. I answered standard questions like when I'd last seen Zarina.

Wade said, "Do you know of any conflicts Zarina may have had?"

I crossed my legs and leaned forward. "Zarina and her ex were in a debate over their daughter and visitation."

"Husband or boyfriend? Where is the daughter now?"

"Husband. Zarina has been living with her mother in Charleston. She's been working and saving up money to move to Heyward Beach. Then this guy pops back into her life wanting a second chance and confusing her."

Marc said, "I've helped Zarina on a legal matter and can get her mother's contact information. It's on my laptop, which is in the truck."

"Good. You can text the information to me." Wade frowned. "Andi Grace, is there anything else?"

"Do you know Marvin Graves?" I waited until Wade nodded. "He was angry with Zarina over her photography business. He kinda threatened her earlier today, and I saw him near the Old Kitchen in a heated discussion with his son a few minutes before I found Zarina's body."

Marc squeezed my hand.

"Thanks, you've been helpful. Do you mind if I question some others in your office? It'll save time compared to driving into town and meeting at the department."

"Help yourself, but it might be more comfortable up at the main house. Plus, it's possible the dogs will get upset if you have a lot of people traipsing in and out. If they start barking, it could disturb you. But if it's easier to use my office, there are Cokes in the mini fridge." Oh, dear. I was rambling.

"Point taken. I'll reach out to Juliet." He left us alone in my office.

Marc stood and opened his arms to me.

I fell into his embrace. "I can't believe she's gone."

"Me, either. She was so young and talented with a bright future." His voice cracked.

The tears I'd held back during Wade's questions flowed free, wetting Marc's crisp cotton button-up.

"Oh, honey. Let it out."

I sobbed. This wasn't the first dead body I'd discovered, but Zarina had found a special place in my heart. Her death hurt.

"Excuse me." Doc Hewitt cleared his voice.

I pulled away from Marc and swiped at my tears. "Hi, Doc."

"Hate to interrupt, but the young woman who died, well, she might have some pictures of the con man, or woman, behind Operation Tail-wagger."

I waved the veterinarian into the office, and he shut the door.

Marc said, "Catch me up. What are you talking about? Operation Tail-wagger?"

Doc said, "It's supposed to be a nonprofit that raises money to pay veterinarians to perform surgery on dogs. They raise money on social media, because not everyone can afford to pay vet bills. In fact, I was supposed to perform a surgery today, but no one ever showed up with the dog. Zarina called me this afternoon. She said you two had a conversation about scams." He pointed at me.

"Yes, sir. Zarina told me that her brother fell for a scam, and it ruined his life." I moved to the little refrigerator and removed three Cokes. "Let's sit."

Marc and I returned to the chairs where we'd sat earlier, and Doc settled behind my desk. He folded his hands. "This young woman who was murdered said she searched through social media sites. She felt sure that the person behind the dog operation was a woman. Zarina believed the woman would be here tonight and that she was involved in more than one con."

The hair on my neck jumped up. "Then there's possibly a connection between Zarina's murder and the scam?"

Doc rubbed his bald head. "I believe it's possible."

"The sheriff needs to know."

Doc popped the top on his can and guzzled it. "Yep. I thought it prudent to tell you first in case Sheriff Stone wanted me to keep the information to myself."

Despite the tragedy, I couldn't stop myself from smiling at my friend. "Thanks, Doc."

"I'll see you two later." He exited my office.

Marc stared at me. "You better start taking notes. We've got another murder to investigate."

"You don't mind?"

"There's no need to waste time and energy worrying about me. My only request is to be careful. I'll help as much as possible."

"I've already taken a few notes." I circled around my desk and pulled out a fresh journal, not that I'd expected another murder, but I'd begun to journal my spiritual journey. So, it made sense to keep a couple extras around. "If Doc's hunch is correct, I need to dig into the scam. For now, I have three persons of interest."

"Who?"

"Zarina's ex-husband—"

"His name is J. T. Green." One side of his mouth quirked up. "Sometimes I know things."

"Nice. Next is Marvin Graves. Also, the person behind the fraud, and somebody I haven't considered." I wrote down all of the names.

"Seems like four there. Where will you start?"

"Let's see if we can find J. T. Green. Zarina thought he'd be here tonight." I searched for his face on a search engine. "Oh, he's nice-looking. Good teeth and a great smile. It's easy to see why Zarina fell for the guy." I turned the screen for Marc to see.

"Yep, but you never know what's going on inside a person."

"True." I'd been fooled by a couple of men years earlier.

"I need to talk to you about the mystery wedding gift we got."

I turned my focus to Marc. "Yes, the turquoise lacquer tray?"

"That's the one. It came from Chris and Carol Williams."

Marc's compressed lips quelled my desire to go outside and look for J. T. Green. "Right. You told me to let you handle the thank-you note. Do you know those people?"

"Kinda." He turned his hands palms-up. "They're on the way to Charleston and want to meet me before the wedding."

Our wedding was small enough that I knew everyone we'd invited, and they weren't on the list. "Wait a minute, they have the same last name as you. I thought it was a coincidence because you don't have any living relatives."

Redness crept up Marc's neck, jawbone, then cheeks.

I swallowed hard. It took a lot to rattle my fiancé, and whoever these people were seemed to have unsettled him. "Are they related to you?"

He heaved a big sigh. "They claim to be my grandparents."

Chapter Four

"YOUR GRANDPARENTS? Where have they been all this time?" I scooted my chair closer to his and held his hands in mine. Marc's parents had died when he was young, resulting in him being placed in foster care. Only one placement had been good. It'd been an older couple, but the man's health complications ended their time with Marc.

"When the accident happened, the authorities conducted a search for my family but came up empty. Chris and Carol Williams were missionaries in a small village in Africa. While there, they pretty much lost contact with the rest of the world. They didn't learn until they returned to the States ten years later that my parents had been killed in a car crash."

"Why didn't they try to find you when they got back?"

He shrugged. "Carol had dengue fever and let it go too long. That's actually why they left Africa. Some friends in Kentucky let them stay in a cabin for free. Chris was focused on helping Carol get well and adjusting to life in America. I think finding me was more than they could deal with at the time. What would've been a hurdle for some was a mountain for them back then."

It didn't escape my notice that he referred to them by their first names. "Do you believe them? Why reach out now?" Were they trying to scam Marc?

"Once we do blood tests, I'll be surer of my answer. I'm willing to meet them tomorrow, if you don't mind. The wedding is days away, so it'd be understandable if you want me to stay."

"Of course I want you to stay, but if this is an opportunity to meet your family, you should go. I'll come, too."

"Somebody needs to hold down the fort. You need to stay here."

"Then ask Lincoln or Nate to go."

"That sounds like a good idea." He brushed his lips against mine. "Now, let's go outside and look for J. T. Green."

With our hands clasped together, we walked out of the barn.

Near the house people stood in clusters, talking softly among themselves. Hannah's speech had been canceled, but some attendees stood around her. The musicians had quit, but Juliet had easy listening music playing on wireless patio speakers.

Poor Belle. She'd been so excited about tonight's gig. "Looks like the Moonbeams won't perform."

"Hold up." Marc pulled his phone from his pocket. "Look over there at Belle with the other band members."

"Okay, but what do you want me to notice?"

Marc snapped pictures. "Lincoln's around here somewhere. I'm sending these to him. It seems to me that older man is a music agent or something. If he's talking to Belle, Lincoln should know about it."

"Wait, Belle keeps telling me she wants to make it on her own."

"Too late, but consider this. What if that guy is a sleazebag who takes advantage of young singers? She's only seventeen. What if I knew and didn't speak up? I couldn't live with myself if Belle was taken advantage of."

My hero. He always looked out for others, even when he was in pain. "You're right."

Lincoln appeared and slapped Marc's shoulder. "Thanks for the warning. That scumbag is Ben Lowe. I'm going to meander over and see what happens. With a little luck, you won't have to bail me out of jail tomorrow morning." Lincoln stalked toward the group.

"Is he kidding?"

"Probably not when it comes to his daughter. She created a stage name for herself. Belle Peach. She doesn't want people to know she's Lincoln's daughter."

"Hopefully her pride won't get her into trouble."

"Ain't that the truth. Let's resume our search."

We skirted around the people gathered.

A man leaned against a tree.

"Marc, look. That guy resembles J. T. Green."

"You're right. Stay calm when we approach. We know nothing about him."

"Good advice." As much as I wanted to run over and question the guy, my steps matched Marc's slow stride.

When we were a few feet away, Marc said, "Hey there. How's it going?"

The tall young man narrowed his eyes, but he remained glued to the massive oak. "Been better. Did you know the sheriff won't let anyone leave until they are questioned? If I knew my way around these parts, I might escape through the woods. But with my luck they'd impound my truck."

"I'm Marc Williams and a local attorney. I can pretty much guarantee you they'd hold your truck until they got their answers."

"Figured as much." He crossed his long scrawny arms.

"I'm Andi Grace Scott, a friend of Zarina's."

His head jerked back. "Zarina." The name came out as a moan.

"My guess is you're J. T. Green."

"Yeah. I can't believe she's gone." He moaned.

"Zarina told me you were coming tonight to discuss custody arrangements. In fact, she admitted that she didn't know if she could trust you."

"That's the thing." He pushed off the tree. "I'm not the same guy as before. I've been through anger management sessions at the church. With hard work and prayer, I worked through my issues. I wanted a second chance with Zarina but was afraid she'd refuse."

Marc said, "Why ask for time with the child?"

"I had a plan, man. Phase one was to get talking to Zarina. Best topic was Sarah. More visitation would mean more contact with Zarina. In my mind, if she saw I was a good father then she'd think I was a better man. Phase two was to slowly prove I was worthy of dating her. The next phase involved a proposal then happily ever after this time. I screwed up the first time we got married."

Marc grimaced. "Sorry it didn't work out."

"Me too." I studied the tall young man. Did I buy his story? He seemed sincere, but I'd been fooled before. "What time did you arrive, J.T.?"

"I'm not sure exactly. The jazz band was playing. I walked around looking for Zarina but never found her."

"Did you speak to people?"

"I asked a few people if they'd seen her. I parked by a dude who was dressed in black slacks and a white shirt. I think he was a server because he muttered something about not being allowed to have a cell phone while working. He opened the door to his clunker and slid it under the seat."

"Can you describe him?"

"Frizzy red hair, kinda tall, not skinny but not fat either. I think his car was an old Buick." He glanced toward the crowd and pointed. "That's him, but why does it matter?"

With my phone I snapped a picture of the young man serving food. "You know the police will consider you to be a person of interest."

His eyes widened. "Why? Because I'm one of the few Black guys here?"

"No. It's because you're Zarina's love interest, you have a child together, and no matter how nice your plan was to woo her back, you were in a disagreement about time with Sarah."

"What should I do?" His shoulders slumped.

"Be honest with the sheriff or deputy when you're questioned."

Marc removed a business card from his wallet. "You can always say you want your attorney present."

J.T. studied the card. "I can't afford you."

"Zarina was special to us, and I won't charge you. It might be a good idea to start building your case though. Tomorrow's Friday. Can you come to my office in the morning?"

He rolled his head back. "I need to call my boss, but yeah, maybe. Honestly, if he gets wind of this, he'll probably fire me."

Marc crossed his arms. "We'll handle one problem at a time."

Like a ball in a tennis match, my mind zipped back and forth. J.T. was most likely a suspect. The kid appeared innocent. He was bigger than Zarina. Way bigger. But he truly appeared to love her.

"Thanks, man."

I said, "Did Zarina mention being scared about anything?"

J.T. half smiled. "Nah, she was spunky."

"How about anything she was concerned about?"

"Obviously she didn't believe I was a changed man."

"Besides that?"

He rubbed his chin and closed his eyes. "Zarina really didn't want me to come tonight. She asked me to wait until she got back to her mom's house to meet up. At the time I thought she just wanted Momma Mills to be there for support."

"But?"

"I'm trying to remember exactly what she said." He paced around the massive oak and returned to us. "I think she said something about a dog. Yeah, that's it. I remember now because I thought she wanted to adopt a dog."

Was her dog comment to J.T. related to what she'd told Doc about suspecting a scam? "Can you think of anything else?"

"Not right now." His voice shook and he stared at the crowd. "How can she be gone?"

My stomach tightened at the sight of his grief. I wanted to believe he loved Zarina, but was he a good actor and tricking me?

Deputy Denise Harris approached us. She was the first Black deputy in our area, and she walked with authority. "J. T. Green?"

"Yes, ma'am."

"Please come with me. I have a few questions for you."

Marc said, "You good, J.T.?"

"Yes, sir. I'll call if I need you."

Marc passed his business card to the deputy. "I'm J.T.'s attorney, and he's voluntarily agreeing to answer your questions."

Deputy Harris took his card. "Good to know, Mr. Williams. If he asks for you, I'll follow proper protocol."

"I appreciate it."

J.T. followed the deputy into the main house.

I said, "Should we question the waiter?"

"How about you question him, and I'll check on Lincoln and Belle?"

"Divide and conquer? I like it." After a quick kiss, I headed into the crowd. I found the redheaded waiter. "Excuse me, can I ask you a quick question?"

The young man held the tray closer to me. "Help yourself."

"Thanks." I took a petite ham and cheese biscuit and a napkin. "I'm Andi Grace Scott. Did you see anyone when you parked tonight?"

"Well, yeah. Why?" His eyes narrowed.

"Sometimes I unofficially help the sheriff solve murders. I was trying to decide if someone had an alibi."

He stepped closer. "There was a dude driving a white Chevy truck. He parked in the field next to me."

"Do you remember the time?"

"Six fifty-five. I remember for sure because I was afraid of being late by the time I reached the kitchen. Ms. Reed is great, but she doesn't like it if you're late."

I laughed. "Understood. Can I get your name?"

"Howie Brown. Do you think he killed the photographer?"

"I don't think so." Howie's story made me feel better about J.T. "Thanks for your help."

"Sure. I hope they catch the killer."

"Me, too. See you later." I ate the flaky biscuit and wandered around. Was Zarina's killer still here and acting like nothing had happened?

My phone vibrated.

It was a text from David. *Lacey Jane's in labor. Meet us at the hospital.*

Yes! I hurried to find Marc, then we needed the sheriff's permission to leave. My sister better not have her baby before I got there.

Chapter Five

EARLY FRIDAY MORNING, I sat in my sister's hospital room and held my niece. A sense of inadequacy filled me at the eight-pound miracle in my arms. "Elizabeth Christine Wayne, you're beautiful."

Lacey Jane smiled. "She is beautiful. We're going to call her Lizzy."

"I like that." I couldn't hold back the happy tears leaking from my eyes. "Hey, I'm so sorry Marc had to leave with Lincoln and go to Charleston."

"I know Marc cares about me, but what's so important in Charleston?"

Lacey Jane had worked for Marc, and he treated her like a sister. "They're going to meet Marc's grandparents for breakfast near the Battery. Make that alleged grandparents. They're going to do blood work to confirm."

David entered the room, carrying two cups of coffee from Daily Java and a bag of pastries. "Erin sent Griffin over with these."

Griffin Reed was Juliet's brother and possibly Erin's new boyfriend. If they were dating, it was low-keyed.

Lacey Jane's eyes sparkled. "Andi Grace will have to drink my coffee, but I'll definitely eat whatever is in the bag."

I continued to hold the baby while they devoured their breakfast. We discussed the nursery in their new home. Marc and I had been blessed with property, and we'd given Lacey Jane and David Marc's house on the property next to the farm. In order to be fair, we'd given much of the farm and the main house to my brother and Juliet. Marc and I kept Stay and Play and the boathouse on the Waccamaw River. We'd also kept a parcel in case I was able to build an official dog shelter one day. So far, it was all working out.

David tossed his napkin into the wastebasket. "I couldn't help but overhear your conversation regarding Marc's family. You know, even if they are related, it doesn't mean they won't try to take advantage of him financially. Y'all need to stay alert."

"I tend to agree." I met his gaze. "The timing seems wrong. Why reach out to him a week before our wedding? Do they plan to get donations from the wedding guests for a mission trip? Or do they think we'll get so many cash gifts that we'll feel generous and hand over a large sum of money?"

"Oh, maybe an investment scheme." Lacey Jane licked a crumb off her finger. "Hold on, I'm getting as bad as you two. I didn't used to be so suspicious. Maybe they only want to be part of Marc's special day. They're getting older, and they may realize time's running out to meet their grandson. Despite the emotions that rocked my world, I'm happy Ike found me. My life is better with my biological dad in it. Hopefully, these people will make life more fulfilling for Marc."

I met David's gaze, but neither one of us wanted to debate the issue with my sister.

Lizzy began to fuss, and I glanced at my watch. "It's been almost exactly three hours since the last feeding."

David yawned. "I guess we need to learn to live on very little sleep if she's going to eat every three hours."

I took the baby to my sister and accepted the cup of coffee. We all chatted for a while longer, then I headed home for a nap. As I drove past Marc's office, I saw J. T. Green leaning against a white pickup truck in the empty parking lot.

Slowing my Highlander, I pulled into the lot.

J.T. walked to me, and I lowered the window. "Hey there. We were at the hospital all night. Did Marc know you'd be here this morning?"

"I thought he wanted to talk to me, but we didn't set a definite time."

"Marc's in Charleston on another family matter. We're getting married next Saturday, and my sister had a baby early this morning, and our lives are pretty hectic. I promise you that Marc wants to help you, though. How'd your conversation go with Deputy Harris?"

He crossed his arms. "Not great, but I didn't get arrested. She was actually pretty cool about Mr. Williams, though. She suggested I should meet with him. Said he was a good person to have on my side."

"Marc is definitely a good friend and attorney. Did you have trouble taking off work?"

J.T. huffed. "I got canned."

"No way. That's terrible. What kind of work do you do?"

"They had me cutting yards, but I've had training as a landscaper with my uncle. Unfortunately, my uncle had a stroke. He's been in rehab so long that my aunt sold the business to help pay the bills."

"Hey, my brother's a landscaper. Would you like to meet him? I can't promise you a job, but Nate might have an opening."

"Can't hurt to talk to him."

I sent Nate a text before asking my next question. "Have you thought of who might have killed Zarina?"

"I keep trying to remember what she said about the dog. That seemed to have really riled her up. Maybe someone connected to that?"

"Did she mention surgery for the dog?"

My phone vibrated with a message from Nate. *I'm working at the farm today. Send him over.*

"J.T., my brother said to send you to Kennady Bed-and-Breakfast."

"Cool." He straightened and retrieved keys from the pocket of his baggy jeans.

"Look for guys working on the grounds and ask for Nate. Also, I'll let Marc know he missed you."

"Thanks." He headed for his truck, and I drove home.

Before allowing myself to nap, I pulled the murder journal out of my backpack. J. T. Green had won me over. No longer was he a suspect.

Gloria had hinted at a mystery woman who wore disguises and arrived with cash and dogs needing surgery.

My eyes burned, and I yawned. This could wait. Lack of sleep would lead to mistakes, and the last thing I wanted to do was waste time following false leads.

Chapter Six

My phone's ringtone pulled me from a deep sleep. I swiped it. "'lo." I cleared my throat. "Hello."

"Hey, sis. You awake?" My brother's voice sounded upbeat.

"Kinda." Nate and Juliet had been at the hospital for Lizzy's birth, but they'd gone home and gotten a little sleep. "You sound chipper."

He laughed. "Why not? I'm about to marry Juliet. You're gonna marry Marc, and we have a new niece. Life is good."

I elbowed my way to a sitting position and glanced around for Sunny, my faithful German shepherd. Oh, yeah. I'd taken her and Chubb to Stay and Play yesterday, and we'd left them when we went to the hospital. "You're right. What's up?"

"J.T. is great. He really knows his stuff. Thanks for sending him my way."

I rubbed my eyes. "You're welcome, but is there something else?"

"Maybe. You can decide. I heard J.T. talking to Theo."

"Marvin's son?"

"Yeah. So the guys started talking about Zarina."

He had my full attention now. "Keep going."

"Theo was planting pansies yesterday, and Zarina stepped on a flat of the flowers. She was taking pictures and didn't notice them. Theo yelled at her, then he felt bad and apologized. She apologized too. It's not like Theo to get flustered like that. He's the definition of calm and levelheaded."

"I heard him arguing with his dad in the afternoon. Marvin's not the easiest guy to get along with. Maybe he was still affected by that. Did Theo mention what time he saw Zarina?"

"Nah, you'll have to ask him. He felt bad about Zarina. When he learned J.T. had been married to her, he offered to share his apartment until J.T. can find a place to live. J.T. took him up on the offer."

"That was nice. How long will y'all be working at the farm?"

"The rest of the day, easily."

It was the middle of the afternoon. "I'll head your way after a quick shower. I'd like to talk to Theo."

"Message received. Don't let him leave until you get here."

I smiled. "Thanks, Nate."

Between a quick shower, a messy bun, and throwing on a T-shirt and jeans, I was out of the house in less than fifteen minutes. I chugged a Coke on the way to the bed-and-breakfast and felt alert by the time I arrived.

I parked my SUV by the barn and dashed to the Old Kitchen, where the work crew was busy. We planned to have wedding pictures taken here, and it was where we'd get dressed for the wedding if bad weather didn't change our plans. "Hey there, little brother."

Nate stopped spreading pine straw. "You made good time."

"You motivated me. Where's J.T.?"

"He's working on the wedding arch with Theo."

"Perfect." I took off and found the guys at one of the barns on the property. Stay and Play was housed in the largest and sturdiest barn, but some of the other structures were in decent shape.

J.T. and Theo worked quietly, building the rustic arch inside the shadowy building.

"Hi, guys. How's it going?" I swiped away a spiderweb.

J.T. smiled. "Working for Nate is going to be much better than my old job. Thanks for suggesting it."

"Sure." I turned my attention to Theo. He was on the short side, but muscular. Standing near J.T. made the poor guy seem even shorter. Or Theo made J.T. seem even taller. "Nate knows I have a couple of questions for you, but I'll be brief. Do you remember what time Zarina stepped on the flowers?"

"Pansies, ma'am. It was around five. The event hadn't started, but she was dressed in nice clothes. Work clothes probably." He removed his hat with Nate's landscaping logo and ran a hand through his blond hair.

"Nate said she was taking pictures and not paying attention to what you were doing."

"Right, right, right. She had a real nice backpack, maybe brown leather, and a tripod was attached to it. Reckon the pack had her other equipment in it."

J.T. crossed his arms. "Sounds like her work bag. Lots of compartments for different lenses, and she always carried a backup camera."

I made a note on my phone. "Good to know. So, Theo, what was Zarina taking pictures of? A dog?"

"Nah, it was people. The kids were younger than me. If I had to guess, it was the band. One of the dudes had drumsticks in his hands and kept twirling them around."

"The Moonbeams is a band with three guys and a girl, and they were supposed to perform last night. Did they know she was taking their picture?"

"No way." Theo frowned. "I think it's part of the reason I scared her so bad when she stepped on the pansies. She was completely focused on the people."

"I don't understand why she didn't ask to take their photo. She was so talented, and it would've been good for their social media." There must've been a good reason. Wait a second. Marc had warned Lincoln about Ben Lowe by taking discreet pictures, and Lincoln had been concerned about his daughter. "Was it a man?"

"Nah. A tall woman. I only glanced that way, but it was definitely a woman. Two women and three guys."

"No dogs?"

"Just people."

J.T. raised his eyebrows. "I see where you're going, Andi Grace. Maybe I'm off base on the importance of her dog comment. Maybe she only wanted to adopt a pup for Sarah."

He'd seemed so sure the last time we'd spoken.

Theo said, "If you don't mind, I'd like to finish up here."

"Just one more question. Your dad and Zarina had an argument yesterday. Did they have a history of not getting along?"

"You'd have to ask him that, ma'am. My dad doesn't get along with many people, including his son." Theo turned back to the structure and hammered a nail into place.

J.T. lifted his hands. "I should get back to work too."

"Thanks, guys." I walked out of the barn.

My thoughts shifted at the sound of barking, and I walked to Stay and Play. What had happened to Scout? Was the dog in this area? Or had he been left somewhere along the way?

I called Gloria Voigt.

"Andi Grace, did you find Scout?"

I laughed at Doc's bookkeeper. She was perfect for him, and it was too bad he was blind to the love she offered. "No, I was calling to see if you knew where he was."

"I'm sorry to tell you we still are clueless about the dog's whereabouts."

"Can you tell me how to contact John Graystone?"

There was a lengthy pause. "Let me call him. If's he's agreeable to talk to you, I'll give him your number."

"Sounds good." I ended the call and entered the barn.

Sunny stood in a play area watching over a young litter of golden doodles.

I entered the space. "Hey, girl. I missed you." My German shepherd leapt toward me, and I rubbed her sides.

Belle appeared. "Hi, Andi Grace. I think the new food we're giving Sunny is helping her energy."

"I've been thinking the same thing. She's got a sparkle in her eyes."

Chubb barked at me from the next play area.

"I'll take these two home with me tonight, but for now, let's put Sunny over there with Chubb."

"Sounds like a good idea. The puppies probably need a nap."

After we shuffled dogs around, I motioned for Belle to follow me to my office. I closed the door after she sat. "Who was the lady talking to your group yesterday before Zarina's murder? It would've been around five o'clock."

Belle frowned. "Destiny Howard is probably who you mean."

I pulled Cokes out of the mini fridge and handed one to Belle before I sat in my chair. "Her name sounds familiar."

"She used to be a model, but she told us she has a farm close to Charleston."

I did a quick online search and found the woman in question. "If I ask anything you're uncomfortable answering, just let me know."

The young lady laughed. "After the lecture I got on the way home last night, I'll always walk away from uncomfortable situations."

"What happened?" I'd get back to Destiny Howard later.

"A big-time music manager offered to represent us. He guaranteed shows in Charleston, Atlanta, Charlotte, Knoxville, and Greenville. The only catch was he needed each of us to give him five thousand dollars." Belle's eyebrows lifted. "It seemed reasonable to me, but Dad came over and listened in on the conversation. He pulled me out of the group so fast, I didn't even get to protest."

"I guess it's not legit?"

"Nope. Er, I mean, no, ma'am. Daddy said it's a common scam in the music business. They call it a pay-to-perform scam."

Another scam? "Interesting. Did you get the manager's name?"

"Ben something. Dad knows him, and he warned me not to say anything to the others just yet. The guys in my band think Ben heard us when we were warming up, you know, before anyone discovered Zarina had been murdered. Anyhow, Dad asked me to avoid talking to the guys until he could deal with the situation."

I tried to remember what Marc had told me. Wasn't Lincoln having trouble with a music contract? If it was also connected to this Ben person, it could explain why Lincoln freaked out so bad the night before. Why didn't Marc recognize him though? Had he only discussed Ben and never seen him?

"Andi Grace?" Belle waved her hand. "Did I lose you?"

My face warmed. "Sorry about that. You're smart to trust your dad over some unknown manager. I understand you want to succeed on your own merits, but your dad knows a lot. You don't have to use his connections, but I'm proud of you for listening to what he had to say."

Belle sat up straighter. "Thanks. That means a lot."

"What about Destiny? Was last night the first time you met her?"

"Yeah. She said her dog had a litter of Labrador retrievers, and she asked if we were interested in buying one. It's a good thing I adopted Lady, or else I might have been tempted." Lady had been one of our clients' dogs, but when the schnoodle needed a new home, Belle took her.

"Wonder why Destiny was here last night? Did she say anything about Hannah's election?"

"No."

There was a loud knock at my door. Melanie, my groomer, burst right in. "Juliet found an injured dog. Hurry."

Chapter Seven

Melanie's tiny legs ran faster than I would've imagined. "She's on the front porch."

A dog howled, and I increased my speed. One perk to walking dogs for a career was it kept me in good shape. I pulled away from Melanie and Belle and beat them to the front porch, where Juliet sat on the steps holding a black-and-white mutt. "Juliet, what's going on?"

Nate's dog Bo stood at attention near the bottom of the steps.

"Grr." The mutt emitted a weak growl.

Belle and Melanie appeared but came to an abrupt stop. Belle said, "Would you like us to take Bo and Pinky to the barn?"

Juliet nodded. "Thanks."

Belle led Bo with a leash, and Melanie carried the little brown, white, and black dog.

"It's okay, Scout." Juliet spoke softly before turning her gaze to me. "I took Bo for a walk because Nate's been so busy lately. I know y'all don't mind walking Pinky and Bo, but I had some free time and decided a little fresh air and exercise would do me good."

"All right. Tell me more. How do you know this is Scout?"

"His name is on his collar. There's a phone number too, but I didn't want to call the owner in case Scout has been abused."

"Aw, that's sweet, but I believe he's the dog who was supposed to be brought here for surgery. If so, he has a tumor and we need to call Doc right away."

"Okay. I don't want him to be in pain." She rubbed the back of the black-and-white mutt's head. "I can call Doc if you want to reach out to the number on the collar."

I switched my phone setting to hide my identity before calling Scout's owner. When the call was answered I said, "Is this John Graystone?"

"Yes, do you have my dog?" His voice cracked.

"I believe we do. My friend is calling Doc Hewitt now."

"That's the vet who was going to perform Scout's surgery."

"Right. Hold on a second." I paused for Juliet, who'd laid her phone to the side. "Well?"

"Doc's on the way. He doesn't want to take a chance on us hurting Scout more."

I huffed. "That's offensive."

"Lady?"

"Oops." I held the phone back to my ear. "Sorry, Mr. Graystone. Doc Hewitt is coming to examine Scout. We're not sure if your dog hurt himself while he was missing."

The man said a bad word. "Pardon my French. I've got a buddy who'll bring me there, but can you give me directions to the clinic?"

We exchanged information. At the appropriate time, I had a truckload of questions for the man. Until then, we'd make sure Scout was given the attention he needed.

• • •

Five hours later, I was sitting in Doc's office with Gloria, going over all the information we had on Operation Tail-wagger.

There was a knock on the door, and Caleb Fisher stuck his head in. "Doc just finished the surgery. Scout's in recovery now." His appearance was clean, and he had a nice smile.

Gloria nodded. "Thanks for informing us."

"Hold up, Caleb. You may not remember me. I'm Andi Grace Scott."

"The dog walker. I remember you."

"Well, I'm concerned about Operation Tail-wagger losing Scout. We're lucky to have found him."

"It was scary for sure." He stepped back as if to leave.

I stood. "It's my understanding you're the one who suggested Doc partner up with the organization. They need to be held accountable. How do I get in touch with the charity?"

"Uh, well, I can tell the, er, uh, director you'd like to have a conversation."

"The sooner the better. I'd like someone to contact me tonight." I glanced at my watch. It was already seven o'clock. Where had the time gone? I wrote my cell number on a sticky note and handed it to the student.

Caleb's face reddened. "Not sure I can make that happen."

"First thing tomorrow morning, I'm calling Sheriff Stone if I don't hear from the director. What'd you say his name is?"

"He likes to stay under the radar. It's easier for him to find causes to support. If he made his name public, people would bombard him with requests."

Gloria cleared her throat. "It makes sense, but why pay us cash? Most of the money is raised online, so it seems like electronic payments would make more sense."

It'd also be easier to account for where all the funds went. Paying Doc in cash opened the door to stealing money raised for pet surgeries.

"I've got nothing to do with that. I only want to help pets in need." He backed away and closed the door.

Gloria opened her mouth.

"Shh," I whispered. "Caleb might try to listen to our conversation."

We returned to the desk and continued looking into Operation Tail-wagger. I read over Gloria's notes while she went over the accounting. Her notes included dates and times as well as her impressions, including her belief a woman had worn various disguises when appearing with the animals in need of surgery.

"Now what?" Gloria pushed a strand of brown hair behind her ear.

I pushed the notes she'd made to her.

"What do you want me to do with this?"

I kept my voice low. "Read over your notes and see if they jog a memory. I'm going to search social media again."

She moved her reading glasses from the top of her head to her nose and opened the notebook.

Instead of beginning with Operation Tail-wagger, I searched for information on Caleb Fisher, age twenty-six, and a veterinary student.

Chapter Eight

RAISED VOICES IN THE HALL CAPTURED MY ATTENTION. I slipped on my flip-flops and glanced at Gloria. "I'm going to see what the commotion is all about."

"Right behind you, hon." She removed her glasses and followed me.

Two angry men stood glaring at my favorite veterinarian.

Doc ran a hand over his bald head. "Guys, I promise you Scout's in good shape."

A stocky man with jet-black hair pulled neatly into a long ponytail frowned. "I need to see him, Dr. Hewitt. It's not that I think you're lying, but we've been through a lot ever since I released him to be brought to you for the surgery."

"If you can calm yourself down, I'll take you back." Doc shifted his gaze to the other man. "But you'll have to go to the waiting room."

The gentleman with combed-back gray hair and a gray goatee pressed his lips together. "John, you good with that?"

John inhaled deeply. "Yeah. I'm calm now. Sorry for my outburst, Dr. Hewitt."

"Just call me Doc. Follow me."

Gloria approached the other man. "Sir, can I get you a cup of coffee? We finally splurged on a nice coffee maker."

"Sounds good."

I pointed to the waiting room. "Why don't I hang out with you while Gloria fixes the coffee?"

We walked to the front room. Ignoring the chairs lined up around the walls, the man remained standing. "It was a hard, long drive from Spartanburg. We only stopped once for gas."

"That must have been tiring. I'm Andi Grace Scott, and I imagine you're John's good buddy."

"Vince Murray. Pleased to meetcha."

"Scout was found near my property. My best friend is the one who discovered him. What can you tell me about the situation?"

Vince ran his fingers along his beard. "I was with John when we gave Scout to Claire Rowe. From the very beginning, something seemed sketchy."

"How did John feel about the situation?"

"He followed the fundraiser online. Most anyone who knows him donated, and a lot of people all over the web donated too. John is a simple man with no family. Scout is all he has. I know him because John's the maintenance man in the building where I work. No, he's more than that. The building has office space, broadcasting booths, meeting rooms, and a video studio. Most people rent by the day, week, or month. As more people have begun working from home, some genius decided to rent out these spaces on an as-needed flexible schedule."

"I can see how that would be profitable in large cities." It probably came in handy for families with small children clamoring for a working parent's attention. "Sounds like it keeps him busy."

"Boy, does it. There's a community kitchen in the building, and John gets the coffee going every morning. He usually has snacks laid out nicely, and he keeps the building nice and clean. He's also willing to help you move furniture around or carry in your supplies. Yep. John's a great guy. It hurt all of us to see how worried he's been about his dog." Vince pinched the bridge of his nose. "I'm a sports reporter. Sometimes I post stories online, and sometimes I'm on Zoom meetings and podcasts. Whatever I need, John's ready to lend a hand."

"It's obvious you're a good friend. Can you describe this Claire Rowe to me?" I opened the app on my phone for taking notes.

"Why? Are you a cop?"

"Local dog walker at your service."

Gloria entered the room carrying a tray with three mugs and a plate of chocolate chip cookies. She placed the tray on the tall check-in counter. "Don't let Andi Grace fool you. She has a knack for solving crimes. You can trust her."

My face warmed, and I reached for a mug.

"Really? Are you an actual amateur sleuth?"

"I guess so."

He took a cookie and a mug. "The woman was tall. Red hair and green eyes. Slender. She wore an orange sweater and purple pants. I guess they were jeans because they had the holes in them that are so popular."

"Orange and purple? Maybe she's a Clemson fan." Or she was pretending to be a college fan.

"Could be. It could also be part of her disguise or persona to throw us off her identity." He dunked his cookie then bit into it.

"Where did y'all meet Claire?"

"A gas station off I-26. Her red hair and orange sweater clashed to the point you almost needed to squint. She drove a white Camry, but there was a rental car sticker in the back window. Doubtful it's a lead." He ambled over and sat in a chair. "I should've stopped John for turning his dog over to her. She introduced herself as the head of the charity."

I jerked and coffee spilled onto my hand. "Gloria, didn't Caleb just tell us the director was a man?"

She passed paper napkins to me, and I shoved the phone into my pocket and dabbed at the spilled coffee.

Gloria said, "Yes, but don't forget I've met some of the people delivering dogs to Doc. Remember, I thought it was a woman wearing disguises? Vince is telling us the woman he met was a tall slender woman. It could be the same person."

"Ladies, I'm still here. Who's Caleb?"

Gloria looked at the man. "He's a vet student working here. If it wasn't for Caleb, Doc wouldn't be part of this scheme."

Vince frowned. "Is Dr. Hewitt legit?"

"Absolutely," Gloria and I replied in unison then laughed.

"That's a relief." The man placed his empty mug on the tray.

"Why didn't John just drive Scout here himself?"

"John doesn't have a lot of money, and he doesn't have a dependable car. Even if he could've driven here for the surgery, he'd still have faced the cost of gas and lodging. The woman promised to bring the dog here and return Scout when he was healed. She claimed to have done it many times. She even had pictures of other pets and their owners." He was back to touching his beard. "And now that she's disappeared, John's going to get stuck paying for the surgery by himself. We'll have to work something out with the doc."

Doc joined us. "I'm happy to inform you that John feels much better after seeing for himself that Scout is alive. I removed the tumor, and I gave John instructions on how to care for the dog. However, we need to keep an eye on Scout for at least the next twelve hours. Do you fellows have a place to stay?"

"We'll figure something out. Thanks for your understanding with John. That dog is his whole world."

"Nothing to worry about. I completely understand."

My phone vibrated with a message from Marc. He was at my house, playing with Sunny and Chubb. I texted. *Heading your way soon. Please wait.* "Y'all, I've got to go. I'm glad Scout is going to be okay."

Gloria followed me to the office. As we were walking, she said, "I talked to John Graystone and he told me how much they raised through Operation Tail-wagger for Scout's surgery. The thing is, I happen to know it was almost twice as much as Doc agreed to charge. Those people were going to pocket a tidy sum of money. And then they didn't even show up, so where'd that money go?"

So it was a scam. They were definitely skimming money, and lots of it, from the donations.

I stopped in my tracks when we reached the office. "Our stuff has been moved."

She gasped. "It must've been Caleb. Who else would care what we were doing?"

I gathered my items. "Don't confront him by yourself, Gloria. Have Doc or me with you."

"I know how to do karate. Kinda. Sorta, anyway." She lifted her arms in a cartoonish manner. "Yeah, I'll have Doc with me. First, I need to catch him up on what we learned."

"Keep in mind, the dog is safe. Yeah, people might have lost money in the scam, but don't do anything to put yourself in danger." I gave her a hug and left.

It was important to catch Zarina's killer and to stop the dog scam. But at this moment, I couldn't wait to hear about Marc's meeting with Chris and Carol Williams.

Chapter Nine

BECAUSE MARC HAD SPENT MOST OF HIS DAY SITTING, we decided to stroll on the beach. He held my hand, and the full moon made it easy to walk. There wasn't much wind, but I was glad for the hoodie I'd slipped on. The October evening had a brisk bite. "Tell me about your day."

"Chris and Carol met us and said we needed to hurry to make our appointment at the DNA test center. Lincoln and I had discussed the issue on the way to Charleston, and I knew the test would prove if we're related. After that, we went to a little pancake place for brunch."

"What did you think of them as people?"

"Honestly, they were delightful. They've lived an interesting life, and they have a heart for sharing God with others. It's the reason they spent so many years in Africa. They felt it was their responsibility, no, make that privilege, to share about God with the villagers. Due to health issues, it's doubtful they'll travel anymore. Especially not to remote areas away from health care."

I skirted an incoming wave and body-bumped Marc. "Oops, sorry."

He laughed and slid his arm around me. "I'm not sorry."

We strolled a short distance in silence, but I couldn't stand not knowing more. "Why did they reach out now?"

"They were making out their wills. I'll inherit what they have, but the attorney asked questions about me. He helped them investigate me, and they found our wedding announcement. They decided it was time to meet."

I still didn't understand why they'd waited so long.

"Without me asking, they admitted they were embarrassed for not contacting me sooner."

"That I understand."

Two men wearing waders fished in the water. We walked around their beach cart full of fishing gear and chairs.

Marc gave them a longing look. "Looks like they're going to make a night of it."

"We can fish on our honeymoon, if you want."

He wrapped me in his arms. "We're going to hike, explore, maybe kayak if the water's not too cold, and just get to know the area and get to know each other better. No family, no murders, no friends, and no dogs. Just you and me."

"That sounds wonderful." I kissed him. "Just one week until I'm Andi Grace Williams."

"I can't wait." We kissed again.

"Duke!" Sheriff Wade Stone's voice blasted through the pleasant evening. We pulled apart and turned toward Wade.

I clapped my hands to get his mutt's attention. "Hey, Duke. Come here, boy."

The dog ran to me with a happy bark.

Wade approached at a slower pace. "Hi, guys. Sorry for the interruption. I got waylaid at work and didn't get home as early as I'd hoped. Duke is a little wound up."

I rubbed the sweet dog's head. "Anytime you need assistance, give me a call. Normally, I prefer owners to make dog-walking appointments, but you deserve grace, especially during a murder investigation."

Wade snapped a leash onto his dog's harness. "Thanks, but I hated to bother you with your wedding coming up and the baby. I had every intention of getting home earlier."

"I understand. How's your investigation going?"

"One of my best men is taking some time off because his wife just had a baby, but we're plugging along." He grinned. "Congratulations on your niece."

"Wait until you see her. She's a doll."

"I'm looking forward to meeting Elizabeth Christine. Is that right?"

"They're calling her Lizzy."

"Good to know. Say, if you truly want to help—"

"Yes?"

"Can I bring Duke to Stay and Play tomorrow? Just in case I lose track of time again."

"Sure. I'll let the others know to expect her."

Marc said, "One of us can drive Duke out to the farm for you."

"Y'all are amazing. Thanks."

I didn't want to spoil the moment, but I had to learn something about the investigation. "Wade, have you found Zarina's camera bag?"

His smile dimmed. "We haven't been looking for it. Tell me what you know."

"She has a backpack camera bag. It contains her other camera and different lenses. She also keeps notes in there. I learned that from J. T. Green. Theo Graves said she'd secretly taken pictures of the Moonbeams and a woman he didn't recognize. At least he believes it was a secret because of the way she hid behind trees and bushes and snapped pictures from a distance.

Did he tell you that?"

Wade shook his head. "I'll never cease to be amazed at how people spill their guts to you and clam up with me. Maybe the three of us should have a little talk in the morning. I'll bring Duke with me to your house. Is seven thirty too early?"

Marc said, "It works for me. I'll pick up muffins on my way."

I nodded. "The coffee will be ready when you two get there."

Wade left us standing in the moonlight. I glanced at Marc. "He really interrupted our evening. Let's get back to discussing you and your grandparents."

"They had pictures of Dad when he was a child. There were also some of my parents' wedding and me as a baby. I hardly have any photos from my childhood."

"I bet their photos are special. What does your gut tell you about Chris and Carol?"

He took my hands in his and released a big sigh. "I've been rejected most of my life. Not looking for sympathy, it's just a fact. My protective instinct is to not get my hopes up. Why don't we wait until we get the results back from the DNA tests? Then I can better answer your question."

"Okay. We're going to have an early morning. Maybe we should go." I didn't push for more than he was ready to share yet. It was a peaceful walk back to the house, then he left me and the dogs for a late-night meeting with Lincoln.

I found my journal and added notes on the dog scam and what I'd learned from Theo and Vince.

My heart sped up when I reviewed what Theo had said about the Moonbeams and the strange woman. A tall woman. Was there any possible way the woman speaking to the band was involved in the fundraising fraud for the dogs? Belle had said the woman asked if anyone wanted to adopt one of her new puppies.

What about Lincoln? He'd raced to see who the band was talking to the night of the rally. When he discovered it was Ben Lowe, he pulled Belle away.

Despite my desire to go to my office and research, I struggled to keep my eyes open. It was time to sleep.

The mysteries could wait until tomorrow.

Chapter Ten

ON SATURDAY MORNING I FELT MORE RESTED. Wade, Marc, and I sat on the back patio drinking coffee and comparing notes on Zarina's murder. Sunny, Chubb, and Duke played in the backyard. The new dog food really did seem to help Sunny's energy level.

"Officially, you need to stay away from my murder investigation." Wade took pictures of the pages in my journal.

"Do you believe there might be a connection between the dog scam and Zarina's murder? She mentioned a dog to J.T."

"The ex-husband was my first suspect—"

"I think he's innocent. He was trying to win Zarina back. He even attended anger management classes."

Wade clicked his pen. "I spoke to Zarina's mother and tend to agree with your analysis."

"Good." I relaxed back into my chair. "I don't suppose you'd share your suspect list with me."

"Nope." Wade's gaze bounced from Marc to me. "You two focus on your wedding. I've got the murder case."

Marc stood. "Not a problem."

Wade also rose to his feet, and we said our goodbyes.

Marc took me in his arms. "I need to scoot, but I can take the dogs to Stay and Play."

I hooked my hands together behind his neck. "No need. Dylan is taking over all my dog-walking appointments from today until we return from our honeymoon." Dylan had worked with me before I hired Belle. Though he worked for Griffin now, he still lived in the barn's studio apartment and didn't mind pitching in. "I need to meet with Juliet and review our wedding plans. We need to make sure we're all on the same page."

Marc sighed. "I hope we don't regret not hiring a wedding planner."

"Me, too. Juliet has helped others plan their big day, especially small weddings at the B and B. She knows what she's doing."

"Except this is a double wedding and her wedding. I've got a full day of making up for appointments I missed yesterday. My trip to meet Chris and Carol really threw me behind. Rylee's going to be at the office with me, and with a little luck we'll cruise through the day. Because it's Saturday, we won't have to answer the phone."

Rylee Prosser was an efficient office manager, but she tended to guard

Marc's time. She didn't like it when he changed the schedule for any reason. "I hope you have a good day. Love you."

He gave me a quick kiss. "Love you too."

It didn't take long to clean up from breakfast, and soon I was cruising down the road with all three dogs in my SUV. I parked near the Stay and Play barn and noticed Ike Gage's vehicle.

The retired Marine exited the barn and helped me get the dogs out. "Andi Grace, how's it going?"

"Good. Are you ready to walk me down the aisle next Saturday?" Ike was Lacey Jane's biological father, and we'd bonded over our love for my sister. Because my dad had died years earlier, it seemed fitting to ask Ike to give me away.

"Yes, ma'am, and I'm ready for the rehearsal dinner."

We spoke to Belle and Melanie before getting the dogs settled. I confirmed they knew Duke belonged to the sheriff before turning my attention to Ike. "Lacey Jane and David get to bring Lizzy home today. I'm so excited for them."

"Too bad the hospital had an early flu outbreak."

"Yeah. I mean I'm glad they want to protect the babies and patients, but it was a bummer." Although, if I'd spent more time at the hospital, I wouldn't know as much about the dog scam.

"I was thinking about giving Lizzy a puppy. What do you think?"

"Now?" My voice squeaked.

"Yeah. I thought it'd be fun for her to grow up with a dog." He looked hopeful.

"Well, what if you get a puppy and train it? I'm not sure Lacey Jane and David can handle a new baby and a puppy at the same time."

"Good point. Where do you suggest I look?"

My mind raced. "I've got a brilliant idea, but who's watching your store?"

"Jeremiah Prichard. Why?"

"There's a woman by the name of Destiny Howard. I heard she has a litter of puppies she's trying to sell."

Ike tilted his head. "I hear a *but* coming."

I explained the situation to him. "I want to make sure she's not involved in the puppy surgery scheme. How would you feel about going undercover and checking out her farm? Does she legitimately have puppies for sale? Is she running a puppy mill? Or was she talking to the Moonbeams for another reason? If you could take pictures of the puppies, pretend like you need a picture to show your family, but get Destiny in the photo. And can you try to gauge her height?"

"Gage is my name." He laughed at his joke. "Seriously, take a breath. I'm happy to go undercover, but how do I get in touch with the woman?"

"I'll find out. Don't go anywhere." I left him and tracked down Belle. "Hey, did Destiny leave you any contact information?"

"Tyler got her number. He wants to give his girlfriend a puppy. Do you want me to text him?"

"Yes, please." I paced while she contacted Tyler.

In less than a minute, Belle had the information I needed. I took the number to Ike. "If she agrees to meet you, do you want me to go with you in disguise?"

He shook his head. "I've participated in undercover ops before. Once a Marine, always a Marine. Don't worry."

"Me, worry? Just kidding. I trust you to handle the mission."

"I'll let you know what happens."

"Thanks, Ike." I gave him a quick hug, then he walked away.

On my way to the main house, I called Jeremiah at Beach Mart and scheduled a time to meet him at the farm. It was past time to find Zarina's camera bag. He agreed to meet me at his apartment complex when he got off work. Jeremiah managed to get to most places on his bicycle, but the farm was way too far to bike, especially if he was carrying his metal detector.

I continued walking to the main house, and Juliet met me in the back. "Let's look over the area where the wedding will take place."

"Okay. The weather report looks good for next weekend, but it's a week away. Should we rent one of those big tents in case it rains?"

Juliet crossed her arms. "Those things are crazy expensive. I trust the weather report."

"Okay, no tent." Her reaction surprised me, but if the weather turned, maybe it wouldn't be too late to rent an event tent. "I'm bringing Jeremiah back tonight to search for Zarina's camera bag. If any of your guests mention finding one—"

She lifted a slim hand. "I'll be sure to let the sheriff know. You really have no business trying to solve a murder this close to the wedding. One of the many things we need to focus on is finding a wedding photographer. I really don't want to ask Marvin Graves."

"Ugh, me either. Let me ask Skylar Marshall."

"We can trust her not to cause any trouble at the ceremony." Juliet's tone was confident.

"I didn't think she would, but why are you so sure?"

"She and Wade are cousins."

Whoa. "How do you know?"

"She stayed here while waiting for renovations on her house to be completed. Her previous home was in a bad neighborhood in Charleston, and Wade convinced her to move here. She's also in the process of transitioning from writing for a newspaper to starting her own podcast and blog. We had a lot of conversations over breakfasts."

"All right then, it sounds like you approve."

"Yeah, let's hope she says yes."

Chapter Eleven

Late Saturday afternoon, I returned to Kennady Bed-and-Breakfast with Jeremiah riding shotgun. We parked next to a blue Jeep with bumper stickers covering the back. A sticker proclaiming freedom of speech pretty much convinced me the vehicle belonged to Skylar Marshall.

Jeremiah hopped out and slammed my Highlander's door. I met him at the front of my SUV. He said, "I know the lay of the land. Meetcha back here in an hour?"

"Is there enough light?"

"I always carry a solid flashlight. Starting where you found her body seems like a good place to begin. Work my ways backward. Know what I mean?"

"Yes, sir." I watched him head for the back of the house.

"Andi Grace?" A tall woman with braided hair approached me.

"Skylar, thanks for meeting me."

"Juliet and I became friends while I transitioned to life at Heyward Beach, and Wade assured me you're a good person. How can I help you?"

"Next Saturday, I'm getting married. In fact, it's a double wedding. Juliet is marrying my brother."

Skylar squinted as the setting sun hit her eyes. "Yeah, she mentioned it to me."

"Zarina Mills was our photographer." A bubble of emotion swelled up, and my throat tightened.

"She was so talented. Nice too." Her smile stiffened.

"Would you possibly be able to be our photographer?"

She shook her head. "I'm more of a reporter. I only take pictures when absolutely necessary."

"With a week to go, I think we've reached that stage." I looked around to make sure we were alone. "I can't ask Marvin Graves. He and Zarina had an argument before she died."

"He's despicable. How about this? I'll take pictures for free, if you'll share what you know about Zarina's murder. I already asked Wade's permission, and he's cool with us collaborating."

I laughed. "Looks like being related to the sheriff has some perks."

"Not many, but a few. What do you say?"

Did I have a choice? "Deal, but don't tell Juliet. She wants me to step away from the murder investigation. Hey, if Wade's okay with us working together, does that mean you'll share what you know too?"

"Of course."

"Great. My notes are in the SUV. Give me a second." But then I realized Juliet might figure out what we were up to. "On second thought, let's go to my office. It's in the barn. I'll drive us over."

"Sounds good."

We passed Jeremiah on the short drive, but he never looked up from his task.

Skylar said, "What's he doing?"

I parked near the barn and met her gaze. "I don't want to endanger my friend. How's this going to work?"

"I won't print anything on my blog or say anything on the podcast without running it past you. If you're worried about someone's safety, I'll leave it out of my reporting."

"Perfect." I got out of the SUV and led her to my office.

Belle and Melanie were feeding the animals, and I waved to them.

"Do you have a pet?" I motioned for Skylar to enter my office.

She sat in the chair for clients, and I sat in the seat behind my desk.

"Ugh, I'd be the worst pet owner. I'm always chasing a story and would be terribly neglectful. However, I adore Duke. He's so much fun."

"He's staying here today. You and Wade must have that in common. Um, the part about focusing on a case, or story, in your situation."

"Yeah, we definitely have some of the same traits. It surprised me when he got a dog. Although I guess he adopted Duke before there was so much crime in the area."

"Peter Roth's murder led to my friendship with Wade." I flattened my hands on the newest journal.

"Let's get down to business. Who do you believe murdered Zarina?" She pressed a button on a digital voice recorder.

My palms grew damp. "I'm not sure, but I feel like J. T. Green is innocent."

"Really? The ex-husband is often guilty."

I shrugged. "He seemed to really love Zarina, and he changed to be worthy of her."

She reached for her fat braid and played with the end. "Say I buy your theory, who did it?"

"Maybe Marvin Graves."

Skylar gasped. "That's an interesting theory. I'm aware that they argued about her doing photography for Hannah Cummins. But what about the missing puppy who'd been brought to Heyward Beach for surgery. I heard Zarina was concerned about that."

The recorder made me uneasy, and I pointed at it. "Skylar, I'm not comfortable with that. Can we just talk it out and later do a recording?"

"I'm likely to make a mistake if I rely on memory."

I passed a pen and piece of paper to the reporter and lifted my eyebrows.

"All right." She turned off the machine. "Tell me more."

"Juliet found the missing puppy, and Doc performed the surgery last night." I thought for a minute. Murder on Thursday. Libby born in the middle of the night. I rested at home on Friday then came here. Yes, my timeline was correct. "Scout's owner drove here from Spartanburg yesterday with a friend."

"It doesn't seem like Scout's owner would be involved in Zarina's murder."

"True. All the man seems interested in is getting his dog well. Do you know Destiny Howard?"

Skylar snapped her fingers. "Yeah, yeah, yeah. The model who became a farmer, and she's married to Ben Lowe, the music guy. Zarina went with me to interview Ben a few weeks ago. We'd planned to tour the farmhouse where they live, but on the way, a dog ran into the road. I nearly ran over the Labrador."

I opened my journal and skimmed the notes. "Destiny has a litter of Labrador retrievers available to sell. She asked the members of the Moonbeams if anyone wanted to buy a puppy. It can't be a coincidence you almost ran over a Lab near their farm."

"We loaded him into the car with us and drove to the house. According to the tag, his name was Blackbeard. Ben saw the dog and promised to find the owner, but he never said the dog belonged to him or Destiny."

I wrote down the information she shared. "I guess it's possible they borrowed the dog to breed with their female retriever. It's also possible the dog was a stray."

"I don't think he was a stray, because Ben never looked at the collar. Isn't that the first thing you'd do?"

"I always look for dog tags. Some collars have the dog's name and a phone number stitched onto the collar. Either way, I look." I rubbed my temples to try and stop the beginning of a headache. "So, Ben didn't look and he didn't act like he recognized the dog."

"Correct."

"Interesting." I looked up from my notes. "Did you get to tour the house?"

"No." She opened her phone. "Ben let us take pictures of the outside, but he said Destiny wasn't feeling well so we couldn't go inside. The guy's very personable. He makes good eye contact, has a nice voice, and he seems to know a lot of people."

The memory of Lincoln rushing to remove Belle from a conversation with Ben sent a shiver down my spine. "Was he believable? No, what I mean is, if you were a musician, would you feel comfortable putting your career in his hands?"

"Maybe, but I'm suspicious by nature. It's probably why I go after the bad guys on my podcast." Skylar studied her phone then passed it to me. "Here are some of the pictures I snapped. I don't know what happened to Zarina's extra photos. A few of her shots are on my website, but she took a ton of pictures."

"Did you see the other dogs or puppies? Oh, and what happened to the dog you found wandering on the road?"

"Ben put the dog in a small kennel near a shed. He said he'd deal with the situation later. I never saw any other dogs."

A loud noise followed by a man's scream ended our conversation.

Chapter Twelve

Skylar and I raced toward the sound.

Juliet and Nate ran out of the house.

A flashlight shone in the undergrowth of the trees, and a moan came from the same direction.

"Stay back," Jeremiah yelled. "I got bit by a snake."

I stopped in my tracks.

Nate said, "I'll help, but who is it?"

"Jeremiah Prichard. He's trying to find Zarina's camera backpack." The sky had darkened. "I'll move my vehicle to shine lights on the area." I jogged to the Highlander and moved it to direct the headlights on the area where Jeremiah lay.

Nate carried the lean man to where I sat parked. Juliet opened the back door, and Nate slid him inside. "Probably a copperhead. You need to get him to the emergency room."

"No insurance." Jeremiah's voice shook. "I twisted my ankle trying to get away from the snake."

I met Nate's gaze in the dome's light. "What do you think?"

"It might need to be X-rayed, plus, if it was a copperhead, he'll need treatment. I'll ride with you."

"Jeremiah, you served our country. There must be some kind of government insurance, but even if there isn't, we're going to get you checked out. Don't argue."

His weak nod worried me greatly, and I stepped on the gas. During our frantic drive to the hospital, Nate texted Marc and kept a conversation going with Jeremiah. My focus remained on the highway.

If I hadn't asked the retired military man to use his metal detector to look for Zarina's bag, this wouldn't have happened. Why didn't I leave the case alone?

"Sis, you okay?" Nate nudged my shoulder.

"This is all my fault. If I hadn't butted into the investigation, Jeremiah would be fine."

"Listen here, girl, I could've said no. Some of my most exhilarating times in the last couple of years have been thanks to you." Jeremiah sighed. "You make me feel alive, and because of you, I'm living in a decent apartment, and I have more friends now than before meeting you. Don't beat yourself up."

A warm tear slid down my face. "Thanks."

Nate pointed to the highway. "Keep your eyes on the road. You can cry when we get to the hospital."

"Leave it to a brother to keep things real."

"Somebody's got to do it." He chuckled.

Before long, I pulled up to the E.R.

Marc stood by with a male nurse gripping a wheelchair. Nate accompanied Jeremiah inside, and Marc claimed the passenger seat. "How are you holding up?"

I gripped the steering wheel and drove to the nearest parking space. "I've been better."

"What happened?"

I shut off the engine and looked at my fiancé, soon to be husband. "There must be something wrong with me. I couldn't simply ignore the murder. No siree. I asked Jeremiah to search for the camera backpack. Not only that, I talked to Skylar Marshall and compared notes with her. It appears we have Wade's blessing to work together, because she and Wade are cousins. Then Ike tells me that he wants a puppy for Lizzy, and I asked him to go undercover and look for a pup at Destiny Howard's farm. He agreed to go and see if he notices anything suspicious."

"Whoa." Marc laughed. "You have been busy today."

My face grew warm. "I did discuss the wedding with Juliet. She doesn't want to go ahead and rent a tent in case it rains. Can you believe that? I agreed because she was acting weird."

"Do you think it's pre-wedding jitters?"

"Maybe. Anyway, I agreed. Right now, the weather forecast looks favorable, but anything can happen. I mean, we're technically still in hurricane season."

Marc took my hand in his. "If a hurricane hits, we'll have more to worry about than wedding details. I know Juliet is your best friend, but this is our wedding too. If you really want a large event tent, we'll pay for it."

His offer touched me. "Aw, thanks. Do you think Juliet has money problems?"

"No idea, but weddings are expensive. Even small ones cost money."

"True, but we've cut out a lot of expenses by having the ceremony and reception on the farm. Although, your theory makes sense. I should talk to her."

"Agreed, but first we need to check on Jeremiah. Nate mentioned a snake bite and twisted ankle."

"Yeah. Did I tell you that it's my fault he was searching for the bag?"

He leaned over and kissed me.

"Oh, nice."

"I don't mind you trying to solve the murder, but if the killer's not caught before the wedding, will you leave town with me for our honeymoon?"

"I'm not going to miss our honeymoon for anything."

"Good to know. Let's check on Jeremiah, then you can catch me up on the murder."

I also needed to tell him about the dog scam and see what he knew about Ben Lowe. But he was right. First, we needed to see about Jeremiah's condition.

Chapter Thirteen

Nate drove Jeremiah back to his apartment in Piney Woods, where a mutual friend, Leroy Peck, also lived and would take care of the injured man. After Jeremiah was settled, Nate took my SUV to the farm.

The doctors had taken care of the snake bite with antivenom and a tetanus shot. They confirmed the ankle was sprained and wrapped it, then gave Jeremiah crutches.

Marc and I went to Lincoln's house when we left the hospital.

Lincoln opened the door. "Come in, guys. What's up? Are you concerned about the songs I plan to play at the wedding and reception?" He led us to the living room, and we sat across from him.

Marc shook his head. "I trust you've got the music handled. Andi Grace has a couple of questions concerning Ben Lowe."

Lincoln's eyes widened. "You didn't tell her?"

"Not my place."

"Right." He leaned forward and propped his arms on his thighs. "I was under the wrong impression that when I moved to South Carolina, I had to get a new manager. One that was licensed in this state."

Marc shook his head. "He never consulted his attorney. Can you imagine?"

I laughed. "Really?"

"Cut it out. There was so much going on with Savannah and our separation. Then there was Thomas and the tabloids, and I did consult you about those issues. On top of all that, Belle wanted to move here, and I was delighted. About the time she moved in, it came to my attention I needed a manager who lived in South Carolina. I was introduced to Ben, who asked if he could be my manager. He seemed nice enough, so I agreed."

"What happened to make you want to keep him away from Belle?" I pulled my journal and pen out of my purse and started taking notes. "This is only for the investigation. I won't share with the press, even though I've discussed the murder with Skylar Marshall."

"I know you won't do anything to hurt me." He rubbed his hands together. "I trusted Ben Lowe with my career, and he almost ruined it. If it wasn't for Marc, I probably would've walked away from country music."

Wow. "I had no idea how bad things had gotten."

"Now you understand why I tried to distance Belle from that no-good swindler."

"Did I hear my name?" Belle's melodic voice reached us before she entered the room.

I pressed my lips together, unwilling to cause a rift between father and daughter.

Lincoln patted the couch cushion beside him. "I was telling Andi Grace a little about Ben Lowe."

She plopped down next to her dad. "Oh, yeah. He was the pay-to-perform guy."

"Did you know Destiny Howard, the woman who asked if you wanted to adopt a puppy, is Ben's wife?"

"Really?" Belle tilted her head. "I've been thinking about her. How do you go from being a well-paid fashion model to running a farm and breeding dogs? Does she have cattle or chicken or does she grow crops? How is her farm sustainable?"

Lincoln chuckled. "Those are all very good questions, for which I have no answer."

"I aced high school accounting and marketing. We talked about the plight some farmers face, so I'm curious. Of course, maybe Ben earns so much that it doesn't matter if his wife loses money."

Marc said, "Maybe she invested wisely. Destiny inherited the farm—"

Belle raised a hand to stop Marc. "Most of the farm boys I went to school with want to go to college and move to a big city. Some want to return to their family farms, but they want to get degrees in business and agriculture. They used to talk a lot about new ways to make a profit off their land. It was pretty interesting." Belle undid her messy bun and rubbed her head. "I'm singing a solo in church tomorrow, so I better hit the hay."

Marc said, "I need to drive Andi Grace home. We'll see you tomorrow."

I gave Belle and Lincoln quick hugs. "Let me know if you think of anything important."

Belle said, "I don't suppose Destiny is running a puppy mill on her farm. It's horrible to imagine."

Chills covered my body. "I sure hope not, but I've got somebody trying to check the farm for anything suspicious. Of course, that's top secret."

We said good nights, and Marc drove me home. It felt weird to enter an empty house. Sunny and Chubb would spend the night at Stay and Play because we'd left them behind in our haste to get treatment for Jeremiah. Wade planned to pick up Duke before heading home.

Marc returned to his office to get ahead on some of his cases before our wedding.

I got ready for bed and snuggled under the covers. Reviewing my notes on Zarina's murder and the dog surgery confusion, I wondered if there could possibly be a link.

I reached for my phone and texted Ike. *Did you meet Destiny? What was the farm like? Do you think she could possibly be linked to Operation Tail-wagger?*

My phone beeped. Ike had already replied.

It's been a long day. Meet at Daily Java at 0700? We'll discuss the case then.

I sent an affirmative reply and set my alarm. Tomorrow was Sunday, and I'd take extra time getting ready, but it was doable. Definitely doable as long as my brain would shut off tonight.

Dogs. Surgery scheme, maybe. Zarina's death. Jeremiah's injury. Carol and Chris Williams. Ben Lowe and his shenanigans with musicians. What was going on with Destiny Howard?

I fluffed my pillows again and turned on my side. This time next week, I'd be married to Marc. That thought alone allowed me to have happy dreams.

Chapter Fourteen

Sunday morning, Marc picked me up. We entered Daily Java to meet Ike at exactly seven o'clock. He waved to us from a table in the corner. Marc said, "Why don't you go on over and I'll place our orders."

"Thanks." I strolled through the nearly empty coffee shop. "Good morning, Ike."

"Morning." He stood and held the chair out for me. "How are the wedding plans coming?"

"I feel confident we're prepared. Don't forget the rehearsal is Friday evening."

He scoffed. "I'm giving away one of the brides. No way I'm forgetting my responsibilities."

Griffin Reed joined us. "Hey, I'm giving away the other bride. We should compare notes to make sure we know what we're doing. Juliet might never forgive me if I duff it up."

Ike stood and shook Griffin's hand, and we chatted until Marc joined us with coffees and muffins.

Griffin said, "I best shove off. Erin's employee called in sick, and I agreed to deliver pastries and coffee to the church."

Erin owned the coffee shop and worked hard to make it thrive. It was nice of Griffin to help her.

Marc chose the empty chair next to mine. "What'd I miss?"

I blew on my coffee. "Actually, nothing. We haven't even begun."

Marc rubbed his hands together. "Su-weet."

Ike said, "I called the number you gave me and scheduled an appointment to see the dogs, and I made a point of arriving early."

"Did you meet Destiny?"

"Yes. She answered the door and led me around the house to a room off the back porch. It was attached to the rest of the house, possibly an addition somewhere along the way. I imagine the house was built in the nineteenth century. Except for needing a good paint job on the outside, it appeared solid. Trees formed a circle around the house, preventing me from seeing much of the land."

"What did you think about Destiny?" I probably sounded like a broken record, but I needed to decide if she was involved with Operation Tail-wagger.

"She was cordial enough, but she wasn't all lovey-dovey with the dogs.

She was matter-of-fact. The pups are either a business or an accident that she needed to deal with. She's younger than you. I'd guess more Lacey Jane's age."

"Was she mean to the dogs?"

"No. They were inside in a playpen area. The place was clean enough. She let me pick a pup to take outside and play with. While we were outside, she had to answer a call and went inside. That was my cue to get nosy. The dog and I wandered through the trees until we came to a clearing. There were sheds, maybe a chicken coop, a swaying barn with pieces of wood missing, and a few dilapidated outbuildings. Destiny found us and admitted she'd inherited the farm from her grandparents. Some of her best memories were times on the farm, but she became a big-city girl and doesn't know what she's doing. Along with the farm came debt. Give her credit for trying to save the place, but she doesn't know what she's doing. Plus, she can't afford to pay someone to do all the work to make it profitable."

I sipped my coffee and reflected on Ike's impressions of Destiny. Had she considered converting the farm into a bed-and-breakfast? Wait. My goal was to decide if Destiny was connected to Operation Tail-wagger. "Did she convince you to adopt a puppy?"

"She's asking twenty-five hundred dollars per pup. I could easily go to the animal shelter and get a dog who needs a home." The fit Marine crossed his arms, leaned back in his chair, and lifted his chin.

"But?" Marc's eyebrows rose.

Ike's gaze darted from Marc to me before leaning forward. "That little mutt grabbed a hold of my heart. I'm such a sucker. I've already picked out a name for him. Marney."

"Marney?"

"Yeah, to represent the Marines."

Oh, boy, Ike had it bad. "Can you afford to buy the dog? I mean, you're opening a new business."

"I'll manage." He pressed his lips together, and the skin around them whitened.

"How can I help?"

"I've had dogs before. Living in the little place behind Beach Mart will make it easy to train him and keep an eye on the little guy so he won't get lonely. But there may be some days when I'd like him to hang out at Stay and Play so he can get a good run in."

"Of course, he's always welcome. I bet you're going to be on the road often visiting your new grandbaby." Lacey Jane and David's land bordered my work property.

"You know that's right." He glanced at his watch. "I'm due back at Destiny's farm around one. It's called Earth's Edge Farmstead. Do you two want to go with me?"

I smiled and glanced at Marc. "What do you think?"

"We should go with Ike."

"Awesome." I glanced at my watch to calculate the time before we left. "Oh, we're going to be late for church."

We tidied our area and left Daily Java with a quick wave to Erin, who was waiting on customers.

She didn't bring up the wedding cake, so I assumed all systems were go. I mentally put aside thoughts of animals and the wedding. It was time to go to church.

Chapter Fifteen

IKE HADN'T EXAGGERATED when he'd declared Destiny's home was circled by trees. Marc and I stood in the shade of a magnolia while Ike rang the doorbell.

On the ride over, we decided our cover story was that we were debating if my new niece was ready for a puppy.

Marc said, "If we get back to the farm in time, I'll use Jeremiah's metal detector and see if we can find Zarina's bag."

"Oh, no. I hate for you to do that. One of Wade's deputies should handle it." I rubbed my temples. "Poor Jeremiah. I shouldn't have asked him."

Marc removed his sunglasses. "We've put him in worse predicaments, but I believe he enjoys helping you."

His words made me feel a bit better.

Ike approached us with a young woman at his side. She was tall, her makeup was perfect, and her messy bun appeared to have been crafted with care, unlike my legitimate messy bun. "Guys, this is Destiny Howard."

I stuck out my hand to shake. "Hi, Destiny. I'm Andi Grace Scott."

"Hi." Her handshake was firmer than I expected.

Marc shook her hand next. "Nice to meet you. I'm Marc Williams."

Ike said, "I want you to meet Marney, and you can help me decide if Lizzy is ready for her own puppy."

Destiny smiled. "I think it's a great idea. Your granddaughter and her puppy can grow up together and be best friends."

There was no way I'd agree to a new dog for Lacey Jane's baby without her approval. "In theory, it's a terrific idea. In reality, my sister might not be thrilled to train a new puppy while adjusting to motherhood. Destiny, do you have any children?"

"Oh, no." Her voice squeaked. "Gracious, I'm only twenty-four. Maybe one day though. Let me introduce you to Marney."

I walked beside Destiny. "You seem familiar. Have we met before?"

She shrugged her thin shoulders. "I used to model for local companies in Charleston and Charlotte. You may have seen me on TV commercials, social media, or print ads."

"That's probably it. Do you still model?"

"I turned down a couple of projects when I first took on the farm, and it's been harder to get back into the business than I'd expected." Destiny turned when we reached the back corner of the house.

"How do you make money on the farm? Is it self-sustaining?" Was that the correct term? If not, she was bound to know what I meant.

A bark of laughter burst out of her. "That is a very good question, and I haven't figured it out yet."

Dogs barked from inside the house, and I smiled. "The pups must sense we're coming."

"Sounds like it." She opened the back door, and a yellow corgi sprinted past us. "Stop, Queenie."

Marc turned. "I'll get her."

Ike said, "I'll help."

I looked at Destiny. "Is Queenie your dog?"

She wrung her hands. "Yes. She's never run off before. I should try to find her too."

"I'll help. Where do you think she'd go?"

Destiny narrowed her eyes. "How would I know?"

I gulped. "Does she have a favorite place. A pond? Or someplace she enjoys playing with you? What about a neighbor with small children or other dogs?"

"I don't know. Why are you asking me these questions?" Destiny whined like a spoiled child.

"Corgis are social and enjoy people and other dogs. Never mind. We can split up and look for her." I jogged away from the woman in search of a dog who deserved better attention than she was getting from her human.

When I reached the wooded area, I slowed my pace. "Queenie. Come here, girl. I've got treats." I almost always carried a zippered container of treats and poop bags.

In the distance, I heard the others calling out for the corgi. There was no whining nearby, so I continued my search.

Back in the sunlight, I saw outbuildings just like Ike had reported, but I didn't see a little kennel like Skylar had described.

I approached one of the small buildings with flaking blue paint. The dirty glass windows prevented me from seeing into the dark interior, and a rusty ladder leaned against a little porch.

My phone vibrated. It was a text from Marc. *Found her.*

I smiled. My fiancé had been a man of very few words when we first met. He'd eventually opened up, but sometimes he was concise. I shot off a reply. *Keep Destiny occupied. I'm going to investigate a building.*

I stepped onto the crumbling concrete porch. The doorknob was rusty, but I tried it anyway. To my surprise, it turned in my hand. I opened the door and took a tentative step inside.

Spiderwebs attacked my hair and face. Yuck. I swiped them away and turned on my phone's flashlight. An atrocious smell made my nose tingle.

There were empty dog crates. Moldy dog beds. Half-empty bags of dog food. I took another step and spotted a plastic shelving unit.

Clear totes filled the shelves. One appeared to contain clothes. Jewelry boxes occupied space in a different tote. Why were clothes, and probably jewelry, in this dirty shed instead of Destiny's spacious house? She didn't have children, so wouldn't she have plenty of room for personal articles?

I did my best to photograph the items in the darkened shed. Dust tickled my nose, and I sneezed.

Marc appeared on the porch. "Andi Grace, get out of there. Destiny's looking for you." Marc's urgent tone sent me backing out of the shed.

"Okay, but there's something weird going on."

He grabbed my hand, and we took off running. "Hurry."

"Wait, we need to shut the door." I raced back and pushed the wooden door shut. "Did something happen?"

"Ben Lowe showed up, and he's not happy to see me."

"Yikes. We better get a move on." I reached for his hand again.

"Yep. That's what I said."

Chapter Sixteen

BEN LOWE. The bad music guy. Marc had helped Lincoln get out of his contract with Ben's management company. Destiny was married to Ben. The thoughts kept track with the whooshing heartbeat in my ears.

We darted through the woods. At the clearing Marc said, "Just walk, and try to act natural."

My labored breathing was more from fear than running. I slowed and kept my hand in Marc's hand.

Ike stood talking to Destiny and Ben. Destiny held Queenie in her arms.

At our approach, Ben turned and glared at us. "Counselor, this is private property, and I'd like you to leave before I call the sheriff."

My pulse leapt. We were in a different county, and I didn't know the sheriff or any law enforcement here. This could be bad.

Marc said, "We're here with Ike to pick up his puppy."

"Are you trying to tell me a grown man needs two helpers to pick up one little dog?" Ben practically growled.

Destiny touched his arm. "They were thinking about buying one of the pups, but Queenie escaped and we never got around to seeing the other dogs."

The man's frown lessened. "Darling, you can find good homes for all the puppies without resorting to Marc Williams."

"All right, honey, but Mr. Gage already paid for one of the pups."

Stiffness returned to Ben's posture. "I suggest Mr. Gage get his dog and leave our property in the next five minutes."

Of all the nerve.

Marc squeezed my hand. "Let's wait in the SUV for Ike."

I lifted my chin and ignored Ben because I couldn't for the life of me think of one single nice thing to say to the man. "Destiny, it was good to meet you."

"You too, Andi Grace." She handed Queenie to Ben and turned her attention to Ike. "Now, let's get your puppy."

Marc and I left the threesome.

An idea flashed through my mind. I texted Ike as we walked to his truck. *Ask to borrow a crate for the ride home.*

"Whatcha doing?"

I pointed to Ike's dark gray 4Runner. "I'll tell you in a minute."

We reached the vehicle, and I slid into the backseat. Once Marc was in the shotgun position, he angled his body and looked at me with a lopsided grin. "Well?"

"I asked Ike to try to borrow a crate for Marney's ride home. There were dog supplies in the blue shed, which wasn't too surprising, despite the odor of mold and mildew. There were also totes of clothes and possibly jewelry."

"We need to analyze the situation logically. Destiny used to be a model, but she's working on a farm now." Marc rubbed his chin.

"An unprofitable farm."

Marc nodded. "True. Are you wondering why she hasn't sold those items?"

"I'd really like to know if she has jewelry in the boxes. The door wasn't locked, so it can't be valuable. Right?"

He shrugged. "Not many people would venture into that shed. Thanks to Ben's appearance, we didn't even get to set foot in the house to analyze the dog situation. What do you believe is going on at Earth's Edge Farmstead?"

"Zarina mentioned a dog to J.T. At first, he thought she wanted a puppy for Sarah. I keep wondering if there's a connection between Operation Tail-wagger and Destiny. Did I mention Zarina rode out here with Skylar? But it was do a story on Ben."

"Interesting that he wouldn't meet them in town." Marc rubbed his jaw. "Is there a link between Zarina's death and Operation Tail-wagger?"

"Yeah, that seems even more far-fetched, but Scout disappeared the same day Zarina was murdered. I don't have much to go on—"

"Yet. But if they are related, you'll figure it out."

I leaned forward and kissed him. "I love that you always believe in me."

"Always have. Always will."

My door opened, and Ike passed a little chocolate Labrador retriever to me. "This is Marney. Ben remained by Destiny's side the entire time once you two left. Not going to lie. It was tense. I didn't dare ask for a crate. It was time to get my dog and retreat."

"Smart move. Sorry to add to your stress."

"No problem, but let's roll." He shut the door and hopped into the driver's seat. Acting like he didn't have a care in the world, Ike drove at a steady speed. If it'd been me, I probably would've spit gravel making my getaway.

Once we pulled onto the windy two-lane road, Marc asked, "Don't suppose you noticed anything odd."

"Ben Lowe's behavior was the only peculiar thing. None of the other pups had been adopted. In fact, Destiny asked me to spread the word that she had more puppies waiting for their forever home."

Marney grew restless and gagged.

"Ike, pull over. Your dog's about to get sick." It wasn't my first experience with a pet and motion sickness.

"Um, there's nowhere to pull off." Ike slowed.

I rolled down my window and held tight to the Labrador. "Maybe fresh air will help."

Marc looked back and forth between me and the road. "Ike, there's a driveway up ahead."

Ike signaled his intention to turn even though the road was virtually deserted. He whipped the SUV onto the lane and parked under an oak tree.

I hopped out with the sick pooch before the SUV came to a complete stop.

Marney vomited on the sandy driveway.

Ike joined me. "Looks like we just made it."

"I'm afraid not. There's a little puke on the inside of your car door."

He took the announcement like a champ. "I've got wipes from a recent fishing trip." He left me with the heaving dog.

Marc rubbed my shoulders. "If I'm not mistaken, this is also Destiny's property. See the cotton field here?"

A few bent stalks dotted the large area of land. "Yeah."

"According to a little research I did, Earth's Edge Farmstead used to grow cotton. Destiny's grandparents also had goats and chickens. I believe they also sold produce at the local farmers' market. The farm wasn't huge, but the Howards made a go of it with their diversity."

I knelt beside Marney and patted his side. "I wonder if Destiny tried those things. She claims the farm is losing money."

Ike rejoined us. "The back's as clean as it's going to get. I couldn't help but overhear you. Destiny said she made goat soap and lotion. She sold it online but didn't make much profit. This is the first time she's tried her hand at dog breeding. If she charges everyone as much as she did me, it's bound to be profitable. Do you think Marney needs water?"

"As soon as you get home, yes. Right now, I think an empty stomach is better. We've got a ways to go before we get there though."

"Makes sense." Ike squatted beside the little brown Labrador. "Hey, buddy. It's going to be okay."

Marc twirled his aviator sunglasses in one hand, and his eyes sparkled with an unspoken challenge. "Apparently, Destiny doesn't grow cotton. And we didn't see any chickens or goats on the property."

I stood and dusted off my hands. "It's fall, but we haven't seen any pumpkins either. Those are always popular."

Ike said, "Might be in a different field. We should probably give Marney a few minutes to settle his stomach."

"Let's go." I smiled at Marc.

He pushed his sunglasses on. "Ike, we won't take long in case Ben shows up."

We darted through the abandoned cotton field and stopped at a grove of trees. "Pecan trees."

Marc picked up a handful of pecans and rolled them between his hands. "The price of cotton fell during the Civil War, and some farmers turned to planting pecan trees."

"I know nothing about harvesting pecan trees, but if I'd inherited this place I would've learned or paid someone to pick them for me." In fact, I'd had a similar experience, and I'd turned my land into the bed-and-breakfast and Stay and Play. One day I still hoped to create an animal shelter, but there were legal hoops to jump through. "Why do you think Destiny hasn't hired people to farm the land for her?"

"Who knows? Maybe she's afraid." He dropped the pecans onto the ground. "But we're not going to get arrested for eating her nuts."

"That's for sure. We should probably head back before our luck runs out."

Marc flashed me a big smile. "Sounds like a smart move, however, I'm shocked you didn't try to convince me to explore that little outbuilding."

I looked in the direction he nodded toward. At the end of the row of pecan trees sat a shed. My pulse leapt.

What was in the leaning shack?

Chapter Seventeen

I TOOK MY FIRST FEW STEPS toward the leaning building at the end of the row of pecan trees.

Ringtones sounded on my phone as well as Marc's cell.

I stopped in my tracks.

Marc said, "Ike says he hears a car coming."

Oh, man. "Okay."

"Hurry."

We ran back to where Ike and Marney waited for us. The 4Runner was running, and the dog rested in Ike's lap. We dove into the backseat, slammed the door, and Ike punched the gas.

The vehicle careened onto the road, and I slid into Marc. A childhood song about buckling up for safety flitted through my mind. I moved over and fastened my seat belt and Marc did the same.

Ike glanced over his shoulder. "I heard sirens in the distance. We'll turn at the next crossroad and travel at a safe speed. If the cops stop us, we got turned around."

"That won't be a lie. I have no idea what direction we're heading."

Marc grumbled. "With navigation apps, I'm not sure any law enforcement will buy that story."

"Blame it on bad reception." Ike slowed at a speed limit sign. "Plan B. We're going to stop for gas and allow Marney to do his business."

A sheriff's car sped by us so fast the SUV rocked.

I leaned forward. "Do you suppose they're after someone else? If Ben had reported that we were on his property, it seems like they'd be looking for your kind of vehicle."

"Not sure what's happening." He eased into the gas station and stopped at a pump.

"I'm heading to the restroom." I breathed a sigh of relief and walked inside. After my trip to the restroom, I looked around the store.

"Can I help you find something?" the older clerk asked.

"Yes, ma'am. Do you sell goat soap?"

"Naw, that's too fancy for us. Across the street, there's a general store, and I use the term loosely, because there's nothing general about it. More like an uppity-up boutique store. They carry fancy products made by locals. You can find goat soap, and wool, and sweaters made from the sheep wool. They even have slippers, but land sakes they're expensive. Close to a hundred bucks for a pair of bedroom slippers, and that's the honest truth."

I held back a smile. "That does sound a bit pricey."

"Only problem is the store is closed on Sundays."

And there went my thunder. "Well, maybe I can peek in the windows. We're in the area to get a puppy from a farm up the road, but if it looks good, I'll have to come back." I walked to the soda fountain and filled three cups full of ice and Coke. I paid the woman with cash, in case the cops questioned her about me later. Not that I was doing anything illegal.

"A puppy, you say? If you got your puppy from Earth's Edge, you paid a pretty penny. I reckon you can afford the pricey items at the general store."

"We came with a friend who wanted a puppy for his granddaughter. He bonded with one of the dogs before he knew how much it cost. By that time, he was a goner."

"A sucker's born every day."

"You say sucker, I say softie. At least when it comes to dogs." I didn't appreciate her hard attitude, but I tended to believe every word she said. "Thanks for your information."

I carried the drinks to the SUV. The men leaned against the side, waiting for me.

Marc moved with his special manly grace that often left me weak in the knees. He opened the door for me. "You two seemed to be in a big conversation."

"Oh, I almost forgot. Destiny may sell her goat products in the store over there." I handed him a drink and put the other two in cupholders. "It's closed, but I want to peek in the windows."

Ike said, "I'll park on the street. Take your time."

Marc and I crossed the street and stopped in front of the General Store.

I elbowed him. "I thought the woman just referred to this place as a regular general store. I didn't realize it was the proper name."

"Not sure if it's a clever name or just laziness." He took a drink of his Coke.

"True." I leaned near the window and shielded my eyes from the afternoon sun. "Look, there's goat soap and lotion. And look at that pretty wool. I wish I could knit. It'd make a beautiful sweater."

"It doesn't get cold here long enough to be worth the effort."

"Good point. We should go. I can't imagine anything here is a clue to the missing dog or Zarina's murder."

"Why don't you take a picture anyway? Otherwise, you'll regret it."

"Oh, Marc. You know me so well." I swiped on my phone and snapped a few pictures with the camera app. "Okay, I'm ready to go."

Ike's 4Runner idled in the nearest parking space on the street.

We settled in the vehicle and headed for home. Marc held the dog in his lap, and we traveled with the windows down.

I mulled over what we'd learned, and we were never pulled over by any deputies. I chalked it up as a win when we arrived at Ike's cottage behind Beach Mart. No sick dog, and no arrests.

Chapter Eighteen

Marc drove us to Stay and Play in his Chevy truck. On the drive, I'd talked to Leroy and found out Jeremiah was doing okay. The ankle gave him a little pain, but the man refused to take anything stronger than ibuprofen.

I also spoke to Lacey Jane. The new mother asked if I'd wait a day or two before visiting. She wanted some time alone with David and Lizzy. Of course, I agreed to her request.

"Who else do you need to call?"

"I may call Doc and see how Scout is doing." My phone vibrated before I dialed. "Oh, it's J.T."

Marc rambled along the property's driveway with his wrist loosely over the steering wheel. "What are you waiting for?" His voice carried a teasing tone.

I ran my finger over the phone. "Hello."

"Andi Grace, this is J. T. Greene. I found something in Sarah's diaper bag. You remember how I told you Zarina was afraid of losing pictures and other information?"

"Yeah."

"There's a memory stick. I'm heading back to Heyward Beach after supper. Do you want to meet?"

"You bet I do. Would you like us to come to your apartment?" My heart raced.

"Yes, ma'am. I'll call you when I get close to town. Don't want to rush my time with Sarah, but I promise to call you."

"Oh, of course you need time with Sarah. No need to rush."

"Also, can you bring a laptop? I don't have a computer anymore. It's fried. But I want to see what's on the stick."

"No problem. Be safe driving."

"Yes, ma'am."

Marc parked near the barn. "Sounds important."

"It could be our biggest clue yet. J.T. found a jump drive in Sarah's diaper bag. He's going to call me when he gets close to town. We're going to all sit down and look at it on my laptop."

"I was going to figure out how to use Jeremiah's metal detector. Should I wait?"

"Let's text Wade and see if they've found Zarina's camera bag. There could be nothing important in it, but there could be a clue." I texted the sheriff.

"While we wait, how about playing with our dogs?"

"That sounds like an amazing plan. I've missed them."

• • •

After we played with Sunny and Chubb, I convinced Marc to go visit Doc Hewitt. We dropped our dogs at my house and left the sheriff's dog at Stay and Play. Next stop was to see Doc.

Gloria greeted us when we entered the building. Her dark curly hair touched her shoulders, and she wore jeans and a white blouse. "Good afternoon. What brings you two out here this afternoon?"

"A better question might be why are you working on a Sunday?" I figured she wanted more time with Doc. The slower weekend pace would allow them some freedom to be themselves.

She shook a finger at me. "Don't start."

"I'll behave. We really came by to see if you learned more about Operation Tail-wagger."

"I'm sorry, hon. We've been busy. John Graystone and his friend Vince Murray are in back visiting with Scout. The poor thing had a seizure last night, and Zach wants to watch him one more day. Hopefully, they'll get to take the dog home tomorrow."

"Great. Do you think we can talk to Vince and John?"

"Have a seat and I'll check."

Marc and I sat in chairs facing the door Gloria had disappeared behind. A few minutes later, Vince appeared.

"Hi, Vince. This is my fiancé, Marc Williams. Do you mind if we ask you a few more questions?"

Marc and Vince shook hands and exchanged greetings. Vince met my gaze. "Fire away."

"Do you remember exactly how John met Claire Rowe?"

"Social media. He posted pictures, and she replied. At first, she made kind comments. Then she began commenting how much she wished she could help. She gave excuses about not having much money herself so she understood how helpless John must feel. A few days later, she offered to start a fundraiser for Scout's surgery. As soon as John showed interest, she pounced. It took off from there. She set a goal, found Doc Hewitt, and put the fundraiser in motion. Next thing I knew, we were meeting her at the gas station I told you about."

Marc said, "We've heard a man is behind this scheme. You're confident Claire was a woman?"

Vince closed his eyes a moment. "Pretty confident. She was tall, with red hair and green eyes. Nothing about her seemed manly. I feel guilty for my part in this mess."

I clenched my hands. "You did nothing wrong. Claire Rowe targeted your friend through his love of Scout. She took advantage of how much he loved his dog. The important thing is that Scout will be okay."

"Still, I wish there'd been a better way to help Scout. You know, a legitimate organization." He pressed his lips together.

"I get it. We can't find anyone connected with Operation Tail-wagger to verify their legitimacy."

Marc placed a hand on Vince's shoulder. "We're getting married Saturday, but when we return from our honeymoon, I have every intention of digging into the alleged nonprofit. Once I find them, if they are legit, we'll get their books audited. Their days are numbered, my friend."

"Good. Let me know if I can be any help. John's a basket case at the moment. As for me? I'm angry." He inhaled a deep breath. "Congratulations on your wedding."

"Thanks." Marc patted his shoulder again before removing his hand.

My phone vibrated in my pocket. I checked, and it was a message from J.T. "I'm sorry, Vince, but we've got an appointment. Please stay in touch."

"You bet." He rubbed his beard. "I only wish I could remember more."

We told him bye and drove to Piney Woods Apartment Complex. I couldn't wait to see what J.T. had found.

Chapter Nineteen

WE MET J.T. at the apartment where he was staying with Theo Graves. A stained sectional sofa took up most of the space in the family room. One of the biggest TVs I'd ever seen hung on a wall.

J.T. pointed to the kitchen counter. "This might be the easiest place to load the drive so we can all see."

Marc took a damp paper towel and wiped off the counter. "Sorry. It's a habit of mine from building boats. I like a clean workspace."

J.T. chuckled. "As a landscaper, I work with dirt. Those crumbs didn't even register with me."

After removing the laptop from my backpack, I turned it on and inserted the jump drive.

Nobody spoke for a few tense moments.

All three of us leaned closer to the screen until it opened.

J.T. said, "It looks like a lot of photos."

My hands hovered over the keyboard. "If it's okay, I'll open the most recent files first."

"Yes, ma'am."

We sorted through photos of engagements, senior pictures, sports teams, and a couple of folders of actor portfolios. "I hope this isn't a waste of time."

J.T. huffed. "It there's even one thing on here that helps catch Zarina's killer, it won't be a waste of time. I know you're getting married soon, but if you loan me your computer, I'll go through all of these files tonight and return your laptop tomorrow morning."

My breathing hitched. "I'm so sorry, J.T. I want to go through everything with you."

Marc slid his arm around my shoulders. "You've had a long day. It might be a good idea if J.T. handles this."

I leaned into Marc. "We should be here for each other. Let's keep going. Zarina had a knack for capturing sweet moments."

J.T. nodded. "So, we good?"

"Yes. Next folder."

We sifted through photos for at least twenty more minutes before hitting pay dirt. "Guys, look at that. Zarina is with Destiny Howard."

"What's so important about her?" J.T. leaned back and rubbed his eyes.

"I'm not positive, but Destiny didn't mention knowing Zarina. However, Skylar Marshall and Zarina went to photograph the house at Earth's Edge

Farmstead." My brain whirred. "Ben was there. Not Destiny. Ben told the women that Destiny had a headache and couldn't be disturbed. That's why I didn't realize Zarina and Destiny knew each other."

The apartment door opened, and I jumped back.

Theo. It was just Theo. This was his apartment.

"Dude." The short young man shut the door. "You having a party on a Sunday night? We've got to be at a worksite early tomorrow."

J.T. said, "Sorry, man. We're going through some of Zarina's pictures."

With a cocky swagger, Theo joined us. "I know Andi Grace is used to solving murders, and I'm aware Zarina was your ex-wife—"

"I still love her. Never stopped. Plus, she's the mother of my child. Her murder is my business."

"Chill. I get it." Theo looked at the computer screen, and elbowed Marc out of the way. "That's the woman I told you about. Zarina took pictures of her and the Moonbeams. Like secret pictures. That's why she stepped on the pansies. She was so focused on the people in her camera lens that she never noticed me or the flowers."

"Are you positive this is the same woman?" I watched his expression.

Theo clicked the appropriate arrow to scroll through the file. "It doesn't make much sense. Why would Zarina take all of these professional photos, but on the night she died she took secret shots?"

I looked at Theo. "There are some selfies, and they look like friends." Zarina and Destiny smiled and laughed in most of the selfies.

"Dang. That reminds me, I got an alert from an online service earlier today. It was something about picture memories from a photo sharing and printing site." J.T. searched his phone. "Zarina was good to combine an account with me so I could see the pictures she took of our daughter."

I kept my mouth shut while he swiped on his phone.

J.T.'s eyes remained glued to the screen. "The thing is, Zarina had it programmed to continually upload the photos she takes on her phone to the app. Then either one of us can order prints from the app. Hold up. Here we go." A few more taps and he held the phone out so we could view the screen.

There were lots of photos of Sarah interspersed with random shots of other people or scenery.

"Huh. Look at the dog." J.T. scratched his head with one hand while holding the phone out. "Maybe she really did want to adopt a puppy for Sarah."

"Can you zoom in or out? It almost appears to be a screenshot."

"Oh, yeah. The edit mode will allow me to go back to the original picture." He held the phone closer to his face and adjusted. "Andi Grace, you're right. It's a screenshot."

He passed the phone to me. "Looks like she copied a post from Operation Tail-wagger. Can you forward these to me? Like anything with a dog or anything that looks the least bit curious? Zarina may have left us a clue and not realized it."

"On it." He had my number. "Do you think we're done with the jump drive?"

Marc raised his hand. "Can I make a copy of the files onto the laptop? We'll delete all the photos not relevant to the case."

"Cool, cool, cool. Knock yourself out."

Marc pulled the laptop closer to where he stood at the counter and went to work. J.T. busied himself with the app and photos downloaded on it from Zarina's phone.

I faced Theo. "You doing okay today?"

He pulled bread, peanut butter, and jelly out and began to make a sandwich. "My old man's a pain. Other than that, everything's just peachy. You hungry?"

"No, but thank you. Why is your dad mad now?"

"A deputy questioned him about the murder. He's worried that you saw him arguing with Zarina and that you and the police suspect him and will never stop hounding him."

Oh. My. Goodness. "Do you think your dad murdered Zarina Mills?"

"I don't get along with my old man but I won't accuse him of murder either."

"I understand." No need to push him. The sheriff could handle it from here.

"Oh, man. Oh, man. Oh, man. You guys aren't gonna believe this." J.T. whistled and turned his phone toward us.

There was a screenshot of Destiny holding a dog that had been posted on social media. Two things jumped out at me. The woman used a different name, and there was no mention of Operation Tail-wagger.

I squeezed Marc's hand. "These pictures prove a solid link between Destiny and Zarina."

"Yeah, but it's not enough. We need motive and some actual proof if you want to accuse Destiny of murdering Zarina."

"I know, but at least we've got more than an uneasy hunch." Doubts assailed me. At some point this week, I'd need to walk away from the murder investigation. The next few days should be nothing but joy. I had a new niece, and I was about to marry Marc. My wedding week should not be shrouded in murder.

Chapter Twenty

First thing Monday morning, I called Gloria at Doc Hewitt's office. Sunny sat beside me on the couch where I nursed a cup of coffee.

Gloria answered right away. "Morning, Andi Grace. I couldn't sleep last night for thinking about the dog scam. I should've just got up, but instead I tried to make myself sleep. It was a complete waste of time. I'm more exhausted than if I'd just gotten out of bed and looked for information on the past cases."

I laughed. "Good morning to you too."

"Oh, sorry. Zach always teases me when I go off on a tangent like this."

"Gloria, are you and Doc dating?"

"I'm not comfortable saying anything yet. The man's a little skittish when it comes to women. Somebody must've really done him wrong in his past."

"Don't give up. I think you two would make a terrific couple."

"You sound like a bride-to-be, wanting everyone to be in love."

I laughed. "I can't deny it. Tell me what you're working on as far as the dog case goes."

"Hold on." Footsteps sounded, and I pictured Gloria walking across the tile floor in her flats. A door closed, more footsteps, and a squeaky chair followed. "None of our problems existed before Caleb started working here. I'm not declaring he's involved, but it can't hurt to stay alert. Here's what I've started working on today. Going back to the first surgery for Operation Tailwagger, it was a German shepherd with a broken leg. He'd been hit by a car and needed surgery. The owner was a single mother, and the dog was part of her family, not to mention her protection from an abusive boyfriend. She works for minimum wage. I believe all the pet owners are legit."

I loved all dogs, but German shepherds held a special place in my heart. "Poor thing. Where does she live?"

"Charlotte."

"It's hard to believe that there are no vets between here and Charlotte that would've given her a discount or payment plan."

Gloria cleared her throat. "Andi Grace, you of all people should understand the struggles of living on limited funds."

I hung my head. When my parents had died in a car crash years earlier, I'd given up dreams of college. Instead of heading to Athens, Georgia, I remained home and raised my siblings. If it hadn't been for many of the kindhearted residents of Heyward Beach, we might not have survived.

"You're right. Doc gave me a job that paid well, and he suggested his clients use me for pet sitting. He deserves credit for me becoming a dog walker."

"See what I mean? He only charges Operation Tail-wagger a very minimum price. In fact, he always loses money when he agrees to a treatment plan with the charity."

"I feel terrible for the woman with the German shepherd. How did she get her dog to you?"

"Operation Tail-wagger convinced a pilot to fly Winne, that's the dog's name, Winnie the Pooh. Caleb offered to meet the pilot at the airport. At the time I thought it was right nice of him to run to the airport. Now, I'm not so sure. He returned with the dog and nothing else. I called the owner and we got her consent for the surgery by faxing papers back and forth. Her name is Mary Beth Strange."

"Did she pick up Winnie later?"

"No. She couldn't take time off work. The same pilot returned to fly the dog home."

"It'd be interesting to know if the pilot got pulled into the scam, or is he part of it?" I thought about offering to assist Gloria in her research. But Marc's admonition from the night before compelled me to let Gloria handle the information gathering.

"I'm going to try to contact the airport about flight schedules. It's been a few months, but the exchange took place at the regional airport. Maybe I'll get lucky. If it'd been Charleston International Airport, I wouldn't even try."

"Gloria, thanks for taking the lead on this. Will you let me know what you find out?"

"For sure. Try to enjoy yourself this week. I've got this covered."

The call ended, and I rubbed Sunny. "It's high tide and you won't enjoy a beach walk. Let's go through the neighborhood, and if we end up at Daily Java, who cares?"

Sunny barked, because of course she understood.

I attached her harness and leash before grabbing my phone and credit card. Soon we were outside in the fresh air. Dark clouds drifted overhead. The wind blew my ponytail. Rough waves pounding the shore could be heard.

It was nearing the end of hurricane season, and I hadn't heard of any disturbances in the Atlantic. I shivered. Didn't we need a backup plan just in case of rain? Juliet had been adamant we didn't need a tent, but Marc had reminded me it was our wedding too.

If the weather turned bad, maybe we could move it inside the big house or the barn. I considered possibilities for plan B, and before I knew it the coffee shop appeared.

Perfect.

Griffin had built a little outdoor area in the shade for dogs to drink water and relax while owners got their coffee fix. I got Sunny situated. "Be right back."

There was a small line inside, and I looked around.

"Excuse me, Andi Grace." Vince Murray touched my elbow. "Do you have a minute to chat?"

"Of course, but my German shepherd is on the patio. Would you mind talking outside? Or if you want privacy, we can go to Marc's office. I'm sure he has an empty conference room available."

Vince looked around. "That might be best."

I shot a text to Marc to expect us soon, because his office manager might try to stop me from bothering Marc.

Erin said, "Good morning. What can I get you?"

"Let's go with two of your daily specials, and I see you're making dog biscuits. I'll take two of them."

"I'm trying to get approval from the county to allow dogs inside. In the meantime, dog treats are on me." She bagged up two bone-shaped treats and prepared two s'mores lattes. "Here you go."

"Thanks. Is there any chance you'd create a coffee for my wedding? Something just for Marc and me?" Sharing a wedding had good points and bad points. Mostly good, but I didn't want to lose focus on the wonderful man I was about to marry.

She patted my hand. "Let me handle it. By now, I know what you two enjoy. In fact, if you're not superstitious about the groom seeing the bride on the wedding day, I'll bring breakfast to y'all."

"Erin, you're so sweet. Thanks."

"I'll be in touch." We finished the transaction, and I turned to find Vince waiting for me at the door.

"It's a short walk." I couldn't imagine what he needed to discuss in private, but I was excited.

Chapter Twenty-one

MARC USHERED VINCE AND ME INTO A QUIET ROOM. "I'm about to begin a conference call, but make yourselves comfortable."

I handed him a cup of coffee. "The daily special."

"Su-weet." His eyes sparkled. "Thanks."

"You're welcome." I gave him a quick kiss, then he leaned in for a longer smooch.

Vince laughed. "It's easy to tell you two are about to get married. Best wishes to you."

"Thanks." With a big smile on his face, Marc left us alone.

"Let's have a seat." A stack of legal pads rested on a sideboard. Because I'd left my journal at the house, I reached for one as well as a pen. I sat cattycorner to Vince, and Sunny stretched out on the floor between us. "What would you like to discuss?"

"The pictures you showed me of Destiny made me feel like she was the same woman as Claire Rowe. As a sports reporter, I do more than report on the games. I also dig into backgrounds on athletes. I asked a buddy of mine who does crime podcasts to investigate Destiny Howard, or whatever her name is."

"Skylar Marshall is also a local reporter with her own blog and podcast. The only problem is her cousin is the sheriff."

He ran a hand through his thick gray hair. "It could also be a positive."

"Maybe. What do you propose to do?"

"I want to disguise myself and go to the farm on the pretext of adopting a puppy. Will you go with me?"

Man, did I want to return to Earth's Edge Farmstead? "How will you explain me?"

He placed his arms on the table and leaned forward. "We can say I'm in town staying at Kennady Bed-and-Breakfast and I struck up a conversation with you about adopting a dog. Naturally, you suggested Destiny's place."

His story could seem plausible or suspicious. "Before I agree to go all the way out there, make sure she's willing to meet you."

He raised a finger. "I'll call her now."

Rylee knocked on the door and gave Vince the kindest smile I'd ever seen. "Is there anything I can get you?"

Holy mackerel.

"You're nice to offer. Would it be too much to ask for a glass of water?"

"No problem at all." Her lipstick appeared fresh, and had she spritzed herself with perfume? My nose tingled at the flowery scent.

Sunny raised her head and sniffed.

"Andi Grace, anything for you?"

"Um, I good. Thanks, Rylee."

The office manager disappeared.

Vince tapped on his phone before holding it to his ear. After a pause, he grinned. "Yes, this is Hunter Grimes, and I heard you've got some Labrador puppies for sale. Would it be possible for me to come see them this morning?"

A long pause followed.

"Okay. We'll see you then." He swiped the screen and lay his phone on the table. "She said it'll be three thousand dollars per dog, and I can stop by this morning."

I gasped. "Yesterday, Ike paid less for his puppy."

"Don't tell me how much, because I'm not backing out now."

Rylee returned with a bottle of water and a napkin. "Here you go."

"I hope you don't mind, but it turns out I need to skedaddle. Do you ladies have a suggestion about a disguise?" He stood and took the water bottle from Rylee. "Thanks."

"You're welcome. There's a nice thrift shop nearby."

Marc appeared. "What's going on?"

Vince shared our plan with the others. "And now I'm off to figure out a disguise. I hope you don't mind if Andi Grace goes with me to see the pups."

"My fiancée has a mind of her own, and I just try to keep up. Rylee, you always have a nice style. Would you like to help Vince shop?"

Her face reddened, and she placed a hand on her chest. "Well, if you can spare me, I'd be happy to help."

Sunny stood and sniffed around the table.

Marc said, "Yeah. Have fun."

I glanced at my watch. "Vince, I'll take Sunny home and meet you back here. I should drive my Highlander so Destiny doesn't try to look you up by your license plate."

"Good idea. I probably need cash too."

"Are you actually going to buy a puppy?"

"I don't plan to, but you never know, and it's good to be prepared."

Rylee touched his arm. "I'll take you to my bank. The ladies there will be happy to help."

"Small-town customer service. I like it." Vince motioned for Rylee to lead the way, then he followed.

"Well, aren't you just the little matchmaker?" Marc wrapped me in his arms.

"If Rylee's happy, our lives will be much easier."

"True, but don't forget he lives around Spartanburg."

"One hurdle at a time, Mr. Williams."

"Speaking of hurdles, please tell Wade you're heading back to Destiny's farm."

I considered his request. It couldn't hurt to notify the sheriff in case I got arrested, or worse. "That's a reasonable request."

Chapter Twenty-two

VINCE MURRAY WAS BARELY RECOGNIZABLE. Not only had Rylee taken him to buy new clothes, she'd gelled his hair into a side part instead of his usually brushed-back style. He'd agreed to shave his beard and mustache, and he walked with a limp. "Your friend taped a pebble in my shoe so I'd limp consistently. After this, I'll probably have a sore hip."

"Ouch, but it's doubtful I would've thought of that. Rylee's smart." I adjusted the temperature in my Highlander. It was one of those days where I couldn't decide if I was hot or cold.

"That she is." He rubbed his freshly shaven face. "I confess that shaving was a real eye-opener. I thought I was better-looking. The beard will return."

"How old are you, Vince?"

"Fifty. I'm retired military and try to stay in good shape. No matter how many crunches, push-ups, or miles you run, you can't take away the wrinkles and scars."

"I won't mention cosmetic surgery, because you don't seem the type."

"Got that right. Instead of obsessing on my looks, I'd rather bring these people to justice who are taking advantage of animal lovers."

"I couldn't agree more." I drove us to Earth's Edge Farmstead and slowed because of the rough entrance. I kept my speed under twenty on the pothole-filled driveway. "Once Destiny sees me, she may tell us to leave."

Vince riffled the cash in his hands. "Money talks. We'll see how desperate she is."

If Destiny had murdered Zarina, what would her motive have been? Zarina had been poor and trying to start her career. Was the charity linked to the murder? Or was there a personal motive?

I parked in the grass. Clouds drifted by, but no rain yet. "I promised to text Sheriff Stone. This will only take a minute."

Vince pushed the door open. "For safety's sake, I'm telling her my name is Hunter Grimes."

"Got it."

"Thanks for humoring me." He stepped out and stretched.

Wade, I'm at Destiny Howard's farm, Earth's Edge Farmstead. It's the next county over, but if I disappear, Marc and Ike can tell you how to get here.

I tucked the phone into my jeans and followed a hobbling Vince, strike that, Hunter Grimes, to the front door of the farmhouse.

Parked in the shade was a white sports car, an SUV, and a black pickup truck. I took a deep breath. Hopefully Ben Lowe was nowhere around.

Vince rang the doorbell, and we waited.

Destiny opened the door and stepped onto the porch. Her hair was styled into a sleek topknot. "Hi, you must be Hunter. I'm Destiny Howard."

"Pleased to meetcha. This here is Andi Grace Scott. I met her at Kennady Bed-and-Breakfast. She's the one who recommended you to me when I asked where to find a dog."

Destiny did a double take, as if she hadn't even focused on me before Vince's introduction. "Yes, I know Andi Grace."

"Hi, Destiny."

"The puppies are in back." She kept her attention on Vince. "They're healthy and shots are current. That's one of the reasons I feel like three thousand dollars is a reasonable fee." She slowed her pace so Vince could keep up with her.

She described the four remaining puppies. "Why are you looking for a dog?"

"Man's best friend and all that. I haven't had a dog for the last few years, and I'm ready to try again. I lost my beagle and my wife back to back." He pounded a fist on his chest. "I was a wreck for months. Years, maybe. It's time to rejoin humanity, and I decided a dog was the answer."

I knew next to nothing about Vince, but his story made me a believer.

Destiny ran a hand along his arm. "Sweetie, I'm going to fix you right up."

We entered the back room. The momma dog and four pups were baby-gated on one side of the room. On the other side were a washer and dryer. In between was a farmhouse sink and long counter. I was impressed with the space.

Three brown dogs jumped up against the white gate, scooting it with their movements. Momma looked bored. One little dog sat in the back, by himself, all alone, and he gazed at Vince. He personified puppy-dog eyes. "I'll wait outside for you, Hunter. Take your time getting to know the dogs."

"Thanks, Andi Grace."

I left the two of them alone and meandered around the backyard. Man, if he didn't adopt the little guy in back, I'd have to come up with three thousand bucks myself. That was a ridiculous price for any puppy, especially when animal shelters housed countless animals needing forever homes. I stopped at the edge of the woods. My heart accelerated. Oh, how I wanted to check out the blue shed again.

No. It'd be reckless. I turned around and walked straight into Ben Lowe. "Ack. Sorry. I didn't expect you."

He frowned. "I bet you didn't. Thought I ran you off yesterday."

"Technically you told Marc to leave. Your wife was happy to take Ike Gage's money for his dog."

"Why are you here?"

The irritation in his voice sent chills up my arms. "One of the vacationers was looking to buy a puppy, and of course I thought about Destiny."

He grabbed my elbow and pulled me with him. "We'll just see about that."

I dug my heels into the ground and yanked my arm away. "Don't you dare touch me again. Your wife and Hunter Grimes know I'm here, and if you lay a hand on me one more time, I will be the one to call the sheriff."

He pointed in the direction of the house. "Go. It's time to clear this up."

Chapter Twenty-three

I GRITTED MY TEETH as Ben and I approached the house. He kept his eye on me, and I was afraid to reach for my phone. Yet.

If this situation went any more sideways, we might have to fight our way out of it.

Vince was fifty, and he seemed to be a young fifty. He claimed to workout. He wasn't one of those obvious muscular men, but if he did all the exercise he claimed, and he'd been in the military, he probably knew some moves to put on Ben and Destiny.

Ben reached for me again at the back porch, but I leapt away from his touch. My heart raced faster than a stallion. "Don't. You. Dare."

"You've got some nerve threatening me when you're on my property." He opened the door to the laundry room. "Destiny, we've got company. Andi Grace Scott is here."

"Yeah, she brought Hunter, er, I'm sorry. What's your last name?"

"Grimes." Vince cleared his throat. "Hunter Grimes." He lowered his voice from a tenor to more of a bass.

"Yeah, that's right." She moved to the porch and stood beside her husband. "He's in the area on vacation and asked Andi Grace where he might find a dog to adopt. She brought him here. Wasn't that nice?"

"Oh, she's a real peach." Sarcasm dripped from his voice.

How did the man have so many clients in the music business? He must have multiple personalities, and the rude person came out whenever I was around. I kept my mouth shut since we were technically on his property, and who knew if he had weapons? No need to put our lives or the puppies in danger.

"Oh, honey, be nice." Destiny swatted playfully at his arm. "She brought us a cash-paying customer."

Ben's frown disappeared. "Appreciate the business, Andi Grace."

"I've brought you customers twice this week, but I'm going to be honest. After the way you treated me today, I don't care how wonderful the puppies are, I don't feel safe coming back." I felt a wave of dizziness, probably from my rapid breathing.

Ben's phone rang, and he stepped away to take the call.

Destiny said, "I'm sorry for whatever happened, but you're not in any danger from us. We're simple people trying to make a living on my farm."

I moved to the porch and sat in a rickety rocker. "That's not exactly true.

Ben is a talent agent in the music industry, and you're a model. Did you know Zarina Mills?"

Puppies barked inside, and Vince walked out holding the dog I would've chosen. He shut the door behind him and sat beside me in another old rocker with peeling paint.

Destiny clenched her hands. "I met Zarina."

"Didn't she take pictures of you?" I was mad, and now that the dizziness had passed, I felt stronger.

"Well, um, yes. The farm is a money pit, and I'm trying to survive financially. Zarina took some pictures for a portfolio to reignite my modeling career."

"Isn't it true you two became friends?"

"I get along with everybody. So, yeah, we were friends."

Vince said, "Andi Grace, why don't you take a picture of me on your phone?"

I met his gaze and tried to decipher if there was an underlying message. "Sure."

I removed my phone and took a few shots of Vince and the dog. Then I swiped it to video mode. I placed the phone on my lap upside down so it could record our conversation without Destiny knowing it.

Vince handed the cash to Destiny. "I'm going to take this little fellow home with me. Andi Grace, I know he can't stay in my accommodations while I'm in town, but if I can secure a place with him at Stay and Play, I'd be much obliged."

"I'm happy to keep him."

Destiny fingered the money and counted it. "You've got the exact right amount, Mr. Grimes. It was a pleasure doing business with you."

"Where's Queenie?" Destiny's yellow corgi hadn't been in the laundry room.

"The puppies stress her out, so she's inside the main part of the house. The Labradors stay in the laundry room for easy access." She shoved the money into her pocket.

I nodded. "It keeps strangers from traipsing through your home, which is a safe move."

Ben rejoined us. "I need to see a client up in Myrtle Beach. Do you want to go with me, Destiny?"

"I'd love to go."

Vince stood up in slow motion. "I'll need to get in better shape to keep up with a dog."

I clutched my phone and rose. "Let me get a leash out of my car so he doesn't escape."

Ben shook his head. "Yeah, I'd hate for us to have to chase your new dog, and it'd be even worse if he made it to the highway."

I might be oversensitive when it came to Ben, but his words sounded like a threat. I jogged to the Highlander and opened the back, where I kept extra dog supplies. Grabbing a small collar, a leash, and a dog treat, I hustled back to the others.

Destiny watched as I attached the collar and leash. She never bent to tell the dog bye or give him one last pat. Odd.

We left before the other two.

Vince looked at me. "This little fellow is Hershey Bar Murray because he looks like a candy bar."

"And I bet he'll be just as sweet." I pulled onto the road. "What do you think? Is Destiny Howard the same person as Claire Rowe?"

"The hair, eyes, and coloring are different, but she can't disguise her mannerisms. Same-shaped hands and height too. They are one and the same person." He held Hershey in his lap and rubbed his head. "What happened with you and Ben?"

"He touched me in a threatening manner, and his tone was rude."

"Good thing I didn't know it before, or else I might have decked the guy."

"Aw, thanks." His words settled my fear down a bit. "What's your next plan?"

"I want to expose the truth. They can't continue to steal money from good people who want to help others. I just need to find a way to safely carry out a plan of action. What about you?"

I didn't want to put Vince in more danger, so I didn't reveal all I knew. "Getting married and solving Zarina's murder are my top priorities this week."

Chapter Twenty-four

I PULLED INTO DOC HEWITT'S CLINIC PARKING LOT. Hershey snoozed peacefully in Vince's lap, and I suspected the man had dozed off as well. It'd been a quiet ride, and it was a relief not to deal with a carsick dog. "Vince, we're here."

He straightened and looked around. "Sorry about that. Some copilot I am."

"You're great. I juggled clues in my mind, making it a quick trip."

"All right. I'm going to have Hershey checked out, then I'll look for John. I drove him over this morning before I ran into you at the coffee shop. If I know my friend, he's hunkering down until Scout is released."

I drummed my thumbs on the steering wheel. "You're going to need a ride back to your car. So I'll pop in and say hi to Gloria. If you're not ready to leave when I am, then call me later and I'll come back."

"Thanks for your help today."

"We made a good team. I hope Hershey gets a glowing health report from Doc."

"Me, too." He hopped out of my SUV and entered the vet clinic with Hershey still in his arms.

I texted Marc and Wade that I was okay. Next, I tried to call Lacey Jane, but it went to voicemail. "Hey, it's me. How are y'all doing? How's David? Lizzy? I want to bring you dinner one night this week. Maybe I can even hold Lizzy while you and David eat. Okay, I love you. Bye."

I inspected my face in the rearview mirror. It wouldn't hurt to run a brush through my hair and redo my ponytail. May as well add lipstick too. I freshened my appearance before going to look for Gloria.

Even though I'd stood up to him, the encounter with Ben left me a little shaky. Once inside, Doc's receptionist waved me back, and I found Gloria in her office.

Her eyes widened when she saw me, and she motioned for me not to speak.

I nodded.

She picked up her cell phone, and we retraced the steps I'd just taken but continued walking to the far end of the parking lot. "Andi Grace, somebody broke into my office this morning."

I gasped. "Are you okay?"

She wrung her hands. "Yes, but they rooted around my desk. It wasn't trashed, and you might not even notice it'd been searched. But I know how I left things. I stayed late last night and had put together a file of information on what I believe may be going on with the dogs and their surgeries. I printed off a copy and locked it in my top drawer."

"Let me guess. It's gone."

"Yes." Her voice warbled.

"Did you make a backup of the file on your computer?"

"Again, yes. Like a big dummy, my password isn't very strong. The person got onto my computer. The file disappeared."

"Gloria, don't blame yourself." I rubbed her shoulder. "It could've happened to anyone."

"But it happened to me. You trusted me to help stop Operation Tailwagger from taking money from innocent people. Now the file is gone."

"We can search the computer's trash can. Or maybe it's still on the cloud."

"Oh, I didn't think of that. Although, to be honest, I'm not sure how to access my cloud. Is it through Windows? Google? Or what?"

Oh, boy. "Let's see what we're working with. Can you get me onto your computer?"

"That's another problem. Caleb is working today."

"Right, and you believe he's involved."

"Caleb is the one who brought the charity to Zach's attention." She crossed her arms.

"I remember. Is there a way to get him out of the office?"

"Not without tipping him off."

"Okay, but if he took the paper file and wiped the document off your computer, he's probably already aware you're investigating him."

Gloria lifted her chin. "Investigating? I like that word."

"The problem is you might be in danger."

"Surely not." She tugged her gold necklace and even wrapped it around her pointer finger.

"Think about it. Say Caleb is part of the scheme to make money off people and their sick and dying pets. Take it a step farther, and say it's been profitable. If he discovers you're investigating him, and he worries the scheme is about to end, who is he going to be mad at?"

"Me," she whispered and tugged her finger out of the necklace. "I was concerned the bad guys would move to another scam before we caught them in this."

A sports car pulled into the parking lot and stopped by the front door instead of parking like Doc's normal clients. The driver tooted the horn. It was Destiny Howard.

Soon, Caleb exited the building with a black poodle. He helped the dog into the car and chatted with Destiny.

Gloria said, "I don't want Caleb to see us together. Let's get in my car."

We crept to Gloria's white sedan and slumped into the seats.

I watched the interaction between Caleb and Destiny. Finally, he stepped back and waved until the car exited the property. Caleb looked around before going back into the clinic.

"Andi Grace." Gloria's trembling hands held a piece of notebook paper. "Look. It was on the dash."

Mind you own business.

"I'm calling the sheriff now. It's not safe."

"No. Wait a second. I want us to look for my research before the authorities confiscate my computer and freeze my account or whatever they'd do."

I considered her request. Doc, John, and Vince were all in the building. None of the men would allow Caleb to harm us. "Okay, but we need to make sure somebody knows we're in your office."

"Oh, dear. Not Zach. He doesn't have a poker face."

"You know what, Vince is still in his disguise. Let me call him." I dialed the number.

"Hello."

"Vince, it's Andi Grace. Have you signed in?"

"Yes, why?"

"Drat. Caleb is Doc's resident, and it's possible he's linked to Destiny."

"Good thing I checked in as Hunter Grimes with my puppy. It probably sounds paranoid, but I didn't want to tip my hand."

"Smart man. Destiny was just here. I'm going to be in Gloria's office. Please, don't leave without me." Although I was his official ride to town.

"I've got your back." He disconnected.

"If you weren't sweet on Doc, that Vince Murray would be a good catch."

"I'm ignoring you. What about this paper?"

"We should take pictures of it with both of our phones then hide it under the seat until we call the sheriff. No need to advertise the fact to Caleb, or whoever the culprit is, that you've seen the threat."

Chapter Twenty-five

GLORIA ASKED the veterinary clinic's receptionist to make her a copy of the security tapes, but she didn't tell the young woman her office had been entered.

My list of suspects for the dog scam were Destiny and Caleb. My suspects for Zarina's murder were Destiny and Marvin Graves. In the past, I'd always had more suspects. This time I'd already ruled out J.T. It could be a record for me removing a person of interest from my list, but he'd convinced me of his love for Zarina. He'd become a better person through counseling and prayer.

We walked down the hall and almost reached Gloria's office, when Caleb popped out of an exam room. "Ladies, what's happening?"

My heart leapt, but I tried to act nonchalant. "I brought y'all a new client today."

"Oh, thanks, Andi Grace. Hershey?"

"Yes, his new owner is vacationing in the area and asked me about adopting a pet. I took him to a farm a little closer to Charleston."

"Really?"

"Yeah, it's called Earth's Edge Farmstead. Destiny Howard runs the place. Maybe you know her?"

"It doesn't sound familiar."

Give Caleb a gold star for his performance. "Okay."

"I mean, why would you think I'd know her?"

I shrugged but found it curious he didn't drop the subject. "You're about to become a veterinarian, and she raises and sells puppies. If you don't know her yet, I bet you'll cross paths one day, especially if you stay in this area."

"Destiny Howard, you say? I'll keep her name in mind." He smiled, but from the sound of jangling metal, he fidgeted with the keys in the pocket of his khakis.

Gloria said, "We should get to work. Caleb, see you around."

"Later, ladies." Hands in his pockets, he strolled away from us.

I followed Gloria into her office and shut the door. "What do you think?"

"The boy's up to something, but I'm not sure what. Plus, there's nothing I can prove at this point."

I pointed at her desk. "Do you want me to see if I can recover any of your notes on Operation Tail-wagger?"

"That'd be wonderful. If anyone questions me on why I was organizing notes, my answer will be for tax purposes. Don't you think that sounds legitimate?"

"Very plausible." I sat in her ergonomic office chair. "This is nice. I wish I'd put one of these on my wedding registry. What's your password to log onto this computer."

"A-B-C."

"I've heard worse. Later, we'll create something stronger." I logged on and began a search in the recycle bin.

The receptionist entered the office and handed a drive to Gloria.

The next few minutes were tense as I launched a desperate search for the missing files.

My phone vibrated, and I glanced over to where it sat on the desk. "Oh, that's Marc. I should take it."

"Fine, hon. Let's switch places so I can pull up the security tapes."

I moved around the desk and answered the call. "Hi, honey. What's up?"

"The DNA test results are in. Chris and Carol want me to go with them so we can learn the results together."

"I'm coming."

"I'm already in the truck. Where are you?"

"Doc Hewitt's clinic."

"On the way." The call ended.

I wanted answers to Operation Tail-wagger, but Marc needed me. He'd been so good to support my desire to solve mysteries. Today was too important to lose focus on him. "Gloria, I've got to run."

"Look here real quick." She angled the computer screen so I could see better. "Whoever broke into my office wore a disguise."

A person dressed in black and wearing a hoodie walked down the hall and looked over his, or her, shoulder, then entered Gloria's office. "Please, call Sheriff Stone. He needs to see this."

"I think it'd be easier to go visit him."

"Be sure to take the threatening note."

"Yes. You're exactly right."

"I'll walk you to your car."

Gloria gathered her belongings and the computer drive.

"Why don't you take the laptop too? Maybe he can help get on your cloud."

"Good idea." Gloria grabbed the computer then locked the door.

"Um, Hunter Grimes needs a ride to Stay and Play. I guess I could loan him my SUV." I kept my voice loud in case Caleb spied on us.

"Doc probably wouldn't mind giving him a ride. Let's ask."

I knew Vince's vehicle was at Daily Java, but I didn't want to tip off Caleb. We found the men and came up with a plan to get Vince and John to their vehicle.

When we left, goose bumps popped up on my arms. Doc Hewitt's animal hospital had always felt like home. Never, before today, had I felt uneasy on this property. Operation Tail-wagger had to be brought down.

Chapter Twenty-six

Country music played in Marc's truck as we cruised along the highway toward Charleston. We hadn't discussed the DNA results yet because he'd been on a business call. I'd even taken over driving so he could take notes on the conversation. At last, he ended the call, and I gave him a few minutes to collect his thoughts.

"Thanks for driving."

"Sure." I smiled but kept my eyes on the road. "What do you think the results will be?"

"I believe my dad favored Chris, but it could also be wishful thinking. They truly believe we're related, and it's hard to imagine they're trying to scam me. We'll know soon enough."

Scam artists came in all shapes, sizes, and ages. As bad as Operation Tail-wagger was, this couple would be worse if they were trying to pull something on Marc. My fiancé was intelligent, but a desire for family was his weak spot. "Are we meeting them at the test site?"

He ran a hand over his face and sighed. "Yeah. It's on this side of the city. We should be there in under twenty minutes."

"No matter what the results are, I'm on your side." I gave his hand a quick squeeze before turning my attention back to the road.

My thoughts drifted to the murder. I'd never heard Zarina speak about her brother before the day of her murder. According to her, Zeke Mills lost everything to a scammer, including his wife. She hadn't seen her brother in five years. Was it possible he'd have a reason to do harm to Zarina?

My photographer friend had provided useful clues in another murder investigation. She was nosy, but so was I. No wonder we had gotten along.

Marc directed me to the office in a strip mall, and I parked. "I need to send Skylar Marshall a quick text. I'm going to ask her to investigate Zarina's brother's life. I only have two suspects for her murder—"

"Who exactly?"

"Destiny Howard and Marvin Graves." I retrieved my phone from my purse. "Operation Tail-wagger has been a distraction, unless there's a connection."

"After seeing the pictures J. T. Green shared, I'd imagine it's possible."

"Exactly." I sent a text to Skylar. "Okay, I'm ready."

There was an older couple in the waiting room, and Marc introduced me to Carol and Chris Williams. Carol informed the receptionist we were all together, and we were taken back to an office with a large desk and four chairs on one side.

A slim Black man, wearing black slacks, a crisp white shirt, and a red bow tie, entered and greeted us. He sat at his desk then glanced at his computer. "We can review the science behind the testing or get right down to the results."

I reached for Marc's hand.

He intertwined his fingers with mine. "I believe we're all good with the science. How about telling us what you found?"

Chris nodded. His blue eyes stood out in his tanned face. White hair put an emphasis on the eyes. Marc's eyes were grayer. If the results showed a relationship, Marc had inherited someone else's eyes. Chris said, "I agree."

Carol and I also nodded but didn't speak.

The man's name tag indicated we were dealing with Noah Jones. He slid two files across the table. "You'll see there is a clear relationship between the three of you. Marc has—"

Carol whimpered. "Oh, I knew it. Marc, I'm so sorry it took us this long to connect with you."

Chris placed a hand on his wife's shoulder. "We've got a lot of making up to do."

Tears and laughter filled the next few minutes along with hugs and kisses. Chris and Carol together hugged Marc for so long, I reached for the tissue box on Noah's desk and blotted my tears. When Noah suggested we move our visit to a coffee shop down the way, we left him.

The next couple of hours were filled with giddy discussions of how to spend time together after the honeymoon.

Carol said, "We're going to find a real estate agent near Heyward Beach and live the remainder of our lives there. Kentucky is too far away. Who knows, maybe we can even lend a hand with our future great-grand-children?"

I laughed. "We'd love to have you live nearby." Marc and I hadn't discussed children beyond knowing we wanted kids.

Marc pulled out a business card and wrote something on the back. "Here's the name of a reputable agent. No pressure, but if you're serious, I can help you in the process. There's also a nice retirement community up the road."

Chris took the card. "That could be the right direction. We're not getting any younger."

Carol elbowed her husband. "Speak for yourself. Although to be fair, I've had my share of health issues. If we can find a place close to Heyward Beach, I'll look."

"I'm glad to hear it." Marc met my gaze, and I nodded. "We'd like to invite you to our wedding. It's this Saturday, and it's a double wedding with Andi Grace's brother and his fiancée."

Carol cried again. "Thank you, Marc, and of course, thank you too, Andi Grace. We'll be there. I won't promise not to cry, because sometimes happiness just spills out."

Marc went over logistics with them for the rehearsal dinner, the wedding, and a place to stay closer to Heyward Beach.

My phone vibrated, and I glanced down. There were several missed calls from Skylar. She could wait until the ride home. The visit with Marc's grandparents was too special to spoil with a conversation about Zarina's murder.

Chapter Twenty-seven

By the time we returned to Heyward Beach, it was nearing suppertime. We took the dogs for a walk on the beach. They needed the exercise, and I'd spent too much time sitting today. The ocean breeze felt good against my skin. Fresh air and plenty of space to walk. It wasn't too hot or too cold, and the beach wasn't crowded. A family played bocce ball, and a few teens surfed the big waves. Other than that, it was only Marc, me, and the dogs.

"Do you think a storm is brewing? Maybe I shouldn't have agreed with Juliet about the tent."

Marc looked out to sea. "There's a tropical disturbance, but it's not been named a storm or hurricane yet. Tomorrow, I'm going to order a tent in case it rains."

"Wait a minute. Let's not upset Juliet. There must be a reason for her insistence on not spending the money."

"It's you I'm concerned about. Renting shelter is one less thing you need to worry about."

"Don't forget the barn. It can be our backup plan."

"We'll need a crew to turn Stay and Play into a wedding venue."

Chubb barked, and Marc threw a ball for him to chase. The golden retriever sprinted after the rubber ball.

"You're right, but I bet Nate will convince his work crew to help. Belle's bandmates might jump in too. Speaking of Belle, I heard from Skylar."

"When?" Chubb returned with the ball, and Marc threw it again.

Sunny stuck to my side, content with our slower pace. "She and I were texting, then I called her from the house while changing clothes. The sheriff confirmed Zeke, Zarina's brother, works for a soup kitchen up in Myrtle Beach. He was at the shelter Thursday night and has an alibi."

"Good to know. What else?" Chubb ran into a wave, dropped his ball, found it, and raced back to us. He shook and sprayed us all with salt water.

"She heard a rumor about Lincoln and financial trouble."

Marc rolled his head back. "What'd you tell her?"

"Nothing, but she was digging for dirt. She mentioned Ben Lowe in connection to Lincoln."

"Thanks for keeping quiet. I need to talk to Linc."

"Then it's a good thing we walked in the direction of his house."

He wrapped his arm around my shoulders and we continued walking. "Something tells me you planned our route."

"I knew you'd want to talk to him when you heard about Skylar."

"Let's roll." Marc texted his friend to warn him we were on the way.

Not many of the walkways from the beach to homes contained security gates, but there was only one Lincoln Zane, country music star. It'd be careless not to protect himself and his daughter. Marc tapped the code in, and we met Lincoln on the deck.

"Hey, guys. I'm grilling chicken because Belle is craving chicken Caesar salad. Care to join us for dinner?" Lincoln stood beside his Weber charcoal grill. One hand was fisted on his hip and the other held a set of grilling tongs.

Chubb barked then stretched out next to the rail.

Marc gave his friend a manly hug. "We won't intrude, but I wanted to tell you a couple of things. First, according to the DNA tests, Chris and Carol Williams are my grandparents."

Lincoln whooped. "That calls for a celebration."

"Thanks, but there's something else. Skylar Marshall is a local reporter, and Sheriff Stone is her cousin. She recently moved to our area, and she told Andi Grace she learned something about you and Ben Lowe."

"For crying out loud." Lincoln ran a hand through his hair and looked at the ground.

Sunny walked to Lincoln and rubbed against his legs. My German shepherd often sensed distress and was eager to offer comfort.

Lincoln knelt and stroked her sides. "What'd you tell her, Andi Grace?"

"Nothing of value. She knows we're friends, and I know you don't want Belle to get involved with Ben, but I didn't mention that to Skylar. Is there anything you'd like me to say? You know, like divert her attention in another direction without lying?"

Marc reached for the tongs and turned the chicken while Lincoln continued to pet Sunny.

"Thanks for the offer, Andi Grace. Maybe I should talk to her, but I honestly don't know what I'd say."

"Ben threatened to call the law on me when we visited the farm for Ike to adopt a puppy. If you tell the reporter anything, you'll need to be very cautious what you say." Marc looked from the meat to his friend. "As your attorney, I'd advise against speaking to any reporter about Ben Lowe."

Lincoln stood. "Of course you're right. I usually avoid the press."

I snapped my fingers for Sunny to come closer to me, and I gave her a treat. "Then why would you consider speaking to a reporter about Ben, especially if it could harm you down the road?"

His gaze met mine. "To warn other musicians about the slimeball. He has all kinds of tricks to separate you from your earnings. He's sly as a fox. In case a singer can learn something from me, maybe I should agree to an interview. There are plenty of unscrupulous talent agents preying on young and inexperienced singers and songwriters. If Marc hadn't alerted me the other night, Belle and the Moonbeams could've been the next victims."

"Hey, I heard my name. You guys surely have better things to discuss than me." Belle joined us on the deck carrying her schnoodle in her arms. Lady was a cutie.

"Honey, the chicken is almost ready." Lincoln walked over and kissed the top of her head.

"Great. I'm starved, but why were you talking about me?" Belle wore her thick dark hair loose, and she propped one bare foot on her other leg.

I said, "We were discussing the talent agent Ben Lowe."

"Oh, Daddy. I meant to tell you, Ben approached the boys and tried to make a deal behind my back. Luckily, they knew you wouldn't let me sign with him. And they're smart enough to realize it's better to stick with me." She raised a hand. "Before you ask, none of the guys told them who I really am."

"Good."

"Do I have time to shower and change before we eat?"

"Sure do." Lincoln manned the grill. Once his daughter disappeared into the beach house, he turned to Marc. "I won't say anything to Skylar about Ben."

"Glad to hear it, buddy. We'll get out of your hair now. Have a good evening."

"Yeah. You, too."

Marc and I took Sunny and Chubb and walked home. I poured food into the dog bowls and gave them fresh water.

Marc said, "I'm really proud of you for letting other people help solve Zarina's murder."

"Thanks. I don't feel on top of this investigation, but that's okay. There are plenty of other issues I want to focus on this week."

"One issue doesn't need to be food. I placed an order at Tony's Pizzeria, and Tony assured me he'd be at the wedding."

My heart warmed. Tony had watched out for me from the day my parents died. Doc had given me a job, and Tony made sure we always had food. "If Ike wasn't in our lives, I probably would've asked Tony to give me away. Oh, should I have asked your grandfather?"

Marc's eyes grew wide. "No, you just met him today. You and Ike have a relationship, and it makes more sense to involve him."

"Okay. Good. While we wait for food, should we discuss the murder investigation?"

"Sounds like a plan."

Chapter Twenty-eight

Sunny nudged me awake. I blinked, and when my German shepherd came into focus, sat up. "Good morning."

My phone buzzed, and I reached for it. "Oh, no. I've missed calls from Marc, Gloria, Belle, and Juliet. When I oversleep, I really do it right. You probably need to go outside."

She barked and moved to the hall but waited for me.

I followed her down the stairs and outside, only pausing to grab a Coke out of the refrigerator. Sunny headed for her favorite spot, and I sat down and called Marc first. "Good morning, sweetie."

"Good morning. I wanted to give you a heads-up. Chris and Carol somehow convinced Juliet to let them stay at Kennady Bed-and-Breakfast this week."

"Wow. Are you okay with that?" I gulped. "I mean, we knew they were coming to Heyward Beach to be closer to the activities. But at the farm they'll be right there for everything."

"They keep saying they want to make up for lost time, and their actions match their words. It's cool by me."

Man, I wished Marc was right here so I could read his expression. "Okay, but like you keep telling me, this is your wedding too."

He chuckled. "Touché."

"Anything else?"

"No, I've got a client waiting in the conference room, so I better get at it. I love you."

"Love you too, Marc."

I sipped my Coke and dialed Belle.

"Hey, Andi Grace. Thanks for calling me back. That woman from Thursday night, Destiny Howard, sent me a private message on social media. She asked again if I was interested in adopting a puppy. She said she knows I work at Stay and Play and thinks I should adopt one of her dogs or at least help her find a good owner. Isn't it creepy that she researched me? Thank goodness I haven't posted pictures of Dad and me. I don't think she's figured out who I am."

"Take a breath. Did you answer her?"

"No, but what if she comes out here? It freaked me out how pushy she is. I'm still a kid. She needs to find her own people to buy the puppies. But you know what? Maybe I should buy the puppies just to make sure they're safe.

Oh, and what about the mother? Maybe I should buy all the dogs. Dad would probably loan me the money, but it's doubtful he'd let me bring them all home."

I'd never heard Belle so hyper. "Did you tell your dad?"

"Not yet. He might blow a gasket."

"How about you call him, and I can let Sheriff Stone know about the situation."

She gasped. "Do you think I'm in danger?"

"No. Between the bed-and-breakfast and Stay and Play, there are lots of people around. Still, it can't hurt to tell the sheriff." I paused for her to answer, but there was only silence. "If you're not comfortable with that, at least let me tell Nate. I bet somebody is around from his crew. It'd be smart for them to keep their eyes open for strangers."

"Okay, that sounds good."

"Promise me you'll tell your dad."

"Yes, ma'am."

The call ended, and I went inside to fix a bowl of fruit and yogurt. There was a lot to accomplish today, but I'd learned skipping breakfast wasn't a good option for me.

While eating, I texted Nate about the situation with Belle.

A low continuous barking drew me away from the phone and to the backyard. Sunny wasn't happy about something.

"Hey, girl."

Sunny stood at the back gate and continued her aggressive barking. Her upright body leaned forward. Quick low barks.

Chills zipped up my spine.

I ran into the house and called the sheriff. "Wade, I think someone's trying to get into my backyard."

"I can hear Sunny, and I'm close by. Give me a minute." Sirens sounded as soon as the call ended.

I returned to my dog, who'd transitioned to a warning growl.

"Good girl. You scared away the bad people. Let's go inside and get you a delicious breakfast." Sunny glanced at me.

The sirens grew louder.

An engine started, and tires squealed.

At last, Sunny's posture relaxed. She trotted to me, and we went into the kitchen. I poured her new fancy food into a bowl and refilled her water. "You're such a good girl."

The doorbell rang.

"It's probably Wade." I hurried to answer, and Sunny matched my pace. I opened the door to the sheriff.

Woof, woof. Sunny's mid-tone greeting assured me she'd recovered from the previous danger. My dog returned to the kitchen.

"Hi, Wade. Sorry to bother you." I waved him in.

He held up a hand. "I passed a black truck on your street. It was a woman driver who was going too fast, at least until she saw me. If you're okay, I'm going to look for her."

"I'm fine. Thanks." I locked the door and ran upstairs to find my murder journal.

Why would anyone try to get in the back? Was it a scare tactic, or did they mean to harm me? And why?

My investigation into Zarina's death was going nowhere fast.

Except, Wade said a woman was driving a truck. Destiny Howard had a black pickup truck at her farm. Destiny had also contacted Belle earlier today. If she'd wanted to speak to me, why not ring the front doorbell?

There was a connection between Destiny and Zarina, and there seemed to be a strong possibility Destiny might be involved in Operation Tail-wagger.

Was it possible Destiny was involved with both? If I knew the motive, it'd be much easier to catch the killer.

Chapter Twenty-nine

AFTER GETTING READY FOR THE DAY, I left Sunny at home to rest after her active morning as my security guard. I drove to Doc's clinic and knocked on Gloria's office door.

Doc opened it. "Andi Grace, this is a nice surprise. Shouldn't you be doing wedding stuff?"

I hugged him. "As long as the weather cooperates, we're doing fine."

Gloria gave me a little wave from where she sat.

Doc stuffed his hands into the pockets of his khakis. "I wouldn't worry too much about the disturbance out in the Atlantic."

"I'm trying not to let it bother me."

"Smart girl. I've got a cat to see. You and Gloria stay out of trouble." His tone was serious, and the sparkle in his eyes dimmed.

"We'll be careful, Doc."

He walked out and closed the door.

Gloria said, "Deputy Harris helped retrieve my files from the cloud. She has a copy but told me the department is focused on Zarina's murder. She'll look at my information the first chance she gets."

I sat across from her. "We can't ask for more than that."

She slid a manilla envelope across the desk. "This copy is for you. Doc has a copy in his safe, and I have one in a locked file cabinet. It's a crying shame that someone took what should've been a good deed and turned it into their evil gain."

"Yeah, I agree. Is there information on Destiny Howard in here?"

"Some."

"I'm going to look harder into her life." Gloria had already received a threat. I wouldn't share anything that would endanger her more. "Did you feel safe last night?"

Her face reddened. "I was frightened, and Zach insisted I stay in his guest room. I packed a bag and once I got to his house, all the anxiety left me. Andy and Barney, Zach's Boykin spaniels, slept in my room."

"That was nice of Doc." I reached for the envelope. "Thanks for this."

"You're welcome. We need to get to the bottom of the scam, but I understand solving a murder comes first." Gloria stood. "I'll walk you out."

A frenzy of barking sounded from the reception area, and I quickened my steps in case I could help. A glimpse through the door revealed Destiny Howard. "You won't believe who is here."

Gloria scooted around me. "Well, well, well. What do you know?"

I folded the envelope and stuffed it in the back of my jeans and fluffed my T-shirt over it before joining the ruckus.

"M.D. has no energy." Destiny practically yelled at the receptionist to be heard over the three remaining puppies.

I reached for one of the leashed puppies. "Did you say the mom's name is Maddie?"

Her eyes widened in surprise, but she handed me all three leashes. "No. M.D. for Momma Dog."

Gloria squatted beside the chocolate Labrador curled up in front of an empty chair. She ran a hand along her side. "She may be dehydrated and malnourished. Best let Doc Hewitt examine her."

Destiny held Queenie, her yellow corgi. "Can he check on Queenie, too? Plus, she needs her nails trimmed."

The receptionist picked up the phone and communicated with someone.

Caleb appeared, but his steps faltered the moment he appeared to realize Destiny was the client. "Um, how can I help?"

A strange look passed between the two of them.

"Queenie needs a checkup. I haven't been happy with her last veterinarian and decided to give Dr. Hewitt a try."

"Okay. Does she have any conditions we need to be aware of? Thyroid? Heart issues?"

Destiny passed the corgi to him and explained her desire to the last detail. "Can I trust you with my best friend?"

"Yes, ma'am. I'll make sure Queenie is well taken care of." Caleb's dark hair appeared windblown, and his shirt was wrinkled, as if he'd slept in it.

Gloria said, "I think Momma Dog needs to be seen first, but we can take both of them back."

"I'd prefer Queenie be seen first." Destiny's whiny voice grated on my nerves.

Caleb mumbled his response.

The coworkers headed to the exam rooms, and Destiny turned to me. "We need to talk." She raised her voice to be heard over the Labs.

"The puppies are upsetting the other animals. Why don't we take them outside?" The two I had snipped at each other and tried to run in circles around my legs.

"Fine by me." She stalked to the door, but at least had the grace to hold it open until the puppies and I made it outside. "Andi Grace, you need to find homes for these pups. They're driving me crazy."

Of all the things I'd imagine Destiny might say, this wasn't on my radar. "Say what?"

"I need you to sell the Lab puppies for me."

"I don't sell animals. Never have. Never will." I returned the leashes to her and left. If Destiny had created a scheme to find a sucker to sell her dogs, she'd need to find someone else.

Chapter Thirty

ON MY WAY TO STAY AND PLAY, Gloria called to tell me Destiny had hung notices on Doc's community bulletin board. Puppies for sale. No prices listed, but a phone number was provided. I double-checked the number, and it belonged to Destiny.

Upon entering the barn, I searched for Belle.

She was in a pen, playing with Bo and Pinky.

I observed before speaking. "Belle, did you tell your dad about Destiny?"

"Yeah. He's coming over later this afternoon to go over the sound system for the wedding. After that, he'll follow me home to make sure I'm safe. He's trying to write a new song today but said for me to call if anything else happens."

"If Bo is here, does that mean Nate's working around the farm?"

"Yes, ma'am." She gave each dog a treat and rubbed their heads.

"By the way, I ran into Destiny at Doc's animal clinic. She wants me to sell her dogs, and I declined."

Belle snickered. "She is one wackadoodle."

"Yep. Best for you to steer clear of her. I'll be in my office if you need me."

"Thanks."

I pulled a cold Coke out of the mini fridge and reviewed the work schedule at Stay and Play for the next two weeks. Sunny and Chubb were staying here while we honeymooned. Juliet and Nate weren't taking a honeymoon for a while in order to save money. After assuring myself everything was organized, I opened the envelope Gloria had given me earlier.

Starting from the top, I began to call the families selected by Operation Tail-wagger. Every person had a similar story, and I took notes on them all.

Either a tall, slender woman or a thin man had worked with the families to get the needed surgeries. Never had a family member reached out to Operation Tail-wagger. Instead, they'd all been approached with an offer of assistance. The recipients were overjoyed there was a way to save their beloved pets.

My phone vibrated with a text from Juliet. *Come to the kitchen.*

I quit making calls and jogged to the house.

A vehicle rumbled over the driveway from the front of the house.

Juliet met me on the back porch. "Thanks for coming. Your hair needs attention."

I pulled my ponytail to the front and studied the follicles. "You're right. There are some split ends."

"Come on. You're due for a trim, and I want to give you some subtle highlights." Before Juliet took over running Kennady Bed-and-Breakfast, she'd been a beautician. She linked her arm in mine and steered me toward her living quarters. It was a glorified suite attached to the main house. She was there for guests but had separation for privacy. "Don't try to argue with me. You want to look beautiful on your wedding day."

"Hey, I was right in the middle of a project, but you're right. Thanks for thinking of me, but what about you?"

"I've got a friend coming over from Georgetown. It's a splurge, but, oh well, I think it'll be worth it." She opened the door to her suite, where she'd already set up a place for me to sit.

"I should pay you for today, then you can afford to pay your friend." I sat in the chair.

"It's not the same. You're my best friend." She draped a cape around my shoulders and snapped it around my neck.

"I appreciate it." Money was a touchy subject with most people, but Juliet and I had survived many lean times together. "Remember when we used to eat peanut butter and jelly sandwiches?"

"Day after day we ate them. When the day-old-bread store was in town, we must've been their best customers." She brushed my hair and mixed up some concoction.

"That store always smelled good." I smiled at the memory. "Are you having any money issues because of the wedding? It doesn't seem fair that you've closed this week to paying customers."

"It seemed important to focus on the wedding. Oh, by the way, Chris and Carol Williams are here. I made an exception for them." She sectioned my hair, folded a foil into place, and painted the strand with the lightening solution.

"Thanks. What do you think of them?"

"They're sweet. The love they feel for each other is genuine, and I hope Nate and I are as in love as they are when we're eighty."

"Girl, you've loved my brother even when he was too shy to make a move. I've never seen him so happy and confident. There's no doubt in my mind your love will last."

"He does make me happy." She patted my shoulder. "Chris and Carol have faced some bumps in the road, but they want to be around for Marc for the rest of their lives. None of us have a big family. I hope you two can open your hearts to them."

My friend was right. When my parents had died, there was nobody to raise my siblings, except for me or the government. I was happy to do it, but Marc hadn't been as lucky. He'd been a child when his parents and younger sister were killed in a car accident. A fireman had saved him, and foster care had raised him. "It's all so new and sudden. Unexpected even. After the honeymoon, we'll get to know them better. Have you and Nate discussed your honeymoon?"

"We've been meaning to talk to you and Marc, but there always seems to be something else happening."

I laughed. "Yeah. Murders. Births. Long-lost grandparents. What's on your mind?"

"Nate and I have discussed ways to improve the bed-and-breakfast. Instead of being a place to stay when you're in the area, we'd like to find ways to make it more of a destination. We've done little things toward reaching our goal, but we want to do more. The river is on our border, and we hardly utilize it at all. Nate wants to either sell Nate's Landscaping and Design or hire someone to run it for him. That would give him time to devote to growing this business."

It made sense that Nate would want to sink his roots into the farm instead of running all over the Low Country to make beautiful landscapes for other families.

Juliet said, "We heard about a family who wants to sell a cottage on Heyward Beach. We'd only need to come up with the money to move it here."

I thought about the two-lane road leading to the farm. "Will it fit on River Road?"

"Nate talked to a company who has done this before. Once they get the permits, the front porch and back deck will need to be taken off. Then there are some issues about announcing our intent to move the house and traffic delays and blah, blah, blah. Nate is so excited, and I am too, but the logistics make my head swim."

Juliet was all about beauty and lofty goals. She cared about money, but she was artistic. "If Nate believes it can be done, what are you waiting for?"

"Do you mind if we expand?"

"It's your land, and I'm all for you growing your business." Our conversation solved the mystery of Juliet's finances.

"Thanks. We want to make good financial decisions now in hopes it'll pay off in the long run." She finished the last section and set a timer. "I'll be right back."

My thoughts drifted from the wedding, to the farm, to the murder. A flash of movement outside caught my attention, and I figured it was Juliet. When she didn't appear, I texted her. *Where are you?*

Be right back with cookies.

Hmm. Whoever I'd seen, it wasn't Juliet. Maybe it'd been Belle or Melanie outside with one of the dogs.

Juliet appeared with a plate of cookies and two water bottles. "Oatmeal raisin. Carol asked if she could help me bake cookies. She said this had been her son's favorite, and she wanted to make a batch for Marc."

"She really is trying."

"Come on over to the sink. You can eat after I rinse your hair." The timer beeped, and she pushed the button. "Perfect timing."

An hour later, I walked outside with a lighter shade of hair, a new style, and a bounce in my step. "Thanks, Juliet. I always forget how good it feels to get my hair done."

"You're welcome. I'll talk to you later." She hugged me and walked toward the kitchen entrance.

I headed to Stay and Play until spotting a woman in the distance near the trees. Her head was bent down as if she was looking for a treasure. It didn't take much time to realize who was treasure hunting on our farm. Destiny Howard.

Chapter Thirty-one

"Destiny, what are you doing?" I kept my voice calm despite my anger.

She squealed and jumped back. "You startled me."

"This isn't your property, and your husband was quick to threaten us when we were at your farm. Before I call the sheriff, do you want to explain what you're doing?"

"I'd like for you to reconsider taking the dogs. I can't do anything with them."

"They're just puppies. You can pay me to train them." After all her shenanigans, I'd take the Labs just to prevent them from suffering at her hands, but I wanted to see how the situation might play out. "I know you can afford it because you just sold two dogs."

Her shoulders hunched, and she pointed her finger at me. "You have no idea what I can afford. The farm is bleeding me dry instead of being an opportunity to make money as my own boss."

"Then why do you want to give the last three puppies to me when you could make a few thousand off selling them?"

"They are putting a strain on my marriage." She pouted. "You've got to help me."

"Listen, I don't have to help you do anything. If I take the puppies, I'll find good homes for them. Free of charge. There will be no money exchanged between the two of us, and I'll want Momma Dog."

"Do you plan to pay her vet bill?"

She was really pushing it, but I knew I'd end up paying to get Momma Dog checked out anyway, so I agreed.

Destiny pointed to a black truck. "I've got the puppies with me, and I'll tell the vet's office to give Momma Dog to you."

"You're driving that black truck?"

"Yeah. It was my grandfather's truck."

"Were you at my house today?"

Even in the shade of the trees, it was obvious her face reddened. "Don't be silly. How would I know where you live?"

"It's a small town. People talk, and it wouldn't be hard to get my address."

She stalked away, and I followed. She opened the truck's passenger door, grabbed the tangled leashes, and passed them to me. "They're yours."

My pulse accelerated at the thought of one of the clamoring puppies getting hurt. "Help me get them out so they don't fall."

"All right." She huffed but lowered one of the chocolate Labrador retrievers to the grass. I reached for the second one, and Destiny assisted with the third puppy. "There."

"You're welcome." I took the innocent puppies by their leashes and looked at her. "You never told me what you were looking for. I know you were here Thursday night. The same night Zarina Mills was murdered."

"A lot of people were here that night. If you must know, I lost my ring, er, watch." She flashed her hand at me with a huge diamond ring.

She was lying, and she wasn't convincing. If I had to guess, I'd say she was trying to find Zarina's camera bag. Why hadn't anyone come across it yet?

"I'll discuss it with the staff. If we find your watch, we'll call you."

"Okay. I suppose you'd like me to leave."

"Yes, please."

She got into the truck, and I stepped out of her way with the puppies. It didn't make sense that she'd give me the puppies for free, no strings attached.

Ike and Vince were bound to be aggravated that they'd spent a bundle on their dogs and I got these three for free. Although to be fair, they'd probably be relieved to know all the dogs were safe.

After I felt confident Destiny had left the property, I texted Marc. *We need to find Zarina's camera bag. I'm at the farm.*

He called. "Hey, it sounds like something happened."

"Oh, boy. You won't believe it." I updated him on my day.

"Okay. Well, I've got a little news of my own. Rylee has a date with Vince. She already cut out of here. Let me tie up a couple of loose threads, and I'll head your way. Do you want me to bring Sunny?"

"Yes, please. She's probably ready for some fun."

"Let's think about some logical places Zarina may have hidden her bag instead of randomly looking everywhere. I don't mind using a metal detector if needed, but it might be more time-efficient to try strategic places."

"Good point. Now that you mention it, Zarina took pictures of Hannah. She went inside the house to rest a few minutes and change clothes. I'll talk to Juliet. Maybe she has an idea."

"Okay. I'll see you soon."

"Oh, one more thing. Lincoln's going to come out and do a sound check so he can follow Belle home. If you offer him a ride here, then he could drive her home afterward instead of following her."

"You always think of nice things to do for others. I'll call him and offer a ride."

I texted Wade. *Destiny Howard came to Stay and Play in a black truck. She didn't answer when I asked about being at my house.*

The puppies barked and tousled with each other. It was time to get them off their leashes. I took them to the barn and introduced them to the girls.

Melanie lived on the property, in a small apartment in the Old Kitchen. "They're adorable. I can look after them."

I texted Gloria and informed her I was now responsible for Momma Dog. She agreed to contact me when it was time to pick her up.

My head spun with everything I needed to keep straight. Next up was to warn Juliet about Destiny and ask for ideas about where Zarina may have hidden the camera bag.

I found Juliet in the sunroom, chatting with Carol.

Carol spotted me first. "Come in, Andi Grace. We were just discussing the wedding." She patted the empty spot on the love seat beside her.

"Thanks." I sat where she indicated. "Sorry to interrupt, but I wanted to warn you about Destiny Howard. She was on the property, and I'm suspicious she's looking for Zarina's camera bag. I told her to leave, right after I agreed to take her puppies."

Juliet gasped. "You what?"

"Yep." I laughed. "I also agreed to take in Momma Dog and pay for her vet bill. Destiny caught me at a weak moment."

Carol said, "What about the mother?"

I met her gaze. "She's the sweetest thing. Would you be interested? They were calling her Momma Dog, or M.D. for short."

"Chris and I need a permanent place, and if we choose the retirement community, it'd have to be a place that allows pets."

I pointed to Juliet. "What do you think?"

"I think you should put Carol's name at the top of the list for the mother. She's family."

Carol placed a hand on her chest. "Family. It feels so good to be thought of as family. Thank you, Juliet."

I placed a finger over my top lip to keep me from crying over the sweet emotion. "Okay. In the meantime, we'll keep them at Stay and Play. Once Momma Dog is released by Doc Hewitt, you'll have time to get to know her. My guess is you'll fall in love."

"I'll share a little secret with you. Chris has a soft spot for dogs." Her smile dimmed. "He's walking around the property. Do you think he's safe with that woman on the prowl?"

"She should be gone by now, but it couldn't hurt to alert him."

With shaky hands, Carol said, "It's easier to call. Excuse me, girls." She walked into the breakfast room.

I leaned toward Juliet. "Do you have any idea where Zarina may have hidden her camera bag? Like, what room did she change clothes in?"

"Come on. Let's look around." Juliet told Carol we'd be right back, and we began our search for the bag.

Chapter Thirty-two

OUR SEARCH OF THE BED-AND-BREAKFAST turned up nothing. By the time Juliet and I finished, the men had converged on the property. Marc, Nate, Lincoln, and Chris all sat in the sunroom eating oatmeal raisin cookies, drinking lemonade, and chatting with Carol.

We stopped at the doorway, and Juliet elbowed me. "Now there's a happy grandmother."

I studied Marc's expression. His eyes looked hopeful. There were no frown lines. In fact, his posture was relaxed.

With Chris and Carol being in their mid-eighties, there was no telling how long Marc would have to enjoy their part in his life. If anyone knew how fragile life could be, it was me. Days ago, Zarina's vibrant life had been snuffed out. We never knew how much time we had left on earth.

I crossed the room and slid my arm around Marc's shoulders. I wanted to support Marc through the adjustment period of accepting his grandparents. "Hey, those cookies look good."

"It's the strangest thing. As soon as I took a bite, a memory of eating these with my dad surfaced."

"Food memory. I'll need to create some food specialties for our kids to remember when they grow up."

"Children? I'm looking forward to it."

We'd never discussed when to have children, but Marc would make a terrific father when the time came.

My phone vibrated, and I pulled it from my pocket. "It's J.T."

Do you know where Zarina's car is? She got a new one. Silver Mazda. Four doors.

I looked at Juliet. "J.T. is asking about Zarina's car. Is it on the property?"

She shook her head. "I don't know. Between my guests and Stay and Play visitors, I can't really account for all the vehicles."

Nate said, "Plus, I've had employees here getting the grounds prepared for the wedding."

Chris stood and looked out the window. "I saw a Mazda when I was walking earlier. It was silver, four doors, and one of the newer models."

My heart leapt. "I wonder if the deputies searched it for clues."

Marc reached for my hand. "You need to contact Wade before searching it."

"Of course. I'll text him before answering J.T." I sent the question to the sheriff.

Juliet reached for a cookie then sat in the chair closest to Nate. "Andi Grace and I were trying to find Zarina's backpack. If anyone comes across a brown leather bag, please let us know."

Chris raised his hands. "I wish I could say I've seen it, but the car is the only help I can provide."

Carol smiled at her husband. "You know finding the car could provide a clue to the poor girl's murder."

My phone vibrated. After reading Wade's reply, I updated the others. "Wade says one of the deputies examined the car. We're free to go through it." I sent a quick message to Zarina's ex-husband to inform him the car was on the property and I wanted to look through it.

Lincoln rose. "Mrs. Williams, thank you so much for the cookies and lemonade. I'm gonna mosey out to the wedding site and reception area and decide the best place to set up."

"You're welcome. Are you part of the ceremony?"

"Yes, ma'am. You should know your grandson is a man of many talents. He's written a few songs. I'm going to sing one at the wedding, and there's a cheesy one that'll be perfect for the reception. It's called 'As Long as We're Together I'm Happy.' Now isn't that the sappiest thing you ever heard? Of course, it could be the sweetest thing ever too." He pulled his ball cap out of the back pocket of his jeans.

I said, "I used to have a Neil Diamond song for a ringtone until I discovered Marc had written a hit song for Lincoln. Now it's my ringtone."

Carol leaned back into the couch. "We really do have a lot to learn about each other. If someone could text me the titles of these songs, I want to hear them."

Marc's face turned red. "I'll be happy to send them to you."

"Thank you, dear."

Chris pulled his phone out. "We should get a music app so we can listen to them whenever we want."

Lincoln nodded. "I'm confident Marc can download an app and add his songs onto it. I've got to shove off, but I'll see y'all later."

I glanced at Marc. "Why don't you continue your visit with Carol and Chris. I'll be outside looking around."

"I'll go with you." He turned to his grandparents. "If you'll excuse me, maybe we can talk later, and I'll download the app and songs."

Juliet said, "I'll fix a quick dinner for all of us."

"Thanks. I'm going to grab some gloves from your supply. Put it on my tab." I knew she'd never charge me. I took two pair of food service gloves, stuffed them in my pocket, and we headed outside.

Marc reached for my hand. "Chubb and Sunny are in the barn, and I suppose we're going to search Zarina's car."

"Ding, ding, ding. You guessed correctly."

He chuckled. "It wasn't hard to figure out what you wanted."

My phone vibrated, and I pulled it out of my pocket with my free hand. "How would you feel about a phone-free honeymoon?"

"I'm all for it, but you're the one continually receiving messages and calls. Whatcha got there?"

"J.T.'s finishing up at a new home, but he and Theo would like to check out the Mazda. Their friendship seems to be working, but it'd be great if he could get an apartment of his own."

"True, but I'm sure he knows his financial situation better than we do."

We walked to the side of the main house and found the car.

I squeezed Marc's hand. "Suddenly, I'm nervous."

Marc felt my forehead. "That doesn't sound like you. Are you ill?"

My shoulders relaxed a bit. "No, I'm just being silly. Let's see what we can find."

We walked to the driver's side, and I reached for the door handle.

"Guys, I've got something to tell you," Lincoln shouted and jogged to us.

What could be more important than finding Zarina's car? I couldn't imagine, but I was about to find out.

Chapter Thirty-three

Marc, Lincoln, and I stood in the shade of the pines.

Lincoln propped his hands on his hips. "I was just on the phone with Ben. He's got an investment opportunity for me."

Marc tensed. "After we just fought him over your management contract?"

"Yep."

"What'd he specifically want?" Anger laced Marc's tone.

Lincoln ignored Marc's mood like only a close friend could do. "Ben says he's gathered a group of investors to start a new company to sell tickets to concerts. In the beginning they'll focus on country music, but they have plans to branch out. He named some big-time musicians and businessmen who are on board."

"You're not tempted to invest, are you?" Marc crossed his arms.

"Believe me, Ben makes it sound too good to be true. Return on investment will be immediate and big. It'll just keep growing. He wants me to get in on the ground floor to make up for the previous misunderstanding." Lincoln removed a hand from his hip and ran his fingers over the brim of his hat. "I agreed to meet him to discuss it further."

"Man, have you lost your mind?" Marc frowned.

"Hear me out. Ben is married to Destiny. Andi Grace believes Destiny may be involved in that Tail-wagger group. He approached the Moonbeams with a pay-for-play scam. I have no intention of signing with Ben, but maybe we can expose him. Wouldn't you like to bring him down?"

Marc's shoulders appeared to relax. "You know I would. This is happening at the worst possible time though."

"I know. That's why I asked him to meet us for breakfast." Lincoln clapped Marc's shoulder.

"Hold up. Ben agreed to meet the both of us?"

For the first time, Lincoln smiled. "I'm more than just a pretty face. I've done a few music videos, and I can act. A little. My plan is to meet Ben at Daily Java. You two will be there already. Be sure to sit at a big table. I'll manage to sit down with y'all and suggest to Ben that he share the opportunity with all of us."

Lincoln looked proud of himself, and I had to laugh. "You came up with that plan mighty fast."

Marc said, "It seems there are all kinds of chances for this to go sideways."

Lincoln grew serious. "Ben Lowe must be stopped. If it wasn't for my experience, he would've taken advantage of Belle and her bandmates."

"Fine. We'll be at Daily Java tomorrow morning. What time?"

"I'm supposed to meet him at seven."

"We'll be drinking coffee by then."

"Thanks, friend." Lincoln jogged away.

I hugged Marc. "It's obvious you don't want to do this."

"Yeah, but he's my best friend, and I gotta have his back. You don't have to participate though. It's awfully early."

"Hey, mister." I pulled back. "You know me well enough to know I'll be there with you."

"I figured as much. Let's check Zarina's car." He reached over and touched a strand of my hair. "You look pretty. Er, I mean you always look pretty, but whatever you did to your hair makes you look even nicer."

"Thanks. Juliet fixed it today. Highlights and a trim for the wedding."

Marc's gaze met mine, and he smiled. "Saturday can't get here soon enough. In the meantime, let's look at the car."

I removed the gloves from my pocket and handed a pair to Marc. After gloving up, I reached for the door handle. It moved and the door came open. "Nice of the deputy not to lock it."

"Yep." Marc walked around and got in the passenger side. "What are we looking for?"

I sat down and adjusted the driver's seat to accommodate my longer legs. "Clues."

He tweaked my nose. "Feeling sassy with your new hairdo, aren't ya?"

"Ha. Ha. Ha." I tried to be sarcastic, but Marc was so stinking cute. I was ready to be his wife. "Honestly, I do like the new color and style. Is it too late to elope?"

A burst of laughter shot out of him. "Pretty sure that train has blown past."

"I was afraid you'd say that. Let's see what we can find."

Marc rooted through the glove compartment. "This is a nice car."

"Yeah, it is, but I need to stick with SUVs or vans as long as I'm a dog walker."

"Understood." He removed an owner's manual and some deposit slips. "I guess she didn't have direct deposit since most of her jobs were independent. I remember giving her a check for our engagement pictures."

"Right. I think she had some kind of credit card reader on her phone, but it saved her money to get paid by cash or check." I reached under my seat and pulled out a wad of papers, including a burger wrapper. "I guess Wade has Zarina's phone. Maybe I should check."

"Let's focus on this before you bother Wade. There may be something the deputies missed." He stopped sorting through the papers from the glove compartment. "*Winnie the Pooh* is written on the back of this grocery receipt."

"Oh, that's the name of the first dog Gloria and I found participating in Operation Tail-wagger. At least it's the first dog Doc treated."

Marc lay it beside the little stack of deposit receipts.

I turned my attention back to the papers and trash I'd found. Random names and times were written on yellow sticky notes.

Marc said, "Queenie's name is on this paper. Isn't that the name of Destiny's dog?"

"Yes, she's a yellow corgi."

"Right. If you pop the trunk, I'll look for the camera bag. How crazy would it be to find it sitting here all this time?"

"I'd love for you to find it." I felt around and found the trunk lever and pulled it.

Marc hopped out but left the door open.

I finished sorting and moved to the backseat. On the floorboard behind the driver's seat was a pair of rain boots. The rest of the floorboard was littered with wadded up papers and empty paper cups. Well, she did drive back and forth to Charleston and probably needed caffeinated drinks to keep her awake.

The humidity made my hair stick to the back of my neck, but I wasn't ready to pull it into a ponytail after Juliet had styled it.

A small dollar-store notepad caught my eye. I lifted my hair and fanned myself with the notepad until my neck didn't feel damp. I sat back and flipped through the pages. Times, names, and dates. It seemed odd that Zarina wouldn't just keep her appointments on her phone.

The day before her murder, Zarina had planned to meet high school students for group photos. There was a meeting scheduled with Hannah, no doubt to plan their time before the political rally. Two more people were listed, but I didn't know them. Last on the list was Destiny's name. I took pictures of the schedule with my phone. Wade would want to see this.

A person appeared and cleared their throat. I looked up.

Skylar Marshall.

Had Wade told her about Zarina's car? Why else would she happen to show up at the exact time Marc and I were investigating? I palmed my phone and the notepad and stepped toward her. Yes, I'd share the information with the proper authorities, but I didn't know Skylar well enough to trust her with all the clues I'd gathered. On the other hand, I'd agreed to work with her in return for taking wedding photos. What kind of a mess had I gotten myself into?

Chapter Thirty-four

"Hi, Skylar. Why are you here?" My tone didn't sound friendly. Shame on me. "Sorry, I didn't mean to be rude. So, why?"

"Probably the same as you. I wanted to see if there were any clues to Zarina's murder." The edge to her tone made me shiver.

Marc shut the trunk and joined us. "Hi, there. How can we help you?"

The woman's personality changed as she beamed at Marc. "I'd like to look around the property."

Sweet as can be, I replied, "You'll have to ask Juliet and Nate." The reporter had seemed much nicer the previous times we'd talked. Why was I looking for her to cause trouble?

She shifted her gaze back to me. "It was my understanding you own the place and that Juliet runs the bed-and-breakfast."

I kept my voice on an even keel. "No. Stay and Play is mine, but the bed-and-breakfast belongs to Juliet and Nate. They're the other half of our double wedding."

"I've met them. Remember? While waiting to move into my house." She crossed her arms. "Are you sure you want me to be the photographer?"

"Yes, of course we do. But we still need to ask Juliet about you looking for clues."

"Fine, but I thought we were going to work the case together, Andi Grace."

I took a deep breath and counted to ten in French to myself. "Sorry if I was offensive. It's probably pre-wedding jitters, but I promise not to be a bridezilla."

Her brow crinkled. "Remember photography is secondary to my reporting. I agreed because you're in a pinch."

"We appreciate you so much. As far as the case goes, have you made any progress?"

"A little. I went back over my notes on the interview with Ben Lowe. There's something odd, but I haven't figured it out." She smiled. "Yet. But I will."

Marc pointed to a truck ambling up the drive. "Looks like our guests have arrived. Skylar, we'll walk with you to the main house, where you can discuss your plans with Juliet."

We closed the car doors and headed toward the house.

Skylar said, "I suppose that's Zarina's car?"

"Yes. I plan to contact Wade and share what we found. Do you want to join us for the conversation?"

"Yes, thanks. Let me know when he arrives. I'm off to find Juliet."

I sent a message to the sheriff. *Wade, we found a couple of things in Zarina's car. Need to share with you. Can Skylar join us?*

About the time we reached the back of the house, J.T. and Theo intercepted us. I introduced the guys to Skylar, then she entered the kitchen to look for Juliet.

My phone buzzed. I stepped away from Marc and the guys and answered. "I guess you got my message."

"Yes, ma'am. Before I agree to Skylar joining us, what did you find?"

"Zarina's schedule and a few notes. We haven't found the camera bag or her phone."

"Don't worry about the phone. We're trying to hack into it. Any chance you know her password?"

"No, but J.T.'s here and might have some clues about Zarina's code."

"Great. I'm on the way. As far as Skylar goes, I'd like to have a conversation with you before determining what to share."

"Uh, she's going to blame me."

"I'll handle Skylar. Why don't you take J.T. to the car, and I'll meet you at your office." Wade's gravelly voice made me wonder if he'd had much sleep.

"Wade, if you're in town, why don't you pick up Duke and bring him with you? He can spend a couple of days with us, free of charge."

"Thanks. I hate to neglect him when I get a murder case. If it wasn't for you, I'd probably have to give him to somebody else, and that'd break my heart."

"That's not going to happen. We'll expect to see you and Duke soon." This case must really be getting to the sheriff for him to share a tender moment about his dog with me. I returned to Marc and the guys. "Hey, we can take J.T. home later if Theo doesn't want to stick around."

"If it's okay, I'd like to walk over to where I was planting the pansies. Maybe it'll jog a memory. The more J.T. tells me about Zarina, the more determined I am to help you guys catch the killer."

Marc looked at the other men. "How about we divide and conquer? I'll go with Theo, and you two go to the car."

"That sounds like a good plan. Oh, and Wade is going to talk to Skylar."

"Beautiful."

I got gloves for J.T. and we walked to the car.

J.T.'s legs were long, and I hustled to keep up with him. He opened the door and got into the driver's seat, sliding it back as far as it would go. "Zarina always kept mints in the glove box. She used to joke about needing them to disguise her coffee breath. Some days I swear she lived on coffee and mints."

His words and tone revealed how much he cared about Zarina. I stood beside him and pointed to the dash. "Sorry but that's all we found. No mints or candy."

"Okay, okay. Maybe they're in her camera bag. She also kept crackers in the car in case Sarah got hungry."

"You know what's odd? There's no car seat or even a base."

"Zarina's mom had the seat and base, but Zarina was scattered. No telling what you'd find in her car on any given day."

"I'm going to give you some breathing room." I leaned against the hood while he rummaged through the car.

When J.T. finished inspecting the front seat area, he climbed into the back, then got into the trunk. At last, he stood in front of me. His long fluffy hair blew in the breeze. "No backpack. I didn't find a link to Destiny Howard or that dog scam. Where does that leave us?"

"The jump drive you shared provided some clues. I found this in the car." I passed the notepad to him. "See what you think."

He glanced at the pages. "Interesting."

"Did Zarina have an electronic calendar? Maybe on her phone or computer?"

"Nah, she's artistic. See how she doodles and draws caricatures? She's old school about some things. Not her photography, but other stuff."

"Okay. I suppose we should head over to meet the sheriff."

He frowned. "This isn't a setup, is it?"

"What do you mean?"

"Play me until the sheriff gathers enough evidence to arrest me."

"No, J.T." I met his gaze. "I believe in you. This is no setup."

He stared at me a moment longer then nodded. "Appreciate it." He stuffed his hands into his pockets, and we walked in silence to the Stay and Play barn.

Chapter Thirty-five

J.T. and I joined Marc and Theo in the barn. They were playing with the dogs in one of the play areas.

Theo walked over to us and put his hand on J.T.'s shoulder. "Sorry, man. I didn't remember anything else."

His shoulders slumped. "Hey, thanks for trying. Let me walk you to your truck."

Once they left us alone, I wrapped my arms around Marc. "Poor guy."

"I take it you two didn't have much luck."

"No. I still feel like the camera bag is the key."

"Hang on. I just had a thought." Marc ran toward the other guys.

I played with Sunny and Chubb until Marc returned.

He said, "Theo agreed to use Jeremiah's metal detector in the area where he spotted Zarina. He'll draw us a grid of the areas where he searches so I don't waste time retracing his steps."

"That's wonderful."

Belle entered the barn with Bo and Yoyo on leashes and Griffin's three-legged mutt, Shadow, followed without restraints. Shadow was one of the best-behaved dogs I knew. Except for Sunny, of course. "Hey, guys. Dad said I'd find you around here."

Marc turned and faced Belle. "How's your new dog?"

Belle had recently adopted a black-and-white schnoodle. "Lady's great."

Sheriff Stone entered the barn with his faithful companion Duke. "Thanks for offering to keep Duke for a few days. He loves Belle."

She smiled and reached for the dog's leash. "I love him too. He's got a lot of energy and is just fun to play with."

"Yeah, he'll play chase as long as you'll let him."

Belle disappeared with the four dogs.

Wade's smile disappeared. "Shall we talk in your office?" He motioned for me to lead the way.

Before we'd all gotten seated, J.T. joined us. "Sheriff Stone, I heard you're having a challenge unlocking Zarina's phone. To my knowledge, it won't lock you out no matter how many times you try."

"Good to know."

J.T. crossed his arms. "Zarina was a creative person, not a techie. The password will be something she could easily remember because she was juggling a lot. Have you tried her birthday?"

"Yes." Wade pulled his little notebook from his uniform's shirt pocket. "We also tried Sarah's date of birth."

"What about her momma's? Or her address?"

Wade pulled a phone zipped in a plastic evidence bag out of his pants pocket. He swiped the screen. "Give me some numbers. Marc, will you write down what we try?"

"No problem." Marc picked up Wade's pad and pen.

J.T. rubbed his hands together. "Of course, it's six digits. Let's start with the last six of her social security number."

I sat down and watched the two of them. Like a tennis match, J.T. would spit out a number, and Wade tried it.

Finally J.T. said, "I'm running out of ideas. Let's try my birthday. If that doesn't work, we'll try our wedding day."

Anticipation tightened my muscles. *Please, Lord, let this work.*

"Why are you being so helpful?" Wade stared at J.T.

"Sheriff, I believe when you read the messages Zarina and I sent each other, you'll understand how much I loved her. I'd never do anything to hurt her, much less kill her."

Wade pressed his lips together and nodded. "Fair enough."

"Bingo. J.T., your wedding anniversary is the code. I'll have our tech guys analyze this. If you plan to leave town, please contact me directly."

Marc placed a hand on J.T.'s shoulder. "We'll be sure to let you know, Sheriff Stone. How long do you suppose it'll take to go through Zarina's phone messages? I assume you'll read all of her messages, not just the ones from J.T."

"I've never run a sloppy investigation. No intentions of starting now."

"I didn't mean to imply you would. Sorry."

Wade sauntered away with Zarina's phone in one hand. Once I heard him speak to his dog, I figured it was safe to talk.

"Um, I'll let you guys have some privacy. I'll either look for Skylar or check on Theo." I left and shut the office door on my way out. I shot off a text to Skylar and headed out of the barn.

Belle and Melanie were handling the dogs, but there was no sign of the sheriff.

My phone vibrated. Skylar had replied. *Meet you on the patio of the main house.*

I sent a thumbs-up and headed her way.

"Slow down there. Got a quick question for you." Wade leaned against his official black-and-tan Ford Explorer.

"Sure, Wade. What's up?" His serious expression sent butterflies swirling through my belly.

"I need to share something confidential."

I held my hands out to stop him. "Except for Marc. I refuse to start my marriage by keeping secrets from him. What I mean to say is, never will I keep secrets from Marc. It's not good for any relationship."

"Do you understand the meaning of confidential?" His tone rankled my nerves.

"Yeah, and that's why I'm being up front with you. No secrets from Marc."

The sheriff sighed and removed his hat. "Fine, but it goes no farther than Marc."

"Agreed." What was so important that he wanted to share with me?

Chapter Thirty-six

"You know Skylar is my cousin." Wade rubbed his chin.

"Right." My pulse thrummed in my neck. "On you mother's side, if I remember correctly." Not that it mattered which side of his family tree connected them.

"Exactly." He sighed. "She's been known to go after the riskiest leads. She's tenacious. And like you, she fights injustice."

Nothing about this seemed like a big secret. "Where are you going with your revelations?"

"Please don't tell Skylar about J.T. helping me with Zarina's phone passcode. I promised Skylar she'd get the first and best interview, but I don't want to tip my hand to the killer. At the appropriate time, I'll give her an exclusive interview."

"Okay. I'm on my way to meet her now. You can trust me."

"Thanks. See you round."

"Bye, Wade." His revelation slowed my approach to Kennady Bed-and-Breakfast. No doubt he'd hidden information from me in the past. He probably had other facts tucked away on the investigation into Zarina's murder. I could respect his need to keep some secrets, and I'd honor his request.

"Andi Grace, over here." Skylar waved to me from a patio table. "I've got us fresh-squeezed lemonade."

I joined her and sat in the empty chair. "Thanks."

"You're welcome." She slid one glass to me. "I saw Theo using a metal detector. He said he's trying to find Zarina's camera bag."

I circled a hand around the glass. "Yeah. The sheriff hasn't found it, and there could be a clue."

She drummed her fingers on the table. "I wonder why Wade doesn't have his people searching."

"Oh, they have searched, but no luck. You know his department is small and the county is spread out. I imagine he asked Theo to contact him as soon as possible if he finds the backpack."

"You're probably right. Zarina was awfully protective of her work. I asked to look at some pictures she'd taken, and she refused."

"What did you want to see?" I sipped the icy, tart lemonade.

"I was working on the story of your local veterinarian, Dr. Hewitt. He's performed surgeries for Operation Tail-wagger. The organization isn't transparent about exactly where the money they raise goes."

"Do you believe it's a legitimate nonprofit?"

"I have doubts. The main issue bothering me is the fact they won't account for how the money is spent. Pilots? Gas? Meds? Dr. Hewitt? Or possibly a vacation to Bermuda? I've watched them raise money on social media, and donors should know where the funds are allocated."

"Hold on a second. Let me check a source." I didn't want to expose Gloria or betray a confidence, so I stepped away from the patio area, ignoring Skylar's quirked eyebrow.

"Andi Grace, how are you, hon?"

"Good. I'm meeting with Skylar Marshall, the reporter and podcaster and blogger—"

"I know who you mean."

I shot a glance Skylar's way, but she appeared to be looking at her phone. Unless she was trying to record my conversation. I walked farther away and kept my voice low. "She's looking into Operation Tail-wagger. How would you feel about me sharing the names of your clients involved?"

"I need to ask their permission first. You know the clients were all grateful for the surgeries despite the possibility it was a scam."

"I see what you mean. Did you learn anything about the pilot for that first surgery for Winnie the Pooh?"

"Hon, I haven't found the time yet, but I will."

"No problem. I completely understand. Thanks, Gloria. I won't mention you or the clients to Skylar." We ended the call, and I walked back to Skylar. "Sorry, but I don't have much to report. What if we run an ad on social media? We can ask people to respond if they feel like they've been ripped off by Operation Tail-wagger."

Skylar typed on her phone. "Let's start off with a vague question. I'll even do a podcast and blog on it. Victims of money scams."

"Perfect. If it's okay, I'll put you in charge. If my source shares information that I can pass along, I'll be sure to give it to you immediately."

"Take it easy, Andi Grace. I understand sometimes it's necessary to protect our sources." Her smile seemed genuine.

"Thanks. I also have someone trying to nail down the pilot who flies some of the animals to their surgeries."

"Maybe I can help with that." She typed more on her phone.

I relaxed into the chair beside her and drank my lemonade. "Scout, the mutt with the tumor who got lost, was driven to Heyward Beach."

"I don't know how the group decides the means of transportation. Distance? Urgency? What other vets are involved?"

A manly whoop erupted from the woods.

Skylar grinned. "Do you suppose Theo found the camera bag?"

"I'd say he found something important. Let's go."

Chapter Thirty-seven

Marc and J.T. arrived seconds after we did.

Theo leaned the metal detector against a scrawny magnolia tree trunk. "Guys, look what I found." He lifted a Canon with his gloved hands.

"That's one of Zarina's cameras." J.T.'s eyes widened. "Good job, man."

I longed to click through Zarina's photos, but Wade needed to examine it first.

Skylar reached out. "Let me see."

Theo began to hand it over.

I stepped forward. "Wait, the sheriff needs to see it first. Too bad I threw away my gloves from earlier."

Marc held his phone screen toward us. "I'm calling Wade now. We can't all get our fingerprints on it."

Theo held the camera close to his body. "I guess it's a good thing I always put work gloves on when I pick up a piece of equipment. Years working as a landscaper has taught me to protect my hands. Sounds like I should hold the camera until Sheriff Stone returns."

"This is Sheriff Stone."

We all glanced toward Wade's voice coming from Marc's phone.

"It's Marc. We've found a Canon camera on the farm property."

"Don't touch it. I'm on the way."

Marc switched off speaker mode and walked away with the phone to his ear.

Skylar frowned. "What can it hurt to look through the photos? Theo can turn on the camera and sort through them wearing his gloves. No harm. No foul."

I understood her logic, but Wade would be ticked.

Theo shook his head. "No way. I'm not going to get arrested for, um, obstructing justice or anything else. It's bad enough the sheriff will know I've been holding the camera."

"Come on, Theo. What can it hurt?" Skylar batted her eyes. "Besides, I'm his cousin. He probably didn't mean me."

J.T. stepped closer to Theo. "We don't know what she'll do. What if she erases an incriminating picture on the camera?"

Skylar gasped. "Are you accusing me of murder?"

"No, ma'am. That's not for me to decide." He looked back at Theo. "She could also report what she sees. Then if the killer learns about the clue, it could help him, or her, get away. I've been questioned just because of my relationship with Zarina. If you disobey a direct order from Sheriff Stone, he's gonna grill you like nobody's business."

Marc rejoined us. "Wade will meet us on the patio. Theo, he knows you have the camera. Keep carrying it."

I followed behind Theo. "Did you find anything else?"

"Not much. There was a metal can. Flat. It's one of those tin cans with strong mints."

I avoided stepping on poison ivy. "Were they near each other?"

Theo looked at the ground and kept walking. "I don't remember."

J.T. said, "Don't sweat it. Main thing is you found a camera."

Marc stopped. "J.T., let's see if we can find the box. It's probably nothing, but you never know."

"Theo, you okay if I go back with Marc?"

Theo's eyes darted from Skylar to me. He looked like he'd rather be anywhere else, but he threw back his muscular shoulders. "It's cool."

It wasn't long after we reached the patio that Wade joined us.

Skylar hopped up and hurried to her cousin. "Hi, Wade. Look what we found. Would you please let me go through the photos Zarina snapped?"

"No. I love you, but I won't give you clues to report." He frowned. "Don't forget I promised to give you the first and longest interview. When I have something official to report, you'll be the first to know."

"Fine. I'll figure out another way to gather info." She plopped down on the chair.

Wade pulled on blue disposable gloves. "Theo, thanks for finding the camera."

"You're welcome." He handed the Canon to the sheriff. "If you don't mind, I'll try to help the others find the box of mints."

"Not sure what you mean, but go ahead." He placed the camera in a big evidence bag, sealed it, and scribbled on the bag. Time. Date. Place. Investigation. "You ladies got anything else for me?"

He'd barely left the property before Theo found the camera. "I've got nothing new to report."

"Should I hang around?" He lifted his eyebrows.

"Maybe. Theo found a metal candy can. It could be something."

Skylar said, "It could also be a waste of time."

Wade's gaze jumped to his cousin. "Come on, Sky. Don't pout. I'll give them a few minutes."

"Sorry. I'll get you something to drink." Skylar disappeared into Juliet's kitchen.

I laughed. "Your cousin certainly knows how to make herself at home."

"Part of her charm. Tell me when you see her coming." He pushed buttons on the camera and looked through the bag at the viewfinder display.

Keeping my eye on the kitchen door, I longed to get a glimpse of what he was seeing. I pressed my lips together to prevent myself from asking.

The door opened and Skylar appeared.

"Wade, she's back."

"Thanks." He crossed an ankle over his knee and made himself look comfortable.

"Here you go." Skylar placed a glass of lemonade and a sandwich in front of him. "Juliet assured me you're probably hungry. Ham and cheese on rye."

"She's right. I missed lunch, and that sandwich looks delicious." Before he could remove his gloves, the guys reappeared.

Theo placed the canister beside Wade. "This is the only other thing I found. Not sure if it's important or not."

"Lots of times we don't know something's important until it is." He bagged it. "May as well test it for fingerprints. I gotta scoot." He guzzled his drink and gathered his belongings, including the sandwich.

Marc said, "Hopefully we found a clue today that'll lead your investigation in a good direction."

"You never know." Wade took off.

Skylar turned to Marc. "Do you know one of the suspects? No. An even better question is are you representing a suspect?"

"If I do represent a person of interest, I'll keep their identity secret."

"Unless it becomes public record." Skylar typed on her phone. "Then I'll reach out to them for an interview."

Marc turned his attention to me. "Honey, are you ready to go?"

"Yes, I am." I reached for his hand and we walked to the barn and gathered our dogs before heading to my Highlander. Once we were all in place, I started the SUV.

Lincoln and Belle were getting into Marc's truck, leaving Belle's car on the property. His protective father instincts wanted to drive them home in a big vehicle, and Marc agreed to pick his truck up later. Belle waved from the passenger seat, and her dad drove away slowly.

I laughed. "Look how slow he's driving. I guess he's setting a good example for his daughter."

"No doubt. Lincoln's crazy about his kids and wants them to be safe. I'm glad he's driving Belle home today."

Out of the corner of my eye, I spotted Theo and J.T. driving away.

And last of all, Skylar hopped into her blue Jeep and left in a cloud of dust.

Marc shook his head. "She is one interesting person. I hope she doesn't turn out to be a burr under Wade's saddle."

"He thought I was annoying in the past. She's going to push him to his limits."

Chapter Thirty-eight

MARC AND I TOOK THE DOGS HOME and ended up at Tony's Pizzeria for dinner. After we ordered and chatted with Tony, we found an empty table in the corner. I opened my notebook and faced Marc. "Let's review our suspects."

"J.T. is out, right?"

"Yes. The fact you're representing him solidifies my belief in his innocence."

"Who else you got?"

"Destiny Howard. Is she involved in Operation Tail-wagger? Did Zarina learn the organization is committing fraud? Did Zarina somehow link Destiny to the scam?"

"Good questions. Who else?" He reached for his Coke.

"Marvin Graves."

"Because?"

"Marvin and Zarina argued the day of the murder." I drew a big star on the page. "I need to look deeper there. I also considered Zeke Mills, Zarina's brother. Skylar said he has an alibi. He was working at the soup kitchen up in Myrtle Beach."

"What do you think about Skylar?"

The aroma of pizza stirred my empty stomach. "She's both helpful and a pain. As far as her being a suspect, no. I mean, she's Wade's cousin."

"Not sure that's a legit excuse, but I know what you mean. She's persistent in her quest to find the truth."

Tony joined us and sat beside me. He glanced at my journal and shook his head. "Please don't tell me you're trying to solve another murder this close to your wedding."

I closed the book. "Thanks for being part of our wedding."

"For you, dear, I'd do almost anything." He gave me a one-armed hug. "I recently started delivering food. It seemed like the slow season was a good time to try it out, instead of when we're inundated with tourists. Marc, I met your grandparents on the phone when they placed an order. Good people."

"Thanks, Tony."

"I imagine meeting them at this stage in your lives must be an adjustment."

Marc's face reddened. "You have no idea, but I'm opening myself up to the relationship."

"Good for you."

"Delivery, you say." I smiled at my friend. "Tony, would you send a pizza and breadsticks to Jeremiah Prichard? My treat. Tell him it's for him and Leroy Peck."

"I know just what he likes. It'll be my pleasure." He stood. "Your order should be ready soon."

A waitress appeared with bruschetta and salads. "This should tide you over for a few minutes."

"Thanks. This looks great." I reached for a thick slice of grilled bread. Chopped tomatoes fell off, and I scooped them back onto the bread with my fingers. Tony used the freshest ingredients for the bruschetta, and I didn't want to miss a bite.

The vegetarian pizza arrived right as we finished our salads. I smiled at Marc. "You'd think after a salad and appetizer, I wouldn't still be hungry."

"Nah. My guess is you haven't eaten anything substantial today."

"Well, I am famished." I accepted the slice Marc forked up for me. After the wedding, I'd begin to eat at regular intervals.

We ate in a comfortable silence, and Marc finished first. He reached for my murder notes. "What do you plan to do next?"

"I'd like to speak to Marvin. Would you look on his Twitter feed and see if you can tell where he is right now? If that doesn't work, we can see if there's a newsworthy event. You know, like a fire or—"

Marc placed his phone on the table and frowned.

My spirits sank. "What? Oh, Marc. Sorry if I was bossy."

"That's not it. Marvin is at the counter picking up an order." Marc pointed toward the counter.

"Be right back." I wiped my hands and mouth and walked to the photographer. "Hi, Marvin. How are you?"

The tan man with a receding hairline did a double take in my direction. "Andi Grace. I'm good, but I hope you're not about to ask me to photograph your wedding."

"No secrets in a small town. I'd like to ask you a couple of questions about the other night."

He paid for his pizza with a credit card then picked up the large box. "You mean the night of the murder."

"Yes. Who do you think murdered Zarina?"

"Skylar Marshall."

"Why?"

"They argued that day. I imagine there is a long list of suspects." He frowned. "Even my son yelled at Zarina the day of the murder. I think she stepped on his flowers or something."

Marvin wasn't going to sidetrack me. Theo had already told me about his altercation and apology. "You also argued with Zarina."

"And you know darn well what we argued about, you were right there. I didn't like that Zarina stole the Hannah Cummins account from me."

The man probably wouldn't believe he'd begun to make Hannah uneasy. Zarina hadn't stolen the account. Marvin lost it on his own. I wouldn't waste my breath arguing with him though. "Do you know what Zarina and Skylar argued about?"

"Something about a surgery." He sighed.

"Surgery? Was that the word, or did they say operation?"

"Maybe. What's it matter?"

"There's an organization called Operation Tail-wagger. I thought maybe they were discussing it."

"I don't know, and my pizza's getting cold. Ask Skylar yourself." He stalked out of Tony's Pizzeria.

I returned to Marc. "That could have gone better. All I learned is he overheard Zarina and Skylar in an argument."

"What next?"

"I can't eat any more, and I want to talk to Skylar."

"I'll pay and get a box to take your leftovers home. I finished my half."

"Uh, just because we split a pizza doesn't mean you can't eat more than half. Do you want more?"

He patted his belly. "I'm full. Be right back."

I pulled my phone from a side pocket in my new canvas purse and dialed Skylar.

"Andi Grace, have you learned anything new?"

"Marvin Graves overheard you and Zarina arguing before her murder."

Silence.

"Skylar, are you there?"

"Yes. Marvin? Are you accusing me of something based on Marvin's word? He's not a nice man."

"Regardless of how we feel about him, he saw you and Zarina argue."

"You know I was investigating Operation Tail-wagger. It came to my attention that Zarina had some photos of Destiny. I wanted her to share them with me. She refused. I tried to find out why. The more I cajoled and pushed, the tighter-lipped she became. It's one of the reasons I was hoping to look at the camera Theo found today."

"Would you like to meet up tomorrow and compare our notes on Operation Tail-wagger?"

"Yes. Why don't I look for flight records? There's got to be a contact at Dr. Hewitt's vet clinic. Where should I begin there?"

"Do you mean a person working with the possible scammer?"

"Yeah."

"Let me save you some time. Doc Hewitt is an honorable man. He's all about what's best for the animals. He'd never do anything underhanded."

"Well, it sounds like I touched a nerve."

I took a deep breath and decided to go out on a limb. "I've known Doc for years, and it's not him. The newest employee I've met at the clinic is a vet student by the name of Caleb, give me a second."

"Take your time."

I pulled my notebook from the purse and found what I needed. "Caleb Fisher. Twenty-six years old. He's studying the surgeries Doc performs."

Skylar said, "I'll do a deep dive on Caleb Fisher and leave your friend alone. I haven't found anything on the pilot yet, but I'll continue to dig. Wonder if it was always the same pilot or different people?"

"Don't forget sometimes the animals arrived by car. I'm not sure how many surgeries Doc performed for the organization."

"Don't worry about it. Let's meet for coffee tomorrow after I have more answers. This time I'm expecting you to share also. Don't be going behind my back and hide information."

"If the sheriff tells me to keep something to myself, I can't go against him." While I admired Skylar's fight for justice, she tended to be a little edgy. Maybe even dangerous. Who knew what she'd put on her blog or podcast? "Also, we need to agree on what's private between the two of us and what's fair game for you to report to the public. There's been one murder—"

"We don't know if Zarina's death is linked to the possible scam."

"True, but until we know they are completely unrelated, I won't put my friends in danger."

"Fair enough. Talk to you tomorrow."

Marc returned with a box. "How'd it go?"

"Maybe okay, but I'd like to warn Gloria that Skylar probably plans to reach out to her about Operation Tail-wagger. I don't want Skylar to trick Gloria into believing I shared more than I did." I placed the remaining pizza slices in the box. "I'll call her on the way home."

"I need to work on a case tonight. How about we swing by Lincoln's place and get my truck. Then I'll follow you home to make sure you're safe, and then I'll go to the office."

"You know there's a perfectly good office for you at the house."

"Yes, and I appreciate how you created it for me. Unfortunately, my files are at the office, and if I stay at your place, I might be too distracted to work."

I reached for his hand. "It's our home."

He kissed me. "You're right. Our home."

Marc had moved most of his clothes into the house, kayaks and paddle boards into the garage, and many books into his home office. I'd even tweaked the bedroom décor to look more like a married couple's bedroom and not a flowery single woman's room. Still, did he feel comfortable like it was his home? If not, we'd move.

In the meantime, I needed to call Gloria and research something. The closer we got to the wedding, the less time I'd have to investigate. Maybe tonight I'd begin with Skylar Marshall's background.

Chapter Thirty-nine

After assuring Gloria I hadn't revealed anything she'd shared with me to Skylar, I settled onto the couch with my laptop. I played one of Skylar's podcasts while skimming through her blog topics.

Her fight for justice was obvious. She'd investigated big cases in South Carolina, and she'd even traveled to Tennessee and Kentucky for a drug case involving college athletes and their doctors. I was impressed.

In high school, I'd wanted to be a newspaper reporter. Circumstances beyond my control changed the direction of my life. If given the opportunity to attend the University of Georgia and major in journalism, would I have turned out like Skylar? I shivered.

I loved working with dogs, and I was close to my siblings. Deciding to stay in Heyward Beach to raise my siblings had been the best decision I could've made.

No looking back. I didn't want to be Skylar. I'd helped solve a handful of local murders, and that was good enough for me. I wouldn't trade my life with Skylar or anyone else. I was blessed.

The doorbell rang, and I hurried to answer it. Sunny and Chubb raced to the door, but neither dog growled. Peeking out, I saw Marc and whipped open the door. "Honey, what's wrong?"

He pointed at a stuffed backpack. "Nothing's wrong, but you're right. Why would I work at my lonely office, when I could be here working with you?"

The dogs circled us and returned to the family room.

I cupped Marc's face in my hands and leaned in for a kiss. "I like the way you think."

After our lengthy kiss in the doorway, Marc laughed and walked inside. "I knew you'd be a distraction, but you're totally worth it."

I entered the front room Griffin Reed had helped convert to Marc's home office. Turning on a lamp, I faced him. "Can I fix you something to drink?"

He removed a Nalgene bottle from the pocket on his backpack then set the bag on his desk. "I'm good."

"Okay, then I'll get back to my research." I couldn't resist giving him one more kiss.

"I've got a surprise for you tomorrow night."

"I like surprises. Any hints?"

"Nope." His eyes twinkled, and his hands rested on top of the backpack. "I best get to work."

"Me too." I left him alone to concentrate on his case. Back in the family room, I returned to sorting through Skylar's blog posts. I'd kinda known another podcaster. Dirk Cutter had a radio show plus a podcast. He'd been murdered, and I'd gotten to learn about him after his death. As I sorted through the posts, my admiration for Skylar grew.

My phone vibrated, and I swiped at the sight of Gloria's name. "Hey."

"Andi Grace, Winnie the Pooh's owner spoke to me, and she agreed to talk to Skylar."

"What'd she say?" I opened my journal and clicked a pen.

"You might remember her name is Mary Beth Strange. She's a single mother who works at a grocery store."

I found the woman's name in my notes. "Got it right here. She said the organization flew her German shepherd to Charleston for Doc to perform the surgery."

"Exactly, but here's what we didn't know. She doesn't think she met the pilot. Mary Beth met a lean man who introduced himself as Dee Rowe."

"Was she positive it was a man?"

"I asked her that very question. Mary Beth wasn't positive because she was so distraught over Winnie. She did say there was something off with Dee."

"Still, she gave her dog to him. It doesn't seem very responsible."

"Desperate times call for desperate measures. She couldn't afford the surgery on her own. Trusting Operation Tail-wagger was the only solution she could find."

"I understand desperation." With a shaky hand I wrote down this new information. "Dee Rowe, and we've got Claire Rowe who met John Graystone and Vince Moore. Why does Mary Beth think Dee wasn't the pilot?"

"Dee took Winnie by the leash and walked her to a little plane. Mary Beth said the sun was in her eyes, but she thinks she saw another figure in the cockpit."

"Can we find out who the pilot was on that specific flight?"

"I can try, hon. Do you want me to tell Skylar?"

"If you and Mary Beth are comfortable with her knowing, it can't hurt. I think Skylar has built up a lot of contacts over the years. She might know just the right person to ask."

"Give me her number again, and I'll call her tonight. The sooner we figure out what's going on, the better."

"I couldn't agree more." I forwarded Skylar's info to Gloria then leaned back on the couch. Operation Tail-wagger stretched farther than most of my murder investigations. And I needed to remember the potential scam might not be linked to Zarina's murder.

Maybe I should let Skylar deal with the scam, and I'd focus on the murder. I yawned and closed my eyes. If the murder and scam were not linked, was Marvin Graves my top person of interest?

Chapter Forty

"Good morning, sleepyhead."

I leapt from the couch and a soft afghan fell off me. "What? Where?"

Marc's hands cupped my shoulders. "Easy. You fell asleep on the couch."

I felt my face for drool. Dry. Good. "Sorry."

"We're supposed to be at Daily Java soon. I've already been out with the dogs."

"Yikes. I'll hurry." I took the stairs by twos. I brushed my teeth and washed my face. My new hairstyle only needed a good brushing. A little mascara, deodorant, along with clean jeans and a fresh T-shirt. I glanced at my watch. This was as good as it'd get this morning. I hurried down and found Marc packing his backpack.

He wore jeans, a blue shirt, and a darker blue Henley. His gaze met mine. "You set a record."

"I know it's important to be on time. One car or two?"

"I'll drive." It didn't take us long to load up and drive to the coffee shop.

Erin greeted us. "Hi, y'all. Can I interest you in avocado toast? I also have a fresh batch of pumpkin muffins."

"Are we your first customers today?" The emptiness surprised me.

"Afraid so. It's been a slow morning so far."

The door's bell tinkled behind us. "Hey now, don't be selling all the muffins before I can place my order."

I smiled over my shoulder at Griffin. Oh, yeah. He was sweet on Erin. "Morning."

He cut his gaze to me. "Morning."

Erin's smile had grown bigger. "I have a dozen muffins boxed up for you and your crew."

"Thanks."

"So, what about you two?" Erin turned to us.

"I'll try the avocado toast and black coffee." Marc waved for me to order.

"I'd like a blueberry muffin and your daily special latte."

"Coming right up." Erin rang us up, and we secured a table for four in the corner. Marc sat beside me, and we had a good view of the door.

Marc leaned close. "You must be rubbing off on me, because I think Griffin has a thing for Erin."

"Told you so."

"It probably didn't hurt when he practically saved her life."

I laughed. "Right, but he was into her before that. It just sped up the relationship."

Griffin appeared, carrying two mugs. "Erin's help is running late, and I offered to deliver these to you. I don't know how she accomplishes so much by herself."

"A friend and I were just talking about how desperation can lead us to do things we'd never dream of in a normal situation."

"I hear that." He set our drinks on the table.

"Thanks, man." Marc leaned back. "Hey, the office space at the house is great. I doubt you need references, but if you do, I'll be happy to sing your praises."

"Appreciate it."

My heart warmed. Marc didn't refer to it as my house. Yay.

Erin walked over and hip-bumped Griffin out of the way. She placed our plates beside our mugs. "Enjoy."

Griffin followed Erin back to the front counter.

"Did you see that?" I kept my voice low. "A hip bump. You don't just do that to anyone."

"I already conceded you're the better person at reading romance."

I buttered my muffin. "How's your avocado toast?"

"Tasty, and I feel healthy for eating it."

Movement in the parking lot snagged my attention. "Heads up. Looks like it's showtime."

"I'll keep my focus on you and our food."

The bell tinkled, but I didn't even look up. "Hey, this has little blueberries like they have in Maine. I hope we get to visit a farmers' market while we're there."

He laughed. "We're going to Maine for our honeymoon so we can hike, kayak, and cuddle in front of a fireplace on crisp nights, and you're thinking about a farmers' market?"

"Yeah, and bookstores, and I'd love to see one of the stores with colorful threads displayed for weavers, and of course I want to buy a throw. Maybe two."

"Why do we need two throws in South Carolina?"

"For snuggling together." I smiled then took a bite of my muffin.

"I won't argue with that."

"Don't worry. We'll do plenty of outdoor activities, but I would enjoy shopping."

He kissed my temple. "If you want to shop, we'll be sure to add it to our itinerary."

"Hey, guys. How's it going?" Lincoln appeared and pointed to the empty chairs across from us.

Marc stood and shook Lincoln's hand. "Good. How about you?"

Ben's step slowed when he must've realized who Lincoln was talking to.

"Great. Andi Grace, have you met Ben Lowe?"

Ben was holding a cup of tea and wrapped the tea bag string around his finger. "We've met."

Marc said, "Would you guys like to join us?"

Ben shook his head. "No—"

Lincoln widened his eyes. "That's a good idea. Ben, you can tell all of us about this moneymaking opportunity. Let's sit."

"Your friends won't be interested. It's more of a musician thing."

"Don't you know? Marc has written many of my songs."

Ben's nostrils flared. "I wasn't aware."

It felt awkward for me to sit while the three men stood.

"Let's hear about Ben's opportunity." Lincoln sat in one chair, and Marc sat beside me.

Ben stood still and kept playing with the tea bag string.

Erin approached. "Your breakfast is ready."

Ben took the remaining seat.

"Sourdough toast with almond butter and a Greek yogurt parfait for you, Lincoln." The parfait glass wobbled, and Ben reached a hand out to steady it until it reached the table. "Sorry about that, Ben. Here's your apple muffin. Can I get you anything else?"

We assured her we were fine, and she left.

Marc propped his arms on the table. "Let's hear about your investment opportunity."

"I've gathered a group of people connected to the music industry. The plan is to create a new way of selling concert tickets. We've got the technology to speed up the process and avoid snafus. I've figured the exact number of people necessary to create this new company. I've already lined up top musicians who've agree for us to sell their tickets. The return on investment will be huge and early."

Lincoln said, "How much are you asking for us to invest?"

"Seventy-five thousand. Again, this is a huge opportunity, and you'll more than make your money back."

My stomach flopped. "Um, we don't have that kind of money."

"Because you're Lincoln's friends, maybe I can make an exception for you. Of course, you won't make as much as Lincoln and the others."

Marc said, "Understood. How soon do you need the money?"

Again, my stomach flopped.

Ben leaned over the table. "The sooner the better. We've got to move fast."

Lincoln ate a spoonful of yogurt.

"Are you ready to join me in this great opportunity?" Ben speared Marc with his gaze.

"I need to look into this."

Lincoln continued eating.

I nudged him with my foot. He needed to help Marc get out of this. Nope. He ignored me and kept spooning up yogurt.

"There's nothing really to investigate. This is my baby, and there's nothing to research." Ben tapped his head. "All of the information is right up here. What questions do you have?"

I placed my hand on Marc's arm. "Honey, there's another investment opportunity I've been meaning to discuss with you. We just haven't had time, and there's not so much time pressure like Ben's proposal."

Ben frowned at me. "Many millionaires make quick decisions. This is one of those times."

Marc covered my hand with his. "It sounds like we need to have a conversation before we move ahead on either project."

"And we're getting married in a few days. I hate being rushed." I turned my focus to Ben. "Becoming a millionaire isn't my top priority. I prefer to invest in friends and family."

"Even if you lose money?" Ben smirked.

"Yes, even if." My heart pounded so hard, it felt like I was about to have a heart attack. I couldn't handle any more of Ben. "If you gentlemen will excuse me, I'm going to leave."

Marc stood with me. "I'm with her. Sorry, guys."

When we reached the parking lot, I met Marc's gaze. "Were you interested in joining Ben's venture?"

"No, but we're supposed to help Lincoln stop Ben's shenanigans."

My body relaxed. "Of course you're right. Sorry."

"Is there something going on?"

"Juliet and Nate want to grow and improve Kennady Bed-and-Breakfast.

I started to stress that you wanted to give money to Ben."

"Aw, now. You know me better than that. Family first." He bent his knees enough to look me in the eyes. "Even if I thought Ben was presenting a good business opportunity, I'd never invest without discussing it with you. We're on the same page, right? What's mine is yours and vice versa."

"Always. House, cars, boats, and money. And your grandparents may need money to move here. I'm happy for us to help make it a smooth transition if they need financial assistance. Like with my siblings, it'll be a gift. Not a loan."

"I appreciate that." He kissed me then straightened.

"So, now what? I can't go back inside, but you should. I'll walk home."

Marc looked at the cloudy sky and passed his key fob to me. "Take my truck."

"Okay, but call me when you need a ride."

"Or Lincoln can bring me back to your house."

"Our house." I smiled. "I thought we just had this conversation."

"Touché. Our house."

We parted ways, and I drove home, considering my next move. I hadn't seen my new niece for days. Lacey Jane and David had requested time alone to get used to their new family dynamic with a baby. Still, wouldn't they enjoy me stopping by with lunch?

Chapter Forty-one

Before I knew it, the morning was over. Marc had caught a ride with Lincoln, and I delivered lunch to my sister and her family. The offer was appreciated, but they seemed serious about wanting their alone time. As a big sister, it was my duty to respect their wishes.

I left them alone and decided to swing by Stay and Play.

Dylan was scheduled to begin working today, but Belle and Melanie could probably use my help anyway, especially with the new pups we'd inherited from Destiny.

I texted Gloria and asked about picking up Momma Dog.

She must've been holding her phone because her reply was immediate. *Yes, Momma Dog is ready to settle into her new home. She needs lots of TLC and good nutrition.*

I replied with a thumbs-up emoji.

It didn't take long to drive to Stay and Play, but during the short trip I received a call from Vince Murray. I parked near the barn and called Vince back.

"That was fast." His voice sounded lighter than some of our previous conversations.

"Yeah, I was driving and wanted to wait until it was safe to talk. How can I help you?"

"I'm serious about investigating Operation Tail-wagger. While it's true I'm a sports reporter, I have done a few investigative stories."

Honestly, I had forgotten. "Are you still in town?"

"Yes, ma'am. John and I found a hotel where we could keep our dogs with us. Hershey is definitely a puppy, and I hope we don't cause any damages. Scout is calmer. It seemed like John needed a vacation from all the stress, and he's already more relaxed. More like his old self. This ordeal with his dog wrecked him."

I stepped out of the SUV. A muggy breeze blew my hair, and I headed for the barn. "How is Scout doing?"

"For all he's been through, remarkably well. John wants to visit Dr. Hewitt again before we leave town, and I'll make sure it happens."

"Doc's the best." I walked past the dog play areas and headed straight for my office. "Did you learn anything about Operation Tail-wagger?"

"Nothing since we went and saw Destiny Howard. As I said, I'm sure she's Claire Rowe."

I pulled a Coke out of the mini refrigerator in my office. "Hey, Destiny gave me the rest of the dogs in her litter. She said it was too much work and putting a strain on her marriage."

A long pause followed before Vince replied. "That's very interesting. What about Momma Dog?"

"I'll get her too. Although, I've already got a lead on a good home for her. She's at Doc's clinic, and I'm supposed to pick her up today."

"Would you like me to pick her up and bring her to Stay and Play? John and I wanted to come by and discuss a proposition with you."

I shivered. Ben's early morning proposition had left me unsettled. "Do you plan to ask me for money?"

"No, why?"

"Never mind. I'd love to chat with you and John. Bring Scout and Hershey too. We can put your pup in a play area to run off some of his energy. I imagine Scout is still recovering from his surgery."

"Yeah, but we'll most likely bring him with us. John keeps a close watch on his dog."

"Okay. I'll pay for Momma Dog's treatment and let Gloria know you'll be picking her up. Don't say anything private—"

"Because you're suspicious of one of the employees. If I had to guess, it'd be the student shadowing Dr. Hewitt."

I laughed. "Wow, you're good."

"Like I said, investigative sports reporter. We'll see you soon."

"Bye." After the call ended, I contacted Gloria and gave her my credit card information.

The dogs and new pups all seemed happy, so I ambled over to the main house.

Juliet was baking brownies. "Hey, I wasn't expecting to see you today."

"Surprise. The brownies smell amazing."

"I discovered they are Chris's favorite dessert. Those two are the sweetest couple. Carol keeps snooping around the house, hoping to find Zarina's bag." Juliet filled the sink with hot water and soap. "Earlier they visited Waccamaw Retirement Community. They met some residents and staff, and they're sold. Although, I think they'd made up their minds before the visit because they want to live close to you and Marc."

"It's good that they like the place. It's dog-friendly?"

"Yes. Chris wants Marc to read over the contract before signing it, but if Marc approves, they'll be moving here in a few weeks."

"Good. I think they're still nervous around Marc and me. If they live nearby, hopefully they'll relax into a comfortable relationship."

Juliet washed the mixing bowl but paused to look over her shoulder at me. "I told Nate that Carol and Chris seem more at ease around us. When Marc's around, it's almost like they freeze up. You know what I mean?"

"It makes sense. If you reject them, it'd be sad. But if Marc rejects them, it'd be devastating. Pets always help people relax, and Momma Dog is coming here today. It'll be good to have her around." I pulled a clean towel out of a drawer and dried the bowl. "Oh, is this up to code?"

"Don't worry about drying it. I usually handwash the messier dishes then wash them again in the dishwasher. I won't get shut down for a kitchen violation."

Her words stopped me. Shut down for a violation? "Juliet, I wonder if Destiny gave me the dogs because she knew her dog breeding business was about to be inspected? The dogs were in the back room. The space was tight. I wonder if you are required to have a certain amount of space for each dog? And we never found out what happened to the daddy dog."

"Do you know who the dad is?" Juliet finished the last dish and drained the sink.

"No, but Skylar saw the dog. Let me check with her." I hung the towel on a drying rack and passed to bowl to Juliet. "I'll be in the barn if you need me."

"Hey, don't forget there are two things more important than Operation Tail-wagger."

I stopped and faced my friend. "You're right. My wedding is my top priority, then finding Zarina's killer."

Juliet pointed her finger at me. "And you can't get married if the killer comes after you next. Be careful."

I hugged Juliet. "Always."

Her words haunted me on the way to my office in the barn, but once inside the cool structure, I texted Skylar. *Did you find out the owner of the dad dog?*

While waiting for an answer, I played with the dogs.

Juliet had made a good point. My wedding was the most important thing. Second was Zarina's death, then the puppies.

With that in mind, I contacted the pastor, Erin, and Tony. Lincoln had been by to check the sound system for his performances. He was also working on the wedding song. The star wouldn't put on a full concert at the reception, but he was going to sing a couple of songs. The Moonbeams would also perform.

Everyone confirmed they were prepared for the rehearsal, the rehearsal dinner, the wedding, and the reception. It looked like everything was in place.

Thunder rumbled in the distance.

Oh, well. I couldn't control the weather. We'd have to hope and pray for a pretty day.

Chapter Forty-two

Vince and John arrived at the farm with Scout, Hershey, and Momma Dog. I was sitting on a bench near the Old Kitchen and talking on the phone with Skylar. I motioned for them to head into the barn.

"Andi Grace, are you paying attention?" Skylar didn't hide her frustration.

"Yeah, sorry. Some people arrived with dogs, and I pointed them to the barn. You said you found the owner of the male dog."

"Yes. Luckily, I'd snapped a picture of the dog's collar before we got out at Destiny and Ben's farmhouse. Ben hustled to get the dog away from us, but I'm not sure why."

"Tell me more." I crossed my legs.

"I spoke to the wife, and they seem like normal people. They were in town one day, and Destiny introduced herself. Evidently her grandparents were salt of the earth. Destiny told them about her plan to breed Labradors, and she saw their dog and asked if they wanted to partner up. This couple had raised dogs before and had never neutered their dog. His name is Blackbeard. Cute, isn't it?"

She'd told me the dog's name the first time she mentioned the stray dog, but I didn't want to irritate her by pointing that out. "That is a clever name. It sounds like they aren't involved in anything nefarious."

"Exactly. The couple agreed to loan their dog to Destiny for five hundred dollars, on the condition it was no more than thirty days. They also insisted they get paid whether or not Momma Dog got pregnant."

"Sounds like they were smart, considering how flighty Destiny is."

"Destiny is also smart. She had studied about her dog's cycle, and she paid for Blackbeard's services when the couple brought him to her farm."

"Earth's Edge Farmstead."

"Right. By the way, I did a title search, and Destiny has not put Ben's name on the property."

"I wonder why. Maybe in case he got sued for some of his music industry schemes. He tried to pitch one to us this morning."

Skylar gasped. "I want to come back to that conversation, but there's something else. When Zarina and I went to Earth's Edge, we were expecting it to be real nice. You've seen it. The place is run-down. We got a few pictures, then Ben arrived."

I hopped up and paced. "What'd you do with them? What was your plan?"

"That's the thing. I can't find the pictures Zarina took. They must be on one of her other cameras."

"Neither of us has made it inside Destiny's house. It must be nice if she invited you to come take photos. Weird if the inside was nice but not the outside. I got a good look at one of her sheds. Keeping with the theme of Blackbeard, shiver me timbers."

Skylar laughed. She was always so serious, and I'd rarely heard her laugh. "Do you suppose there's any possibility Juliet will allow me back on her property to look for Zarina's camera bag?"

"I'll mention it to her, but Marc and I were planning to search again tonight. Maybe there's something else you can research."

"How about Caleb, uh, what's his last name?"

"Fisher. What about him?"

"He's a student and probably younger than me. At least he looks younger, but you never know. Maybe I can follow him and find a way to hook up and get some information from him."

"You're pretty, and he'd be crazy to ignore you making a pass at him. He's good-looking too, so just don't fall for him."

"I've never fallen for someone I'm interviewing or investigating. I don't plan to start now."

"Hey, you sound just like your cousin."

"Haha. Wish me luck." She ended the call.

"I'm not sure how I feel about you discussing a good-looking man days before our wedding." Marc's smile assured me he was teasing.

"That was Skylar, and I was encouraging her to connect with Caleb Fisher, the vet student. She's hoping to pump him for information on Operation Tail-wagger." I reached for his hand. "Vince and John brought Momma Dog to the barn. Should we get Chris and Carol? See if they bond?"

"This may be a good time to divide and conquer. You go to the barn, and I'll check on my grandparents."

After a quick kiss, we parted ways.

Vince met me at the barn's door. "Everything's good here. Can we talk privately for a minute?"

"Sure. Let's go to my office."

Chapter Forty-three

"Vince, what's on your mind?" I sat at my desk, and he took the chair across from me.

"I can work from anywhere. All I need is an office with the capability of running my podcast. I also need to be close to an airport for when I travel to games." He rested his elbows on the arms of the chair and steepled his fingers together.

"Okay." I'd learned not to rush certain people for information, and I relaxed, giving him time to formulate his thoughts.

He cleared his throat. "I'm usually better at speaking my mind. Here's what I'm considering. John hasn't had an easy life. He's struggled with addictions and depression. He got himself clean, and Scout has been helpful in keeping him sober. It might not make sense to you, but the dog has given John purpose. He doesn't have family, and I barely have any. We've become friends, and I can't help but notice how much better he seems in Heyward Beach. More relaxed."

According to Marc, Vince had also been on a date with Rylee. Was he also happier in Heyward Beach? "What are you thinking?"

"If I could figure out a job for John, and if we could find places to live, I'm noodling with the idea of moving here."

"What does John think?"

"That could be where you come into play. I've noticed you might could use more employees here." He made a circle with one hand.

"Oh, Vince. I'm very careful with who I hire to work with the animals."

"Understood. What if you just observe him with the dogs? Run a background check. I won't say anything to him, but I still think moving here is a good idea."

"With the wedding this week, why doesn't John volunteer here for a couple of days, and I'll watch?" I smiled at Vince. "No promises though."

He stood and headed for the door. "Thanks. I appreciate you."

"You're welcome." I pulled the work schedule up on my computer. Stay and Play was growing, and I could use more help. My dog-walking appointments were fewer in the fall than spring and summer, so that lightened my load. Vince's observation was spot on. I needed more help, and John could fit. He loved animals. He was soft-spoken and gentle. It was worth a shot.

Marc's voice pulled me from my thoughts, and I headed to the main area of the barn. Marc was with his grandparents, pointing out Momma Dog.

I joined them. "Would you like for us to bring her out?"

Chris said, "That sounds like a right nice idea."

I found a leash and attached a harness to the Labrador. It was doubtful she'd run off, but we were new people and this was not her home. No need to take a risk.

Marc pulled some outdoor patio chairs over to the shady bench where I had sat earlier. As I approached, Chris held the back of his hand out for Momma Dog to sniff. Then she moved to Carol and sniffed her hand too. Her tail wagged, and she looked at each of Marc's grandparents.

"It looks promising." I passed the leash to Chris, who seemed the stronger of the two. "Have you had pets before?"

Chris rubbed the Lab's head. "Before we left for the mission field, we had a beagle. That little rascal kept us on our toes. Full of energy and liked to jump fences. We ended up naming him Rascal for all his antics."

Carol laughed and launched into a story of one of Rascal's escapades.

I sat in the chair beside Marc and listened to his grandparents share stories. They loved on the dog while they talked.

Chris said, "Can we take her for a walk?"

"Sure, but she's been through a lot. Keep an eye out for her growing weak."

"Not a problem." Chris stood but waited until his wife was up before strolling away at a slow pace.

"Good news. I may have a new employee." I told him about Vince's proposition.

"Interesting turn of events." He rested his arms on his thighs. "You feel good about it?"

"John doesn't know anything, and I'll watch him the next couple of days. I'll also ask for Dylan's feedback before I go through a background check." My phone vibrated, and I removed it from my pocket. "It's Wade. He says he's headed here and wants to talk to us and J.T."

"I saw J.T. working at the front gate."

"I'll let Wade know." I texted the information to him. "Now what?"

"Do you want to look for Zarina's camera bag?"

"Yes. Let's start in the sunroom." We walked to the house hand in hand and headed straight for the room in question. On the way, I shared about my calls to the wedding vendors.

"Sounds like everything is working out."

"Yeah." I kept my weather concerns to myself. It was only Wednesday, and lots of things could change the forecast. "I wonder where Juliet is."

"She's probably busy doing something for my grandparents, even though she was supposed to take off work this week. It was nice of her to allow them to stay."

"She's a sweetie." I propped my fists on my hips and looked around the room. There was the baby grand piano, bookshelves, comfortable chairs, a coffee table, nooks and crannies galore. "Let's begin with areas big enough to hold the entire backpack camera bag."

"I'll start on this side and we'll meet in the middle."

"Sounds good." I studied the white shelves. They were built-ins and almost reached the ceiling. It didn't seem possible to fit a bag up there without being seen. I wasn't tall enough to test my theory, but if we didn't find it in the lower spaces, we'd look for a ladder.

I inspected every shelf. Nothing hid behind books or pictures. The window seats had comfy pillows, and nothing hid there. Minutes ticked by.

"Nothing on my side."

I jumped at the sound of Marc's voice. "Sorry, I was concentrating."

"Is the piano always closed?"

I shook my head. "I don't think so."

Marc lifted the lid and situated it in place with the lid prop. Strings, plates, hammers, and parts I didn't know the names of were revealed in the light. No hidden camera bag. Marc took a seat on the bench and played a simple tune.

"I knew you played the guitar, but the piano? You've been holding out on me."

He shrugged. "It never came up in conversation, but I only tinker. Music helped me survive some bad days, especially when I couldn't get outside and jump in a kayak."

His favorite foster parent had been Bobby Joe Wilkes, but the man had been older and a heart attack ended the placement. "I remember one time you said that you couldn't understand how a family would fight over money. In fact, you said you'd give any amount of money to have a family."

"It's true, and I'm all for investing in Juliet and Nate's expansion plan."

"That's not where I was going. You've got your grandparents here. DNA proves it, but I feel like you're holding back part of your heart. Don't be afraid to love them with everything you have, and you have a whole lot of love to give. I've seen how you are with my family." I sat on the bench beside him and ran my fingers over the high keys. Treble clef, if my elementary school memories served.

Clink.

I struck the ivory key again.

Clink.

Marc and I met each other's gaze.

"There's no backpack or camera equipment, but let's see what's causing that dreadful note." He moved around and investigated the heart of the piano. "Play the note again. I need to make sure I'm looking at the right place."

I tapped the same key.

Clink.

"Got it." He stuck his hand down and whistled. "What do we have here?"

Chapter Forty-four

"WHAT IS IT?" I moved closer to Marc.

"A photograph." He unfolded the thick paper. "No, it's two pictures."

Our arms touched, and I reached for one. "Oh, it looks like Destiny's farm."

"I agree." He released one to me and held the other near the window. "This shows how overgrown the fields are. You said she was there with Skylar to interview Destiny about her life at the farm."

"I believe it was supposed to focus on her farmhouse style and her life as a wife in the country." I switched photos with Marc. "Oh, another landscape, and it's not pretty."

"Why would she hide these?"

"I don't know. Wade is on the way. It seems like I should check on Carol, Chris, and Momma Dog."

"I can put the pictures in a plastic bag to protect them."

"Sounds like a plan." He returned the photo to me and headed outside.

I called J.T. and entered the kitchen.

"Andi Grace?" The young man's voice sounded confused. "I'm at work."

"This won't take long, and Nate will understand. We found two hidden pictures. They must've been taken by Zarina, but why do you think she'd hide them?"

He sighed. "She was always into notes and hiding her work. Once in high school, she planned to enter a local photography competition. Someone stole her picture and entered it themselves. The flash drive also disappeared, and she didn't believe it was a coincidence. She became paranoid about her work after that. It doesn't surprise me that she hid them."

I found bags in a drawer and sealed each photo in its own bag. "Okay, that makes sense. There's no writing on them. You mentioned notes."

"Yeah, yeah, yeah. She used to pass notes to me in class. Later, she'd leave them in my car, on my pillow, in my lunchbox. She always loved to sneak a note to me."

"It sounds like that was her love language."

"Do you mind me asking what the pictures were?"

"I think they're from Destiny Howard's farm."

"Something about that day freaked her out."

"How do you know?"

"She was upset about the dogs and wanted to protect them somehow."

"Do you believe her death is linked to the day she and Skylar visited Earth's Edge Farmstead?"

"I don't know, but your brother is heading this way, and he doesn't look happy."

"Sorry. I'll tell him it's my fault. Thanks, J.T." I shot off a message to Nate. He'd hired J.T. based on my recommendation, and I'd hate for Nate to fire him because of me.

"Whatcha doing?" Juliet's question startled me.

I jumped and squealed. "Hey, you surprised me. Where have you been?"

She fluffed her blond hair. "I've been in town getting my hair done."

"You look nice."

"Thanks, but you didn't answer my question. Why are you so jumpy?"

"Zarina's murder has me flustered. I found these two photos hidden inside your piano."

"Is this why Wade is here?"

"No, he was already on the way when we found these." I removed my phone and snapped pictures of the photos. "When I was at Destiny's farm, I thought it looked run-down, but I was mostly focused on the dogs and the outbuildings. Do you suppose Zarina spotted something else?"

"Let's see what you've got." Juliet reached for my phone.

"Knock, knock." Wade physically knocked and spoke the words. "I just checked on Duke. Thanks again."

I nodded. "No problem."

Juliet said, "Come in. Can I get you something to drink or eat?"

"No, I'm on a tight schedule." He turned his focus to me. "I just spoke to Marc. Are those the pictures?"

"Yes." I handed the bags to him. "We touched them."

"Good to know. Although, if they were hidden, it's doubtful the killer's fingerprints are on them. But we'll still check. Do you know where this place is?"

I met his gaze. Was he testing me? "I think it's Earth's Edge Farmstead."

He squinted at the photos. "Destiny's place. Please, y'all need to keep this to yourselves. The less people who know, the better."

I crossed my arms. "I won't go around town blabbing."

Juliet reached for a plastic container of cookies and opened them. "Chocolate chip, anyone?"

Wade reached out and took two. "Thanks."

"Wade, I was talking to J.T. earlier. He said Zarina was paranoid about her work. It seems like she'd be double paranoid if she was trying to prove Destiny was doing something wrong, or illegal, with the puppies. Hiding the pictures in the piano was probably a backup plan."

"I hear ya. We need to keep looking for the other cameras, jump drives, and her bag." He bit into a cookie. "Um, these are great."

"Thanks, Wade." Juliet leaned against the kitchen counter.

I said, "What about the metal candy box?"

"There was a handwritten note in it, from Zarina to J.T." He stuffed the rest of the cookie into his mouth.

"Did it help prove his innocence?"

"To save myself some aggravation, I've cycled J.T. off my list of potential suspects." He opened his mouth to say more.

"Stop, I know what you're going to say. I'll keep it to myself."

"Don't even tell J.T. I don't want to tip my hat to the killer."

"I hate for him to suffer longer, but I understand."

"And on that note, I'm outta here. Juliet, thanks for the cookies."

"You're welcome," she answered his retreating back.

I sat at the breakfast table and opened the photo app on my phone. I scrolled through the pictures, searching for anything that might prove helpful. "What did Zarina find that day at the farm?"

Juliet sat close beside me, as only a best friend can do, and looked at the pictures too. "What's popping out at you?"

"I don't know. Here's a picture inside the shed I entered. There are dog supplies. It makes sense, because she's raising puppies. But if she's gone to the trouble to raise and sell puppies, why did she give me the extra pups and Momma Dog?"

"To save her marriage?"

"Yeah, that's what she said. The dogs lived in the back room. So it's possible the dogs disrupted their days and nights."

Juliet pointed at the phone screen. "What's on the shelf?"

"The totes look like they held her clothes. I figured if Destiny was a model, she probably has a lot of clothes."

"Items not suitable for wearing on a farm?"

"Yeah, but the little building was not climate-controlled. I think the smaller boxes may have been full of jewelry."

"The weather wouldn't bother it as much, unless it rusted or got mold on it. If Destiny is strapped for money, why save this stuff? She could consign it or sell at auction and make pretty good money." Juliet used her fingers to enlarge the picture. "Can't tell much."

"Maybe it's an issue of pride. Destiny loved being a model and the perks it provided. Suppose she wasn't ready to give up her pretty things when her grandparents died. She accepted the farm and believed she could turn it around. Maybe to honor their legacy? Or maybe she plans to flip it for bigger money. Did she convert the inside of the farmhouse, and that's why she reached out to Skylar? If Skylar ran a blog post on Destiny, it'd be free publicity. It's possible she was going to announce her desire to sell the place and move back to Charleston." Something nagged at me. What was I missing?

"When I gave up my salon to move here and run the bed-and-breakfast, it was a dream. I enjoy styling hair, and it was fun connecting with people every day. But there's freedom here to bake and care for people on a different level. I've met so many fascinating guests, and some have become friends. It sounds like the place Destiny inherited isn't this nice."

"It's not. Destiny made goat soaps and lotions and sold them at a boutique and online. Although, I've never seen a goat on her farm."

Juliet drummed her fingers on the table. "Let's show her a little grace. Suppose she moved to the farm because she loved her grandparents so much. She tried to make it work, but nothing she experimented with was a good fit. It's hard to imagine she could sell enough goat products to make a profit."

I released my phone and leaned back. "At the prices she charged, the puppies should have been profitable."

"Yes, but don't forget her husband."

"Destiny has a sweet little corgi, so she must like dogs. It's possible she thought breeding dogs would be as easy as owning one." I reached for my phone again and opened the app to take notes. "Let's compare your situation to Destiny's. You and Nate want to move the little beach house to your land to grow your business. It's got to turn a profit to make it worth the trouble. You run the numbers and decide it's a go."

"Right, but Destiny made money as a teen model. Maybe she didn't realize how challenging it would be to make money like normal people."

"Good point." My pulse increased. Were we on the right track? "Juliet, how desperate was Destiny? Had she spent everything she'd ever earned as a model? She was a kid in those days. She's in her early twenties now. Maybe she never saved a penny and doesn't understand how to make a living on a farm. How far would she go to save her farm?"

The back door banged shut, and heavy footsteps crossed the kitchen floor. A shiver slithered up my back. Who had entered the bed-and-breakfast?

Chapter Forty-five

"Andi Grace, you look white as a ghost." Chris hurried to me and touched my shoulder. "Are you okay?"

Relief poured through me. "Yes, I'm fine. Let's chalk it up to an overactive imagination."

Juliet squeezed my arm. "I probably didn't help. All along I tell you don't go looking for trouble. Don't solve murder mysteries. Then I go and question you about Zarina's murder. I'm sorry."

Chris looked from me to Juliet. "I've been known to fix a mean cup of tea. Would either of you care for a cup?"

Juliet laughed. "You're my guest. I should be offering you refreshments. How about it?"

"Maybe in a bit. Carol wanted more time with Marc and walked to the barn with him."

"Let's at least sit in the sunroom where it's more comfortable." Juliet motioned for us to change rooms, and we followed her.

I sat near Marc's grandfather. "Chris, how did you and Carol do with Momma Dog?"

"She's gentle, and I dare say the perfect match for us. Do you mind keeping her at Stay and Play a little longer? We're trying to make this move fast. Thank goodness we don't have a house to sell. Carol and I are so happy to have Marc in our lives, and we're ready to get settled."

"I'd be happy to keep her until you're ready."

"I hear a *but* coming. Let me assure you, we're aware it's our fault for the fractured relationship with Marc. We want to spend as much time together as possible, but we know his most important relationships are with God and with you."

My face heated. "I wasn't going to say that." At this point, I wouldn't say anything else. I'd talked to Marc about opening his heart to his grandparents. "While I might butt into a murder investigation, I intend to treat your relationship with respect."

Marc and Carol entered the room.

Carol fanned herself with her hand. "It's warmer than I expected."

Juliet jumped to her feet. "Sounds like time for lemonade. I'll be right back."

Carol said, "I'd like to freshen up, but I'll return for the refreshments."

"I'll come with you." Chris disappeared with his wife.

Marc pulled a chair over and sat facing me. "I talked to Wade about the note in the mint container. Zarina told J.T. that she wanted to get back together, but she wanted to take it slow. What have you learned?"

I gave him a quick update. "I feel like Destiny is involved with Operation Tail-wagger."

"Lincoln doesn't trust Ben. It's possible he's spreading his wings, and it's also possible Destiny and Ben are in it together."

"Good points, but let's don't forget Caleb Fisher might be part of the fraud."

"Right. You mentioned Skylar was going to check on Caleb."

"Yes. We should focus on another aspect of this case. Right now, Destiny is my primary person of interest. I'm tired of playing tug-of-war with her and this mystery. It's time to catch the prey."

Marc held my hands in his. "Catching the prey typically involves setting a trap. We're getting married in three days. If we're going to set a trap and catch the killer, we need to shift into overdrive. To do that, we're going to need more people involved, and Wade won't be happy."

"True, but the murder happened to our photographer, right here where we are getting married. Zarina was a young woman with a full life ahead of her. And if she was murdered because she wanted to protect dogs and protect people donating to Operation Tail-wagger, it's even worse. We've got to make sure there's justice for Zarina."

Marc nodded. "We need to pull a switcheroo. Destiny and Operation Tail-wagger baited people with sad stories and pictures of pets needing surgeries. We need to figure out how to bait her and get the truth."

"What can we use to lure her?"

Vince entered the room, wearing his Hunter Grimes disguise from our previous visit to Earth's Edge Farmstead. "If you two are discussing Destiny Howard, I may just have a suggestion to your dilemma."

Marc stood and shook Vince's hand. "What's your plan? And why the getup?"

"How about a drive to the country? I'll tell you along the way."

We had just discussed needing more people involved, and Vince showed up. I walked across the room. "Time is of the essence. No offense, but maybe we should discuss your plan first and make sure it's not a wild-goose chase."

Vince narrowed his eyes. "I want to go visit Destiny. The story I plan to pitch her is that I know she's involved in the dog surgery fraud, and I want in. I figure she'll deny the truth, but I'll confess about recognizing her from

Scout's drop-off. I'll insist on her letting me into the organization. That's why you two need to come with me. Andi Grace, you're the dog expert. Marc, you're my attorney."

Marc rubbed his jaw. "I don't see how it'll work. Operation Tail-wagger claims to be a nonprofit."

Vince paced.

Juliet joined us with a tray of drinks. "Sorry it took so long, but Nate called."

"It's okay. Thank you." I reached for a glass.

Juliet looked around the room. "I'm scared to ask about the disguise. Seems like a good time to run refreshments up to Carol and Chris."

"Sounds good."

Marc pinched his lower lip between his fingers. "I may have a better idea. You'll go with an offer to buy her dog-breeding business."

Vince clapped his hands, and the pop echoed through the room. "Excellent plan. Let me give her a quick call to make sure she can meet me."

I took a sip of lemonade. "I'm going to call Skylar."

Marc looked at his phone. "Wade's calling me."

"We should step outside in case Vince gets Destiny to answer the phone. She shouldn't hear us in the background."

"Right." We left Vince alone for our own phone calls.

I sat in a rocker on the front porch and called Skylar.

"Hey, I'm about to head out. I've arranged to meet Caleb on a blind date."

"That was fast."

"Gloria told Caleb she wanted to fix him up, and he went for it. I'm meeting him for drinks at a new bar between here and Myrtle Beach. If it goes well, we're going to dinner."

"Skylar, have you told Wade what you're doing?"

"No because he'll try to stop me. Besides, I'm driving my Jeep. There's no way Caleb can drive me to some deserted patch of woods."

"At least you'll have your own transportation. Do you have a phone tracker on so we can find you if there's any trouble?" I rocked back and forth.

"Is there something I should be aware of?"

"Not really. Just be careful, and don't be afraid to call for help. Oh, and don't leave him alone with your drink. We don't know if Caleb is involved or how deep he's in."

"Right. I've done investigative pieces before. Don't worry."

But had she confronted someone so potentially dangerous? "Be careful, Skylar."

"You too."

The call ended, and I placed the phone in my pocket. I was heading to see Destiny, but Marc and Vince would be with me. We'd have her outnumbered if she tried to pull something, but other factors could shift the odds in her favor. Still, we needed to act, and this seemed to be the best course.

Chapter Forty-six

Vince turned off Highway 17 and onto a shady country road. He drove his old Wagoneer with precision and caution.

Marc rode shotgun. Instead of talking much, he'd been texting Rylee about a client.

I leaned up from the backseat. "You're dressed as Hunter Grimes."

"Yep. I'll be disguised. When John and I met Destiny in Spartanburg, I didn't introduce myself as Vince Murray. Instead, I remained in the background while they conducted business."

Marc's fingers stilled. "If for any reason Destiny questions your real identity, you need a story."

Vince snorted. "You mean besides I'm trying to catch her in a crime?"

Marc's eyes widened. "Well, yeah. That exactly."

"I'm a sports reporter and podcaster. I can claim wanting to promote them on my podcast, but I confess that I needed to investigate them first."

"That could work." I leaned back in the seat. "She's probably trying to find out more about you right this minute."

"It'd be the smartest move she could make. Of course, she won't find me."

Marc said, "What about your friend? Does John know about your plan? Destiny might try to call and trip him up. She might start a plan of her own to stop you."

"John and I had a discussion. We both want to stop these people from harming another dog. Scout ran away, delaying his surgery. He could've been run over, drowned in the river, attacked by wildlife, or anything really. John and I agree, Operation Tail-wagger needs to be stopped. He knows I'm up to something, and we discussed the possibility of Destiny checking me out. He'll only answer his phone to people he knows."

I sighed. "It sounds like you thought of everything."

He signaled then turned onto Earth's Edge Farmstead. "We're about to put our plan into action."

Marc swiped off his phone. "You're here as Hunter Grimes, wanting to convince Destiny to sell the dog-breeding business to you."

"Right, because I'm new to town and need her contacts." He parked beside Destiny's black truck. "Y'all ready to do this?"

My stomach churned, but I opened my door. "Destiny's walking our way. Don't forget your limp."

"The pebble is already in my shoe." He chuckled.

I walked around the old SUV. "Hi, Destiny."

"Andi Grace. Why are you here?" Before I could answer, she turned to Vince. "Mr. Grimes, I didn't realize this was going to be a party."

Vince hobbled to her. "Once you hear my proposition, you may be glad they're here. This is Marc Williams, my new attorney."

"Why do you need him?"

"I was thinking about opening my own dog-breeding business, but I'm new to the area. It seems like buying you out would give me contacts for opening the business. Know what I mean?"

"My business isn't for sale."

"How about we partner up then?"

"I'm sorry, but I'm not interested. Sorry you wasted your time driving out here."

Vince straightened his posture. "Hoped it wouldn't come down to this. Let's go for a little walk."

Destiny's chin lifted, and she looked like a runway model. "Anything you want to say can be said in front of them."

Marc raised his hands and back away. "I trust him not to harm you, but I don't want to witness whatever is about to happen."

Destiny turned toward me.

I shrugged, unsure of my next action. Vince wanted to help stop Operation Tail-wagger from stealing money from generous dog lovers, but how far would he really go? "Um, I'm going with Marc. If you feel unsafe, just holler. We'll be close by." I hurried to Marc.

He took my hand in his. "There aren't any nice sitting areas like at Kennady Bed-and-Breakfast. How about a little stroll?"

"I'd love to go back to the sheds, but if Vince should hurt Destiny, we'd never forgive ourselves. I mean, it's doubtful he'll do any harm, but we don't know him very well."

"True. Just because he loves dogs doesn't mean he wouldn't hurt a human."

We walked to the edge of the woods.

Near the house, Destiny and Vince talked. She flung her hands, and he crossed his arms.

I turned my attention to clouds drifting by, then I shifted my gaze to the towering pine trees and oaks. The pines swayed back and forth in the breeze. "Have you kept an eye on the forecast?"

"There's a disturbance in the Atlantic, but it's supposed to fizzle out in a day or two."

"What if it doesn't? It'll be too late to order event tents. Should we call Griffin and ask for a standby crew?"

"To do what?" Marc lifted his face and watched the clouds.

"Transform the barn into a wedding venue?"

He barked a laugh. "You've gone to a lot of work making it a dog barn. You've got play areas, sleeping quarters, and the dog grooming area. Plus, where would you house all the dogs during the redesign and the wedding?"

My stomach churned. "I don't know. There are a couple of other barns, but they aren't in the best shape."

"Hey!" Destiny waved at us.

Marc squeezed my hand. "Why don't you see what she wants? I'll call Griffin."

I kissed Marc then jogged over to Destiny and Vince. Both frowned. Oh, boy. I'd try to act casual. "What's up?"

"People always talk about how nice you are, Andi Grace. It never occurred to me you'd be involved in a blackmail plot."

"Hold on there. I'm not blackmailing you. I was asked here to share my knowledge about dogs so he could know more about offering to buy your business." What exactly had Vince said to her, and did she know his real identity yet?

Vince waved his hands. "You misunderstood."

Destiny's nostrils flared. "You threatened to expose my involvement in Operation Tail-wagger unless I sold my business to you."

"What's going on? Destiny, are you part of that charity?"

"No. I'm trying to make this farm thrive, and I'm a model. You need to be careful who you associate with. This man isn't Hunter Grimes."

My heart raced in staccato beats. "What?"

"I searched online for Hunter Grimes, and this isn't him."

Vince cleared his throat. "I'm not on social media. There's no crime in that."

"True." I crossed my arms, unsure of our next move. "Destiny, I'm confused. You gave Momma Dog and three puppies to me for free. It seems like you're not going to breed dogs any longer."

"That's not any of your business. You all need to leave my property before I call the sheriff."

"I'm not sure who to believe, but Hunter, are you willing to take Marc and me back to Heyward Beach? Or do you want to give us a ride, Destiny?"

"I'm too busy for that, you can hitchhike for all I care."

"No need. I reckon giving you a ride is the least I can do seeing how you and your fiancé kindly came all this way to help me." He touched the brim of his ball cap. "Destiny, I apologize for the misunderstanding."

"It wasn't a misunderstanding. I know exactly what you said and meant."

Marc strolled across the field with his phone to his ear.

I motioned for him to meet us at Vince's SUV, and it didn't take long for the three of us to leave Destiny's farm.

After we reached the highway, Vince relaxed in his seat. "I'd say we struck a nerve for sure."

"What's next?" My mouth had grown dry, and I would've loved an icy cold Coke.

"Sit back and wait. I predict she'll do something before lunch tomorrow."

"Like what?"

Marc said, "She'll probably reach out to her co-conspirators."

Cloud cover made the road seem ominous. "If she lived in town, it'd be easy to follow her, but out in the country will be a challenge."

Marc glanced back at me. "You can't try to follow Destiny. That didn't come out right. I'm not telling you what you can or can't do, but there's no good place to hide then follow her."

I nodded. "You're right. Plus, I really don't have time. I need to train John on working at Stay and Play. I guess the big question is—"

Vince interrupted me. "Did we learn anything new?"

Chapter Forty-seven

"MARC, WHERE ARE YOU TAKING ME?" I'd changed into a casual dress without knowing the purpose.

"It's a surprise. It's also one of the many reasons I didn't think you'd have time to follow Destiny if she left home tonight." He raised his hand. "I'll never tell you what you're allowed to do or not do. But I do hope we'll have enough respect for each other to voice concerns about dangerous situations."

"Of course. I know you won't ever boss me around, and I do respect your opinion."

Marc pulled into his office parking lot and shut off the truck.

"Work?"

"Trust me." He grinned and jogged around to open my door.

I took his hand. While curious, I trusted Marc enough to know this would be a fun surprise. Country music played. "Thomas Rhett? Do you know more than one country music superstar?"

"No. Lincoln is my only friend in the music industry." He opened the door and led me to the biggest conference room. "Voilà! Isn't that French for ta-da?"

I laughed. "Yes, but you need to give me a little more information." My gaze bounced from the large table pushed to the side with chairs stacked on it. There was also a woman standing beside a boom box.

"This is our dance instructor for the evening. I know you want to dance at the reception, and because I don't dance it seemed like I should take a lesson or two."

I cupped his face in my hands. "You most definitely are the best fiancé in the world. Thanks, Marc."

He introduced me to Floriana Ferrari. The trim woman was older than me. Her thick dark hair was pulled back in an elegant way, and her eye makeup was stunning. I shook her hand and almost wished she'd teach me how to do my makeup instead of teaching us to dance. But Marc would hold me in his arms while we danced, so who cared about makeup tips?

Three hours later, we thanked Floriana for the amazing lesson, then headed to Tony's for a late dinner. If it weren't for Tony, we'd probably starve this week. The man brought us a vegetarian pizza almost as soon as we entered the restaurant. "How were the dance lessons?"

I shook my finger at Marc. "Did you tell everyone what we were doing?"

He slapped his chest. "I did not tell everyone."

Tony's eyes sparkled. "Marc asked me for a recommendation, and I suggested he call my girlfriend."

My heart leapt. "Tony, you've been holding out on me. I hope you'll bring her to the wedding."

"With your blessing, I'd be happy to bring Floriana."

"Most definitely. Do you know how to dance?"

Tony puffed out his chest. "What do you think?"

Marc laughed. "I doubt you'd be dating Floriana if you couldn't dance."

"You're not wrong about that, my friend. Enjoy your dinner."

The restaurant wasn't crowded, so I pointed to the empty chair at our table for four. "Can you join us?"

He looked around the dining room. "Why not? What's the boss going to do? Fire me?"

"There are advantages to being your own boss. Of course, there are headaches too. But if you have an office manager like Rylee Prosser, you don't feel like the boss." Marc placed slices of pizza on two plates. "Tony, are you hungry?"

"I'm good. You two go ahead and eat." He pointed to the pizza. "I've seen your office manager in here with a new man. He's a sports reporter."

"That's right. He also adopted a dog from Destiny Howard and will probably move to our area."

Tony crossed his arms and leaned them on the table. "That makes sense. He had one of those magazines with homes for sale."

Marc said, "Do you know much about Destiny?"

"She's married to an older guy. Old enough to be her dad, but he's in good shape. Muscular, fancy haircut, nice clothes, and he doesn't wear socks with his Italian loafers."

"Ben Lowe is in the music industry and probably interested in keeping up appearances. I imagine he's close to your age."

Tony pointed to his hair. "It'd be hard to compare us with all my gray, but I've earned each and every one."

I patted his arm. "You're authentic, Tony. I'll take that any day over a phony."

"Thanks." He squeezed my hand. "You know they always eat salads and sometimes soup. I've never prepared pizza or pasta for them. It's probably why they're both so skinny. My momma, God bless her soul, would try to fatten them up if she knew them."

"If I didn't move around so much with the animals, I'd probably have to only eat salads." I took a bite of pizza, and my taste buds and stomach lurched in happiness. "Yum."

"Ben is crazy about his wife though. He always checks to make sure she's happy with her order and whatever. And when they're in here, Ben can't quit touching Destiny. I don't mean holding hands. He strokes her face, runs his fingers up her arms, rubs her back, and more. I don't know if it's sweet or creepy."

It sounded more creepy than sweet. "I bet it makes you and the customers uncomfortable."

"Yes, it does."

Customers had been coming in to pick up take-out orders, and a delivery person had come and gone, but not many patrons stayed to eat tonight. Tony looked around the near-empty dining room. "The last time Destiny and Ben were here they met a young man. He had a beard and was taller than the other two. He was friendlier than them too."

Marc said, "You don't know the other guy?"

Tony drummed his fingers on the table. "I'm afraid not, but they seemed to be close. Hugs and laughter. Like family, you know what I mean?"

I gazed at the men. "Do we know if Ben has adult children? Like could the young man be his son?"

Tony said, "I didn't hear him say Dad, but it's possible."

Marc wiped his hands on a paper napkin and scrolled on his phone.

"There was another time just Ben and Destiny were here. They were angry about something, and they were talking about that photographer. Marvin Graves. Yeah, that's it. They were both upset," Tony snapped. "No, Ben was mad. His wife looked scared."

As much as I loved Tony, he tended to gossip. It often helped me, but since solving murders, I tended to use caution with how much I revealed. "Do you think Marvin had compromising photos of Destiny? She used to be a model."

"It's possible. Be right back." Tony crossed the room and greeted Pastor Larry Mays and his wife Phyllis.

Marc passed his phone to me. "It doesn't look like Ben has children, but he's been married before. What do you think about Marvin?"

I glanced at the picture Marc had found of Ben and his ex-wife, who apparently lived in California now. "We'll assume the young man wasn't Ben's son. Let's put that on the back burner for now. I'd like to talk to Marvin again, but how can I get to him?"

Tony's delivery man returned and entered the kitchen.

"Let's order a pizza for Marvin and deliver it. Most people open the door for pizza."

"Great idea." My phone vibrated. "This is Skylar."

"If you want to take her call, I'll order a pizza." He walked away with the casual grace of an athlete that always intrigued me.

I swiped my phone. "Hey, Skylar. Are you okay?"

"Yes. I'm still on my date with Caleb but I came to the restroom to call you. Ben is Caleb's uncle. I'll explain more later but wanted to let you know."

"Thanks. Don't forget to order a fresh drink in case he slipped you a mickey."

"Yes, Mom." She laughed. "Seriously, thanks for watching out for me. I better get back out there."

I found a picture of Caleb on social media then screenshot it. While waiting for Tony and Marc I ate another slice of pizza. The food brought me joy, and I'd hate to be a model and worry about every morsel I put in my mouth. I'd also hate to give up drinking Coke. A dog walker was a good career for me.

The men returned, and I showed Tony the picture of Caleb. "Is this by any chance the man you saw with Ben and Destiny?"

He pulled the phone close then pushed it back until he adjusted it to his vision. "Yes, that's him."

"I just learned Caleb is Ben's nephew."

Chapter Forty-eight

When the doorbell didn't appear to work, we knocked on the front door of Marvin Graves's duplex. The run-down place needed a fresh coat of paint. The grass needed to be cut, and weeds were overtaking the yard. I'd heard Marvin scraped by living as a photographer, and if the looks of the outside of his home were any indication, the rumor was true.

Marc held the pizza box up to hide his face and knocked again. I stood to the side, hoping Marvin wouldn't see me if he looked out the peephole.

In my investigation, I'd learned Marvin didn't get along with too many people. He'd argued with Skylar, Zarina, Ben, Destiny, and his own son.

"Who is it?" a voice on the other side of the door snarled.

"Pizza delivery."

The door whipped open. "I didn't order pizza."

Marc kept the pizza box held high. "This is the address they gave me."

"Is it paid for?"

I stepped out of the shadows. "Yes, it is. We paid for it."

Marc lowered the box. "It's for you, but we'd like to ask a few questions. We won't take much of your time."

"This is about that dead girl, isn't it?"

"Zarina Mills. Yes."

"Do you think I killed her?"

I shook my head. "No, but maybe you can help us figure out who did."

"Come in." He opened the door wider and led us to the kitchen.

The place was neat and clean in stark contrast to the outside.

"Have a seat." He pointed to a scarred round maple table. Still, it was clean. Marvin retrieved a plate from the cabinet and a beer from the fridge.

Marc and I sat across from each other, and the photographer plopped down and chugged his beer before opening the pizza box. "What do you want to know?"

"Let's start with Destiny Howard."

He took a bite of pizza starting with the crust. "Yeah, she's a real piece of work."

"Can you elaborate? And do you mind if I take notes on my phone?"

"Knock yourself out." He took another bite before answering. "Destiny wanted me to take pictures of her puppies and find a reporter to promote her business. I didn't promise a reporter, but I went to her farm. Something about the earth."

"Earth's Edge Farmstead." I didn't look up from my phone.

"Yeah. That's right. When I got there, she was chasing a dog. Turned out to be the sperm donor. I snapped some pictures of her chasing the male dog, then I strolled over to the back of the house. There were two puppies in a pen. In another pen was what I figured was the mother. When Destiny returned, I questioned her about breeding the dog again. She assured me her vet approved the back-to-back breeding. What do I know? I took pictures of everything I saw. Good and bad."

"Was she happy?"

He laughed. "The very opposite. First, she was mad, because I didn't bring a reporter. I tried to tell her I can write decent stories. Second, she didn't want me to publish all the pictures."

"Which ones specifically?"

"Her chasing the daddy dog."

I glanced at Marc. "I wonder if it's the same dog we heard about."

Marvin leaned back in his chair. "I don't know about that. But she said if the owner found out the dog had gotten away from her, their breeding contract would be broken. She was steamed. Even threatened me."

"Like how?"

"Put me out of business. Tell her model friends not to use me. You name it, and she threatened it. I didn't put much stock in her intimidation tactics though. I've been in the business long enough to have established my good reputation."

I wasn't sure *good* was the best word to describe his reputation, but I kept my mouth shut. "You said there wasn't a reporter with you. Did you interview Destiny?"

"Yeah. I calmed her down then we sat on her front porch and began to talk. She kept getting text messages and was distracted. I don't know what was said, but at least one message came from somebody calling himself Fly Boy."

"Did she reveal anything about Fly Boy? Like was she using a pilot to say, maybe, fly the puppies to their new homes?"

Marvin straightened. "I didn't just fall off the turnip truck. It seems to me you really want to know about Fly Boy and Operation Tail-wagger."

My heart leapt. "Did y'all discuss the operation?"

"Not that day." He closed the pizza box, placed it in the refrigerator, and grabbed another beer. "She and Zarina discussed it—no, they argued about it—the day of the murder."

"Do you know any specifics?"

The man remained standing. "Not really."

"You also argued with Zarina, and you seemed more than a little disgruntled."

"Yeah, well, I'm innocent. Zarina was a good kid, but I didn't appreciate her stealing jobs from me." He popped the top and took a drink. "People aren't loyal like in the old days. What can I say? Zarina and I were competitors for photography jobs."

Marvin hadn't taught Zarina photography, so how did loyalty fit the equation? I let his comment go in case I could learn more about the murder. "What do you know about Operation Tail-wagger?"

"I've been reading up on it, and it doesn't seem legit."

"I tend to agree. Who do you think murdered Zarina?"

"I don't know, and I've looked through my photos from the day of the murder. Nothing really jumps out to me as suspicious activity."

"Have you shown the photos to Sheriff Stone?"

"He didn't ask to see them."

"Well, okay then."

"If you think of anything, would you contact us?" Marc handed a business card to the man.

"Yep."

"We'll leave you alone unless there's something else you'd like to share."

"Nope. Thanks for the pizza." He walked to the door.

Marc and I followed and thanked him for his time.

On the way home, I reviewed my notes. "I hope that wasn't a waste of time."

"We learned Destiny has a dark side, and she's secretive. She didn't want people to know she's not good with dogs, and she didn't hesitate to threaten Marvin."

"Good points. I should text Wade and tell him Marvin has photos from the day of the murder."

"I find it hard to believe nobody asked a photographer if they took pictures that day."

"Me, too. Maybe Marvin is lying. Still, I should tell Wade."

"Agreed."

I sent the sheriff a text. "I'm going to sleep on all we've learned today. Maybe I'll be fresh enough in the morning to figure out my next move."

"Sounds like a good plan."

"What about you?"

"I've got a late meeting with Lincoln. He asked me to stop by tonight."

"Is it about the wedding?"

Marc scratched his five o'clock stubble. "I really don't know, but don't worry. If there's a problem, Lincoln will fix it."

I relaxed and trusted Marc. It made me sad to know Zarina had just begun to trust J.T. right before her death. The first thing I planned to do in the morning was to go through Kennady Bed-and-Breakfast and find Zarina's camera bag. There must be a clue in it, and I wouldn't rest until we located it.

Chapter Forty-nine

Early Thursday morning, I entered the kitchen of Kennady Bed-and-Breakfast and bumped into Nate.

He placed his hands on my shoulders. "Steady now. How about a cup of coffee? Juliet prepared a pecan blend."

"Sounds perfect."

Nate pointed to a tray of muffins. "Help yourself to one of those. Marc's grandparents are the only guests here, and they won't eat the entire batch of peach muffins."

"Thanks." I reached for an antique plate with pink roses trimming the edge. "After you guys are married, I hope you convince Juliet to serve food on plates that can go in the dishwasher."

He laughed. "I've tried. She said something about ambience and making guests feel special."

"Juliet mentioned moving the beach house to your property." I pulled up a stool and sat, but Nate leaned against the counter. "Well?"

"Together, I believe Juliet and I can grow this place. When we begin dreaming, it's like the ideas pour from us. I've already paid for the house. The logistics have been worked out to move it here, and I think it'll be a good investment. We'll fix the thing up as a little cottage. The Old Kitchen has been a hit for families and small groups of people. The house is going to be a popular addition."

"What about your landscaping business?" I blew on my coffee before sipping it.

"There's enough property here to satisfy my need for landscaping. Plus, Juliet has big dreams for the bed-and-breakfast. I'll do whatever it takes to support her."

My thoughts drifted to Ben. "But you won't cross the line and do something illegal."

Nate huffed. "Of course not. What in the world?"

"How far do you imagine Ben Lowe would go to protect his wife and her farming dreams?"

"I don't know the man, but I've heard he scammed some country stars and got away with it." He chuckled. "Come to think of it, that could've been the headlines on a grocery store magazine. Oh, well, I better scoot."

"Hey, Nate. Are you concerned about the weather?"

He frowned. "I'm keeping an eye on the reports. You worried about the wedding?"

"Yeah. What if we can't hold the ceremony outside?"

"The only thing I know for sure is come rain or shine, we're getting married on Saturday."

"Marc's going to talk to Griffin about possibly moving the ceremony and reception to the barn."

"That could work. The rehearsal dinner will be smaller. If it rains, we can move Friday's events into the main house. That'll buy us a day."

"True. Changing the subject, have you ever done any work at Earth's Edge Farmstead?"

"No, but the owner asked for bids on the landscape. None of us were hired. One of the guys heard she decided to redecorate the inside of the house first." He scratched his head. "Most farmers are more concerned with the land, crops, and animals."

"Yeah, that makes the most sense. Although, I don't know if her heart is into the farm."

"Then she should sell it."

"True, but I think it could be a sentimental issue. When our house burned down, I was torn up at the thought of losing that connection to Mom and Dad. It wasn't easy to sell the lot for someone else to build on."

"You did the right thing, and your place is terrific."

"Yeah, it is. And I think Marc is starting to feel like it's his home too."

"Good. Now I really need to get busy." Nate gave me a quick hug.

I ate my muffin and considered where to begin my search of the main house.

Juliet entered the kitchen. "Good morning."

"Morning. I'm going to hunt for Zarina's camera bag today. Can you tell me what rooms she was in?"

She sighed. "Zarina cleaned up and changed clothes. She also had a snack, but I honestly don't know where all she went. You already checked the sunroom. Make yourself at home and look around the place."

"Thanks, and I'll be mindful of Marc's grandparents."

"They have a meeting at the retirement community to sign the final papers."

"They aren't wasting any time." At least today they weren't wasting time. It was too bad they couldn't connect with Marc before now. So many wasted years.

"We can only move forward. That goes for all of us. If Nate and I had been braver, we might have gotten together years ago."

"I see what you mean, and I'm glad Carol and Chris are planning to settle down near us."

Juliet gave me a quick hug. "They're good people."

I laughed. My desire to protect Marc from pain was fierce, and a tiny part of me feared his grandparents' ability to hurt him. "I'm doing my best to believe you."

"That's all I ask. I'll be around. If you need me, give a shout."

"Was Zarina in the kitchen?"

"Yeah, she made a sandwich."

"Then my search begins in here." I started with cabinets at eye level. When that didn't produce results, I crawled around and searched the lower cabinets.

Nothing.

The pantry was next. Juliet was organized, and it was easy to determine no camera backpack hid in the small area.

I headed to the breakfast room and ran into Carol. "Hi, Mrs. Williams."

"Good morning, dear. Is Marc with you?"

"No, ma'am. He's at work. Where's your husband?"

"Chris walked to your barn to visit Momma Dog. I hope the dog will be able to distract Chris on the days I'm running behind." She smiled. "I can't wait until we can move into our new home with her. Some of our friends in Kentucky are meeting with movers to send our belongings here. We don't have a lot, but we have enough to begin our new life in Heyward Beach. I'm praying we'll be in our new place by the time you and Marc return from Maine. We'll invite you over to supper."

"That will be nice. Thanks."

"Are you still looking for the camera bag?"

"Yes. I didn't see it in the kitchen, and we didn't find it in the sunroom."

"Let me help you look around the breakfast room."

"Thanks." We divvied up the room and searched until there was nowhere else to look.

Chris appeared. "Sweetheart, we've got a meeting at Waccamaw Retirement Community in less than an hour."

"I only need to grab my pocketbook." Carol winked at me then left the room.

Chris jingled change in his pockets. "Still looking for the camera bag?"

"Yes, sir."

"How'd you get into solving murders?"

"One morning, I came here to walk a friend's dog. You've met Chubb. Marc's dog was a puppy and belonged to my friend at the time. I eventually convinced Marc to adopt Chubb." I swallowed hard. It was still hard to discuss Peter. "To make a long story short, Peter had been murdered. I found the body. Marc found me, standing over the body. A deputy thought I murdered Peter. My parents were killed by a hit-and-run driver who had not been caught, and I hadn't been able to get over their deaths. I figured maybe I could get justice for Peter by finding his killer and proving I was innocent."

"That's some story. I hope you're being careful. It appears to me that the closer you come to catching the guilty person, the more danger you'll be in."

I couldn't deny the truth behind his words.

"Okay, dear. I'm ready, and Andi Grace, feel free to search our room. I've snooped a bit in case that poor girl stashed her bag in there, but you should give it a thorough look."

I thanked her and told them bye. It seemed like their room was the next place to search.

Chapter Fifty

I WALKED DOWN THE BEAUTIFUL STAIRCASE more than a little bummed that I hadn't found Zarina's bag. I'd examined the room where Carol and Chris were staying. I even checked for false panels in the closets.

Zilch.

There was still the living room to consider. I ran my fingers along the shiny wood banister's handrail. I paused on the bottom step. It'd been over two hours since I began the search. What a waste of time. Smart soon-to-be-brides were probably doing girly things at spas. I wasn't exactly sure what they'd do. Facials? Massages? As much bending as I'd done in my search, I could go for a massage.

What options were left? I gripped the newel post and gave it a frustrated shake.

The post moved the slightest bit.

My heart leapt.

No way could Zarina have hidden her camera backpack in the newel post, but what about something else?

I pushed it back and forth, and it moved under my touch. I twisted the top of the newel post. It turned.

"Andi Grace, what are you doing?"

I met Juliet's gaze. "Have you ever removed this?"

"No." She stepped closer. "What's in there?"

I turned the top of the post and kept turning. "Oh, man. It may only be loose."

"Let me try." Juliet turned it but didn't have any luck either.

"I just remembered something Zarina told me. She said this house was part of the Underground Railroad and that there were lots of secret hiding places. I wonder . . ."

I stepped onto the main floor and walked along the side of the rising staircase. The hall was fairly wide, and the floor shone in the sunlight streaming in from the front windows.

The steps rose in an orderly fashion. Each wood step had been polished until it shined. The risers had been painted white, adding to the crispness of the scene. The newel post was followed by spindles all connected on top with the handrail. The bottom of the spindles were secured on the steps.

The wall under the stairs formed a right-angled triangle. The white beadboard leant a casual air to the historical house. I ran my hands along the wall until I felt a prick. More than likely, I was about to be disappointed again. "Juliet, what's this?"

She walked to me. "What?"

"Feel right here." I shone my phone's flashlight on the spot. "Look. There's a little hinge in this groove."

Juliet ran her fingers over the spot. "You're right. There's something here, but I don't want to demolish this wall if it's nothing important."

I laughed. "You know I want to take a sledgehammer to it, or rip down the beadboard. But I'll refrain. If Zarina found one of the secret hiding places and hid her bag behind this wall, there's got to be an easy way to open it. And there's bound to be a good bit of space under the stairs."

We leaned so close our shadows made it hard to see.

Juliet said, "Why don't I shine the light on it and you try to figure out how it opens."

I ran my fingers up and down the grooved area. My fingernail snagged on a different spot, and I worked the area until the latch lifted. "This is it."

"Be careful."

The hidden door opened. The space was dark and went as far back as the wall on the other side of the wide steps. "A small person could fit in here."

Juliet gasped. "Do you think people hid in this space?"

"Maybe. If not people, maybe the home owners hid valuables in here." My pulse throbbed by my temple. "There's nothing visible, but I'm going in."

"I'll shine the light for you."

I ducked my head and entered the hiding spot. The farther I ventured in, the taller the space grew.

My foot hit a hard object.

I knelt and reached for the item.

"There's something here." It felt like nylon with straps and zippers. It had to be Zarina's missing camera backpack. I lifted the heavy bag and made my way to the hall where Juliet waited.

"Oh my stars. You found it."

"Let's not jump to conclusions."

"Are you kidding? Who else would hide a bag under the stairs? Plus, Zarina hid the other photos in the piano." Juliet's voice squeaked.

The sound of a vehicle out front stopped her words.

"Give me a minute. I need a pair of gloves to open it before calling Wade. You know, to make sure it belonged to Zarina."

"Girl, you're going to get us in so much trouble." She glanced over her shoulder. A sedan had parked in front of the house. "I'll see who's in the car. You better call the authorities. Wade or David or somebody."

"I'll be in the kitchen." I hurried but hid the bag in the pantry before placing my call. Some might call me paranoid, but it wouldn't pay to have a stranger touch potential evidence.

Juliet was right. It had to be Zarina's bag. No matter how much I wanted to snoop, I needed to contact the sheriff. So, I sent a quick text to Wade and Marc. *Backpack found at the B&B. Let me know what to do.*

Voices from the front hall sent chills up my spine.

I sent another text. *Hurry. We may be in trouble.*

Chapter Fifty-one

Juliet was speaking to a man in the front hall. Her squeaky shrill voice revealed how uncomfortable she was in the situation.

We needed help. Who could reach us the quickest?

Dylan, John, and Vince should all be at the barn working with the dogs. There was also Belle and Melanie to consider. Their safety was of the utmost importance.

Lacey Jane and David had dodged most of my calls since the baby was born, so it'd be a waste of time to reach out to them. Instead, I called Dylan.

"Hey, boss. We've got this under control."

"Great, but we may have a little problem up here at the main house. I need you and John to stay there and protect the girls and the animals. Would you ask Vince if he'd mind coming over to check on us? Warn him though it could be dangerous."

"Lincoln's here too. We'll figure out a plan to help you and protect the others." The line went dead.

I took a deep breath, tapped the voice recorder app on my phone, and walked into the hall. With a little luck, I'd pull off a casual vibe. "Hey, Juliet. The florist needs to discuss our bouquets."

Juliet's cheeks were red. "Ask if we can call her back. Um, Andi Grace, this is Ben Lowe."

"We've met," Ben practically growled.

"True. You threatened to call the sheriff if I didn't leave your farm. Why are you here?"

"I came to find you. We need to discuss the visit you paid my wife yesterday. Privately."

He'd stumped me. If I left with him, I'd be in danger. If I stayed, Juliet might be in harm's way too. "How about talking on the back patio?"

"The front porch works better for me." From what I knew about him, the man always wanted to be in charge. He took me by the elbow and propelled me in his desired direction.

Juliet leapt in front of us. "Let go of her."

"Mind you own business."

I planted my feet on the hardwood floor and yanked my arm out of his grip. "I refuse to go anywhere with you. Yesterday, I was at your place at the request of a friend who wanted to buy your wife's business. When she asked us to leave, we left. There's nothing more to discuss."

I heard the back door bang shut. The sound rang through the house.

At the same time, Lincoln entered through the front door. "Ladies, what's going on? Are y'all okay?"

I shook my head. "I'm not exactly sure."

"We're all good." Ben lifted his hands in defense and backed away.

Vince entered the hall from the kitchen. He blocked Ben's exit. "What have we got here?"

Lincoln said, "Ben, perhaps we should hear what the ladies have to say."

Juliet stood close to me. "Ben tried to manhandle Andi Grace. He wants to talk to her about something that happened yesterday."

Vince turned on Ben. "Most conversations don't require manhandling."

Ben smiled at us. "I only wanted to have a friendly chat with Andi Grace."

Lincoln's gaze bounced to me. "Well?"

"Nothing friendly about his actions. Ben tried to force me outside for a conversation." My legs shook. Had the shakiness begun when I saw Ben, or was it from the relief of being safe?

Lincoln crossed his arms. "Ben, you're usually much more civilized than that. For example, when you wanted us to invest in your ticket venture."

Vince stood in front of Ben. "Yesterday, Andi Grace joined me in an advisory capacity when I went to make a monetary offer to your wife concerning her dog-breeding business."

Ben was a small man compared to Lincoln and Vince. Never had it been as apparent as right now standing in the wide hall. Ben's nostrils flared. "You three ganged up on her. You scared my wife."

Vince said, "How? I simply made Destiny an offer. My attorney was on the phone most of the time, and Andi Grace was with him."

A siren sounded in the distance.

Vince glared at me. "Did you call the sheriff?"

"Yes, on a different matter." I didn't mention finding the backpack.

Ben pushed past me and elbowed Juliet as he made his escape.

Lincoln paused to check on us before running after Ben.

Vince touched our shoulders. "I don't believe he was carrying a gun, but it's a good thing you called us. No telling what he planned to do."

"Thanks for coming, but I'm worried about Lincoln now. What if Ben pulls a gun on him?" I hurried down the hall and out to the front porch.

The two men stood in the grass near Ben's sleek car. They were close enough for me to hear their conversation, but far enough away that Ben couldn't nab me.

Lincoln pointed. "Man, you've got nowhere to go. The sheriff is almost here, and there's no way to outrun him."

Ben looked in the direction of Wade's official SUV, and his shoulders slumped. "Why does any of this matter to you? We're not working together anymore. Your attorney took care of that."

Chills zipped up my spine again. His words confirmed why Ben seemed to hate Marc.

Chapter Fifty-two

Marc arrived right after a deputy took Ben to the sheriff's department to be questioned. He took me in his arms. "You liked to have scared me to death."

I held tight. "He did frighten us."

Wade coughed. "Break it up, you two. We need to discuss the missing you-know-what."

Marc's eyes widened. "Is it true? You found it?"

Despite the encounter with Ben, I couldn't help smiling. "Yes. Can you believe it?"

"Su-weet." Marc gave me another hug then pulled back. "Where is it?"

"Let's go to the kitchen."

Juliet had prepared a plate of sandwiches and glasses of sweet tea. "I know it's early, but I thought we might need lunch. Besides, it's best when I keep busy."

I hugged my friend. "You really stuck your neck out for me. Thanks."

"You're my best friend, and nobody's going to hurt you if I can stop it."

I'd been in tighter scrapes, but Ben had unnerved me. "I'll always try to protect you too, but hopefully we won't have any more close calls."

"Amen to that." Marc pointed to the food. "Buffet style?"

"Why not?" Juliet pulled out plates and napkins.

J.T. knocked on the door and entered the kitchen. He took off his ball cap advertising Nate's landscaping business. "Sheriff Stone called and asked for me to come over. Ms. Juliet, Nate gave me the okay to take off. Do you know why the sheriff called me?"

Wade entered the kitchen before Juliet responded. He said, "Thanks for coming. Andi Grace found Zarina's bag. We're about to go through it. I'd like your opinion."

J.T. turned the hat in his hands. "If it'll help you catch Zarina's murderer, I'll do anything you need."

"Good answer. You knew Zarina better than any of us. Maybe something will jump out at you that I might skip over." Wade clapped his hands. "Andi Grace, where's the bag?"

"In the pantry." I walked into the small space and picked it up.

Juliet said, "Is anyone hungry? Or would you like me to put these in the refrigerator until later?"

"Don't mind if I do. Thanks." Wade picked up a little ham and cheese sandwich and ate it in two bites.

I reached for a turkey on rye and managed a bite before Wade slipped on his crime scene gloves. "We need to go through this on a clean surface."

"We can spread out at the breakfast room table."

Soon we all sat around the table and watched as the sheriff opened Zarina's missing camera backpack.

J.T. sat on the edge of his chair and bounced his leg. "You're gonna see Zarina's calendars, journal, wallet, probably a drawing from our daughter, definitely at least one photo of our daughter, possibly the latest devotional book she was reading, and stuff women normally keep in their purses."

"Okay." Wade removed each item J.T. had predicted plus more. "Here's her tablet. Do you think it's the same password as her phone?"

"Yes, sir."

Wade tried swiping and pushing buttons. "It's out of juice."

"I have a charging cord that might work. Give me a minute." Juliet left the room.

Marc said, "If I remember from our engagement photos, Zarina could send pictures from her camera to an email address."

"Right. Right. Right. But she preferred to touch up most of the photos before giving them to her customers." J.T. frowned. "She never wanted people to be disappointed in her work. Every so often, she'd capture a sunrise, a rainbow, or Sarah smiling and send it to me from her camera. Most of the time, she transferred them to her tablet or computer and perfected the photos."

"Makes sense. I remember now. It was a few days before we received all the photos." Marc smiled at me.

Wade placed the items he'd gone through in a neat stack and opened the next section. "Whoa. That's a lot of lenses."

"Each one does something a little different. A famous photographer in Georgetown died, and his wife wanted to sell most of his equipment. Zarina got wind of it and reached out to the widow. The woman loved Zarina's story and gave her everything for free because she wanted to support her dreams."

"Cool." Wade removed a camera.

I pointed at it. "I'm no expert, but that looks like the one I saw her using the day she was murdered."

"Let's see what we've got here." Wade pushed buttons. "Oh, here we go. Here are some of the crowds at the rally. Now Hannah and her dog."

Wade and Hannah had dated, and I still believed they could be good together if not for Wade's stubborn pride. "Do you remember Theo Graves said she took pictures of Ben and the Moonbeams? No, it wasn't Ben, it was Destiny, which seems weird because Ben is the one who works with musicians."

Marc said, "According to Belle, Destiny asked them if they wanted any of her puppies."

"Hmm. I don't see anything like that on here." He met my gaze. "Glove up and give it a look while I check another camera."

I pulled blue gloves on and scrolled through the photos on Zarina's camera. "You're right. J.T., did Zarina have a camera that could take pictures digitally and use film at the same time?"

"She tried that once. In her opinion, it was easier to go digital. Although, she said film blends light and colors more naturally. Still, she almost always used digital."

"I use the camera on my phone, and if I don't like a picture, I delete it. Does a camera work the same way?"

"Yes, ma'am."

Wade set the camera on the table. "Whatcha thinking, Andi Grace?"

"Just suppose Zarina took a picture of something that put her in danger. She figured out the significance. What if she sent the photos to someone's email then deleted them off her camera?"

J.T. said, "I haven't checked my email in days, but if it was something dangerous, she'd send it to me and not her momma. The other possibility is she took the pictures with a different memory card. But if she stumbled onto something, it's doubtful she'd go to the trouble to swap out memory cards. No. She'd start snapping away in order not to miss the moment. A camera memory card is small and flat. It could be in the bag."

Wade continued searching the bag. "Can you access your email from anywhere? Like do you know your password?"

Juliet returned to the room with two cords. "One of these is bound to work. Guests often leave their cords behind. When I reach out, they usually say it's cheaper to buy a new one instead of having me mail theirs."

Wade tossed her a pair of gloves. "See what you can do."

She soon had the tablet charging.

J.T. said, "I don't have an email app on my phone. Do you want me to log onto my email from that?"

"No. Juliet, do you have another tablet or laptop J.T. can use?"

"I sure do. Hang on."

Wade emptied the bag. He even held it upside down and shook it. "Unless she found another hiding place, I don't see the memory card."

Juliet returned with her laptop and sat beside J.T. In no time she logged on and passed it to Zarina's ex-husband. "There you go."

His hands hovered over the keyboard and he closed his eyes. "Here goes nothing. Or everything. I'm not sure which."

Chapter Fifty-three

EXCEPT FOR WIND RATTLING THE WINDOWS, the breakfast room grew quiet as J.T. opened his email. Wade stood behind him and watched over his shoulder.

"Here's one." J.T. pointed to the screen and opened the email. "Look at these pictures. It looks like the same dog to me. I think Zarina took a picture of this dog, but this other picture is a screenshot from social media. They look exactly like the same animal."

Wade leaned closer.

I said, "Is the social media post connected to Operation Tail-wagger?"

"Let's see." He pointed to one photo. "They both are from social media, asking for help to save the dog's life by donating to the organization. Here's the kicker though. The first post was three years ago, and it was a different organization. Loving Our Pets."

"Is there anything connecting either group with Destiny Howard?"

J.T. shook his head. "Not in this email."

"See if there are any other emails. We still don't have the missing pictures Zarina took of the band."

J.T. searched. "Yeah, yeah, yeah. It probably got moved to my spam folder. Sometimes emails with a lot of attachments get moved there." He frowned.

"What's in the email?" I wanted to be the one looking over J.T.'s shoulder, but technically I was the dog walker. It had been nice of Wade to include me in this get-together.

"Hot dog. It's the missing pictures from the day of her murder." Wade placed a business card on the table. "I need you to forward those messages to my email."

"Yes, sir."

I looked at the others. "We still need a direct link between Destiny and Operation Tail-wagger. We also need to catch Zarina's murderer. Until Ben showed up today, I suspected Destiny."

"And now?" Marc quirked an eyebrow.

"I'm not sure. Is Ben trying to protect his wife, or did Ben commit the murder?"

A hush fell over the room.

Wade broke the silence. "Y'all need to trust my department to solve the case. Focus on the weddings. Move on with your lives. I'll catch the killer."

J.T. closed the laptop. "I've just got one question. Where is Zarina's tripod?"

I gasped. "Right. Theo said the tripod was attached to her backpack. Let me look in the secret space again."

The others followed me to the hiding place under the stairwell. I turned on my flashlight app and searched the area. "I don't see it."

"Let me look." Wade waited until I exited, then he entered and used a powerful flashlight. It didn't take long for him to return. "Nope. I didn't see it either. Is it important?"

J.T. sighed. "Only because there's a secret compartment in one of the legs where she might have hidden something."

"Of course there's another secret compartment. Let me remind everyone not to discuss what happened today with anyone. Don't mention the bag was found. Don't even tell people the tripod is missing. If you find it, let me know." Wade returned to the breakfast room to gather Zarina's belongings.

J.T. said, "Can I go back to work now?"

"Yep. Just don't tell anyone what happened here today."

"What should I say?"

"You can say I had some questions about Zarina, but I don't believe you're involved."

"Thanks." J.T. left out the front door.

Juliet said, "Wade, let's get you more food."

Marc and I faced each other in the hall.

I reached for his hand. "Do you have to go back to work?"

"I took the rest of the day off. Rylee drove me here so she could spend time with Vince."

I laughed. "It's hard to picture her working with the dogs. You know how I usually like to match people with dogs? I can't picture Rylee with Hershey. Maybe a corgi like Queenie, but not a Labrador."

"Don't be too sure. I've seen a softer side to Rylee in the days since she met Vince. She might be a Labrador lover given the right circumstances."

I laughed. "Each one has a strong personality, and it'll be interesting to watch their relationship."

"Yep, but in the meantime, what do you want to do?"

"Let's walk the property and check for wind damage."

"You surprise me. I figured we'd do something related to the murder."

"I don't want to neglect our wedding."

"And?" His eyes twinkled.

"And I probably need a break from thinking about the murder. It's been such a tug-of-war. Stop Operation Tail-wagger versus solve the murder. Are they related or two random events?"

"Both of us believe they're connected. So? What's it going to be? Wedding or mystery?"

"Wedding first, then check on Sunny and Chubb." I headed to the front door.

"Then we'll get back to solving the murder."

"Perfect." We stepped out into a wind blowing from the south. I couldn't control the weather, but there was no reason I couldn't prepare for it.

Chapter Fifty-four

AFTER INSPECTING THE SITE where we planned to get married overlooking the Waccamaw River, Marc and I met with Lincoln in my office.

We'd gotten sprinkled on. *Windswept* didn't begin to describe how my hair looked after our walk on the property.

Dylan appeared in the doorway. "Hey, guys, Chubb is unsettled. Probably from the weather. I can handle him, but since Marc is here, I was wondering—"

Marc leapt out of his chair. "Say no more. I should have brought his storm jacket thing."

I said, "We have extra ThunderShirts if you want to use one."

"Thanks." Marc disappeared with Dylan.

Lincoln said, "I'm glad Sheriff Stone took Ben in for questioning."

"Yes. Thank you for stepping in earlier. I might could've fought him off, but it was nice to have you on my side."

"Anytime you and Marc need me, I'll be there for you." He propped one foot on the other leg. His jeans shifted up, exposing a brown cowboy boot that hit about mid-calf. "I guess y'all want to discuss the wedding."

Marc and Chubb entered my office. Marc sat, and Chubb propped his chin on Marc's knee. Marc rubbed the golden retriever's head. "What'd I miss?"

Lincoln said, "I was asking about Saturday."

"And I was about to tell him our concerns about the weather."

"Are y'all planning to change venues?"

Marc shook his head. "Not exactly. If we move the event into the barn, would you be able to set up in here?"

"It's been years since I performed at a wedding, especially an indoor ceremony. We'll need a stage. It doesn't need to be as big as the outdoor one. I can make the adjustments. You'll also need a smaller dance floor in here. I know a guy who can help with that. Oh, smaller speakers so we don't deafen your guests. That's also doable. Yeah. We can perform inside the barn. The sooner you decide, the smoother it'll go."

Wow. It never occurred to me that Lincoln didn't perform at weddings anymore. I knew he was a big country superstar, but he'd agreed so easily to our wedding. I figured he often did it for other friends.

"Andi Grace? What do you think?"

I met Marc's gaze. "Let me talk to Juliet. We can't put this off any longer,

I just hope she sees it's the right thing to do."

Marc continued loving on his dog but turned to Lincoln. "How's Belle? Any trouble from Ben or Destiny?"

"No, but I've been keeping close tabs on her since the murder. I'm not saying either one of them murdered Zarina, but Ben and I got sideways. In addition, I didn't invest in his ticket scheme, and I'm hiding the fact that Belle is my daughter. If he learns that, he might take his frustration out on Belle."

"He's angry with Marc too for helping you legally."

Lincoln drummed his fingers on his boot. "Sorry 'bout that. You've helped me out of quite a few predicaments, including the tabloids. Fame isn't all it's cracked up to be. We're planning the next tour now, but between the three of us, it might be my last big tour. I don't mind so much when bad people gun for me, but attacking my friends and family is where I draw the line. My son has suffered because of my fame, and it wreaked havoc on my marriage. Ooh wee. I got off on a tangent. My bad."

Marc smiled. "Hey, I asked. It's hard to see you walking away from performing, but if you need help becoming a normal person, let us know. Have you considered what you'll do?"

Lincoln took a deep breath. "Yeah. You know buying Piney Woods Apartment Complex has given me a lot of satisfaction. I didn't grow up rich, and I enjoy fixing the place. There's no reason low-income residents should live in substandard housing. Know what I mean?"

It'd be impossible to miss the passion in his voice. "Good for you, Lincoln. Heyward Beach is lucky to have you living here."

His face reddened. "Meeting the residents touches my heart. I'm getting back as much as I'm giving."

"I know some of the people living there, and they are great."

Lincoln stood. "Mind if I use one of your notebooks? I'd like to sketch how the barn will look when we move the wedding in here."

Marc chuckled. "Andi Grace always has a journal or notebook."

I pulled one out of my desk drawer along with two pencils and passed them to Lincoln. "Here you go."

After he left, I moved closer to Marc and Chubb. "Hey, boy. Do you feel the storm coming?"

The golden retriever barked, and I gave him a treat. "We'll protect you. Don't worry about a thing."

"You almost always have a treat on you."

"Better get used to it." I tweaked the dog's nose. "What do you think about looking for the tripod at the main house."

"Sounds like a good idea, and I think we need to talk to Juliet and broach the subject of moving the wedding."

My heart sank. "You're right, but she'll probably push back."

"I have faith in your ability to convince her."

I considered his words. What was the best way to approach Juliet on moving the wedding to the barn? "Oh, how crazy would it be to come in with our dogs instead of bouquets of flowers?"

"Pinky is small, and it might work for Juliet. No way you're carrying Sunny."

"True. I'll keep thinking of the best argument to convince Juliet."

"What about Nate?"

"If Juliet and I agree, he'll go along with the plan. He learned years ago that life is easier that way."

"Good to know."

On the way out of Stay and Play, we left Chubb in John's care. Dylan was aware of the dog's anxiety. Dylan also knew John wanted to work for me. This would be a good test, and if John was rough or uncaring, Dylan would step in and take over.

Chapter Fifty-five

THAT AFTERNOON, I pulled my Highlander into the Seagull's View neighborhood, where Skylar lived. It was easy to spot her blue Jeep. Marc rode shotgun, and we'd already dropped Sunny and Chubb at the house.

I pulled up my rain jacket hood and darted to the front porch. Marc joined me before Skylar opened the door.

"Hi, guys. Come in out of the rain." She opened the door wide and took our coats. "Can I get you a warm drink? I've got a fresh pot of coffee."

"No, thanks. We won't take much of your time, but we'd like to hear how your date with Caleb went." I had plenty to keep me busy, but I was curious.

"Let's sit down." The entryway, family room, and dining area were all one large space. "Excuse the mess. I'm working on my blog article and getting ready for the podcast. Andi Grace, can I interview you? Or Marc? Are you interested?"

"Thanks for the offer, but I can't squeeze one more thing into my schedule before the wedding." I sat on a green love seat, and Marc sat beside me.

Skylar sat in a recliner. "Maybe another time."

"Absolutely. What did you think about Caleb?"

"At first, he seemed nice enough. He talked about his love of animals. After he had a few drinks, he began complaining how much it was going to cost to pay off his student loans. We never left the bar. Instead, we ordered multiple appetizers. I asked if he was going to work for Dr. Hewitt when he finished his rotations. Nope. He has bigger plans. He wants to only perform surgeries on pets."

"How'd you learn about his uncle?"

"I asked about family, and he spilled his guts. He admires Ben and even asked his uncle to help with college expenses. Ben refused, but he told Caleb there are always ways to make extra money. He suggested Caleb get creative. After a couple more drinks, Caleb said he and Destiny were in the same boat. They both admire Ben, but neither one of them is financially stable."

"Are Caleb and Destiny close?"

"It didn't occur to me they might have a relationship without Ben. What do you think?" Skylar crossed one long leg over the other.

"I'm not suggesting an affair or anything like that. I don't really know what I meant. Maybe a mutual admiration for Ben bonds them."

"Could be."

Thunder rumbled and the apartment shook.

Marc said, "We probably should check on the dogs."

"Wait. Is there anything you two want to share?" Skylar's tone dared us to move.

I'd been dreading this question, but Wade had been specific. Don't mention the camera bag. "Um, nothing comes to mind right now. Skylar, after the sheriff catches the killer, I'll be happy to answer any questions. It's just, I don't know much."

"Okay. I took your advice and ordered a fresh drink after our call. It's doubtful Caleb would spike my drink, but why chance it?"

"Exactly. I'm glad you're safe."

"Do you want me to take pictures at the rehearsal? And what about the storm? Will you move the wedding?"

We'd made an agreement with Juliet and Nate. "We're arranging the barn now to get married in there."

"Oh. I should check the lighting. Are you sure you don't want a professional photographer?"

Marc said, "No. We appreciate your willingness to jump in at the last minute."

"Sure. It's just so sad about Zarina."

"Yeah, it is. By any chance did Caleb mention Fly Boy?"

"No. Who is that?"

"It could be the pilot for Operation Tail-wagger."

"I'm not getting far into identifying the pilot, but maybe his nickname will help."

A flash of lightning lit the room.

I jumped to my feet. "We should go, and if you have time to come to the rehearsal, it'd be fun to get pictures of it too."

"Alrighty then. I'll see you tomorrow night, if not sooner." She rose and walked us to the coat tree by the front door where she'd hung our coats.

"Thanks, Skylar."

The rain wasn't bad, but the wind was frightening on the drive home. Once inside the house, I looked at Marc. "Tomato soup and grilled cheese sandwiches for lunch?"

"Sounds like the perfect meal for a day like this." He turned on the TV. "I want to see the latest on the storm."

I began warming the soup and prepared the sandwiches."

Marc said, "It's heading toward South Carolina, but it's growing weaker.

They predict we'll have torrential rain but not a hurricane."

"That's something. This will be the first coastal storm your grandparents will experience."

"Maybe. All we know for sure is they were missionaries, they've been living in Kentucky, Carol had dengue fever, and the DNA test proves we're blood relatives."

My spirits sank. "They love you, Marc. I think they regret not knowing about your situation. I also believe Chris and Carol want to show you how much they love you by moving here. Those are three things I know."

Marc muted the television and joined me in the kitchen area. He wrapped his arms around me. "How would I survive without your sunny outlook on life?"

Sunny barked, and we both laughed.

"You'll never have to find out because you're stuck with me for the rest of your life."

"That's music to my ears. Oh, the soup's bubbling." He found a wooden spoon and stirred it.

I flipped the sandwiches. While the other side grilled, my thoughts drifted to J. T. Green. He and Zarina had blown their first shot at happily ever after. It appeared they were getting a second chance when Zarina's life was cut short.

I needed to figure out how to balance solving mysteries and using caution if I wanted a long and happy life with Marc.

Chapter Fifty-six

Later Thursday afternoon, Marc and I drove to Daily Java to meet his grandparents for coffee. We left Sunny and Chubb at my house.

It wasn't storming, but fog and a light drizzle made it dreary. We entered the coffee shop and spotted the couple right away. Chris and Carol waited for us at a table for four. We greeted each other and hugged, then Marc and Chris walked to the counter to give Erin our orders.

Carol patted my hand. "How are the wedding preparations going?"

"Okay, I think. Erin is making the cakes. Marc wanted a regular wedding cake, and I agreed. He asks for so little, and it seemed like the right thing to do."

"That was kind of you. Do you have someone to walk you down the aisle?"

"My family is almost like a patchwork quilt. You know my parents died years ago, but we recently met Lacey Jane's biological father. Ike moved here in order to be close to my sister. In a short time, we've all grown close. I asked Ike to walk me down the aisle. If we weren't having a double wedding, I would've asked Nate."

"I see how that would be appropriate." She avoided eye contact.

Marc and Chris returned, carrying two mugs each.

I leaned toward Marc. "I think you should ask them now."

He lifted his brows, then nodded. "Andi Grace and I have a question for you two."

Chris blew on his hot tea. Earl Gray, according to the tag. "Shoot."

"It's late notice and all—"

Carol held up a freshly manicured hand. "Of course, that's our fault. You can ask us anything."

"Would y'all read the scripture at the wedding? Carol, I'd appreciate it if you'd dance with me for the groom and mother dance."

Her face reddened, and she pressed her lips together. Her answer was a nod.

Chris said, "We'd be honored. We've also got a request for you. Would you call us Grandmother and Granddaddy?"

I ran my hand across Marc's back, as we all awaited his answer.

At last Marc met Chris's gaze. "I haven't really known how to address you since we got the test results. Grandmother and Granddaddy it is."

Erin appeared with pie for everyone. "Can I bring you anything else?"

"It all looks good. Thanks, Erin."

Chris blessed the food before taking the first bite of his pie. "Say, how's the case going? Have you found the dead woman's missing camera bag?"

Yikes. I didn't want Marc to have to lie to his grandparents. "Yesterday the sheriff told us to forget about the murder and focus on our wedding."

"Sounds like good advice, but one day I want to hear more about you two solving murders." Carol cut off a small piece of pie with a fork and slid it into her mouth.

Marc laughed. "Oh, the stories we can tell."

"We've definitely had some harrowing experiences."

Carol's eyes grew wide. "On second thought, maybe I don't want to know."

We all laughed and continued eating our breakfast.

Erin returned. "Do you have a tent for the wedding?"

"No, but we've decided to move it into the barn."

"Oh, Andi Grace. I'm sorry to hear it, but that sounds like a smart plan. It's not supposed to be a hurricane, but we're gonna have some bad weather."

Marc pulled his phone out and looked at his weather app. "She's right. It's worse than the last report I saw."

Erin propped a fist on one hip. "I'm taking care of the cakes, but how can Griffin help?"

"I'm so glad you asked. Please ask him to call one of us. Not his sister. Juliet is still in denial that we won't get married outside." Oops. That didn't sound kind. "I'm not going behind her back, because we did discuss moving the wedding into the barn."

"I love Juliet like a sister, but when she makes up her mind, it can be challenging. I'll ask Griffin to call you."

Marc said, "It'll be easier on Juliet if we move forward and save her the agony."

"Sounds like we've got a plan." She stepped away then turned back. "How about instead of me giving you a wedding gift, I give you a discount?"

"I'm a businesswoman too, and while I appreciate your offer, be fair to yourself." I knew Erin had struggled financially almost from the beginning of Daily Java, and it was only right to pay for her hard work.

"Say, are you helping Sheriff Stone with his murder investigation?"

"Um, a little."

Erin pulled a chair over and sat at the end of our table, shooting a quick glance in the direction of the counter. She hunched over the table, and we all leaned in. "Ben Lowe and his wife, Destiny Howard, the model, do you know who I'm talking about?" Her voice was soft, and I wasn't sure if Marc's grandparents could hear everything Erin said.

"Yeah, I know them." I also kept my voice down so nobody else would accidently overhear our conversation. I could update Chris and Carol later.

"You want to know what I think?"

"Absolutely." I refrained from taking notes.

"Ben is crazy about his wife, until he isn't. He's enamored one minute and the next he's angry with her."

"For instance?"

"One morning they were here, and he ordered black coffee and an avocado-egg sandwich without the bread for both of them. Actually, he orders her the same thing every time they're together."

"No bread?" Carol huffed. "What does she order if she's by herself?"

Erin pointed to Chris's plate. "A cinnamon roll and a latte, but she rarely comes here by herself."

I tried to decide if this was newsworthy. Surely not. "Is there more besides her food order?"

"They've been arguing lately about dogs. Ben thinks Destiny is in over her head. He wants her to get out of the business. I even overheard him say if she'd lose a little weight, she could get back to modeling."

"That's cruel. She's too thin now, but she's beautiful."

Marc fiddled with his phone then passed it to his grandparents. "That's a picture of the woman we're discussing."

Carol gripped the phone. "Her face is angular. There's no softness. Probably because her husband is trying to starve her."

Marc said, "At the prices she charged for the puppies, it's amazing she couldn't make a go of her business."

"True, but how many pups did she sell at those prices? Ike and Vince may have been her only customers, then she gave me Momma Dog and the extra pups."

Chris finished his tea. "Folks, I'm sorry to leave, but it sounds like you have important business to discuss, and that fine piece of pie made me feel like I need a nap. It's been a pleasure."

Carol passed the phone back to Marc. "We'll see you later."

"I'll make a point to look for you at the bed-and-breakfast."

"Thank you." She walked away with her husband.

Erin moved her chair back to its original table and sat across from us. "How much do they know?"

I laughed. "How much do you know?"

"Probably more than you suspect. Let's get back to the dog business. I truly believe Destiny likes dogs, but Ben thinks the business is dangerous."

"He must be afraid of dogs. Some people are. I found out Destiny tried making goat soaps and lotions. It seems like she wants to make the farm sustainable."

Erin nodded. "I get that. If I worked for a big company, I'd make lots more money. My grandmother left the bakery to me. She understood my love of baking. I put my own spin on it by turning this into a coffee shop with a bakery. It's taken time to get to this point, and tomorrow I could go belly up, but I'm following my dream. Perhaps Destiny has happy memories of the farm and wants to make it work instead of returning to modeling."

I'd feel more sympathy for Destiny if I didn't think she was involved in Operation Tail-wagger. "Do you know Caleb Fisher?"

"Hot cappuccino. Sometimes he'll order Americanos for the people he works with. He seems like a nice kid." She snapped and pointed at me. "Let me guess. You're wondering if there's a connection between him and Destiny. She loves dogs, and he's going to be a veterinarian."

"What else?" I loved Erin's energy.

"They've had coffee together. Now, I don't want y'all to think I go around spreading gossip to everyone. But what if I know something that will help catch Zarina's murderer? I might even know something important, and I don't even realize it. So, ask me questions."

I swiped my phone. "I've got to take notes. When Caleb and Destiny were alone, did you overhear their conversations?"

"They're always quiet and there's nothing romantic. I've seen them talk, look at files, and look at their phones. Pictures of dogs when I've been able to catch a quick peek. I offer refills on some drinks."

Marc laughed. "Aren't you sneaky? Criminals wouldn't stand a chance if you and Andi Grace started your own detective agency."

I rubbed his arm. "Hey, give yourself some credit. You're a great assistant."

He laughed. "Thanks."

"That's probably all I've got. If I remember anything else, I'll text you." She gathered the dirty dishes and left us alone.

Just then, I received a text from Gloria. "Marc, I think we need to pay Gloria a visit. Apparently she has some new information."

"Let's roll."

Chapter Fifty-seven

THE RAIN HAD LET UP, and Gloria met us in the clinic's parking lot. Her expression was somber. "Let's walk. That way there's no chance we'll be overheard."

A lady wrangling three black Doberman pinschers walked toward the building.

Marc turned around and opened the door for her.

Gloria shook her head. "She needs to pay for obedience lessons for the dogs and herself."

"Yeah, that's the way it often works." I'd purchased Erin's daily latte on my way out of the coffee shop before heading here. I sipped my maple pecan drink.

Gloria stopped at the far edge of the parking lot. "There's a nice little trail in the woods, and I often walk it on my lunch break. After all the rain last night, it's probably too muddy to be fun."

"We can stand in the parking lot. If Caleb comes out and questions us, we'll make up something about the wedding."

"My Camry is right here." Gloria pointed to a white car, and we walked to it.

Marc met us there. "What did you find out, Gloria?"

"I finally tracked down that pilot who flew some of the dogs here. I called the regional airport again and mentioned that name Fly Boy you told me about, and it worked like a charm. They knew just who I was asking about."

Gloria was turning out to be quite the detective herself.

"So anyway," she went on, "I got his number and called him and asked him what he knew about Operation Tail-wagger. He said all he knew was that they'd hired him a few times to fly dogs down here. Said it was always a woman who hired him, and she paid him cash. He also said that when clients paid cash you knew something sketchy was probably going on, like maybe drugs or something, but you didn't ask questions. He sounded legit to me. He even asked if he'd done something wrong."

"Okay, one less loose end to worry about. We can cross him off our list. Anything else?"

"There is something bothering me." Wind blew her hair, and she grabbed it with one hand. "Caleb came in with a hangover and has been guzzling coffee like there's no tomorrow. This is the second day in a row that he's been in that condition."

"He had a date with Skylar last night." I took notes on my phone with my free hand.

"Yes, I set them up. When I asked him about it, he said there probably wouldn't be a second date. He blamed himself. I didn't push for too much information."

Marc crossed his arms. "You said this was the second day in a row he'd shown up with a hangover."

"He came in that way yesterday too, before he even went on his date with Skylar. Doc won't put up with that kind of behavior. It endangers the animals."

"Even back in the day when I worked here, Doc didn't tolerate hangovers. The animals' safety always came first." A woman carrying a hamster cage walked by us, and I waited until she was in her car before speaking again. "Skylar discovered Ben Lowe is Caleb's uncle. So, we've got that connection but need to decide if it's related to Operation Tail-wagger."

"Or the murder." Marc pointed to the building. "There's Caleb."

Caleb had exited the clinic and pushed on dark sunglasses. He glanced around the parking lot as if he'd forgotten where he'd parked. Finally, he walked toward us. It was easy to tell the moment he spotted us. He threw his shoulders back and walked faster. He pointed at Gloria. "This is all your fault."

Instead of cowering, she lifted her chin. "I didn't tell you to get drunk. You knew when you signed on to work with Dr. Hewitt that he wouldn't tolerate an employee showing up in your condition."

"You set me up with Skylar Marshall. If I hadn't been on a date, I wouldn't have gotten drunk."

"What about the night before? I didn't fix you up with anyone Tuesday night."

"Veterinary training is hard work. I needed to let some steam off."

"Again, that's your problem."

Caleb lunged for her.

Marc was faster and pulled him back. "Take it easy. Your problem isn't with Gloria."

"This is Skylar's fault." He maneuvered away from Marc.

"Man up. You can't blame somebody else for your actions. Do you need a ride home so you can sober up?"

He muttered something ugly then stomped away and jumped into a white sports car.

I snapped a picture of the license plate. "I think that was at Destiny's house the other day."

"He's probably borrowing it, because he's been complaining for days that he can't afford to get his truck fixed." Gloria frowned. "If he didn't buy all those fancy coffees, he might be able to pay for his truck. No offense to the local baristas."

"No telling what I could do if I quit going to Daily Java. I'm frugal in other areas of my life, so I'll keep supporting Erin's coffee shop." I lifted the cup to my lips and took another yummy sip.

Marc said, "So money is tight for Caleb. Did something trigger his excessive drinking?"

"I can't think of anything work-related. Didn't he say he was upset over the date not working out? You'd think a good-looking kid like that would have had lots of experience with pretty women." Gloria tsked.

Marc took my latte. "Would you send a text to Wade about Caleb? Include the tag."

"White sports car?"

"Camaro. Late model."

I sent the information to Wade. "Thanks, Gloria. Stay clear of Caleb. If you see him coming, call the sheriff."

"Honey child, when Zachary hears about Caleb's behavior, he'll probably notify the veterinary college. There's no way he'll continue to allow Caleb to work here."

"I'm not surprised. The safety of his animals is Doc's primary goal."

"That's the truth. Y'all be careful too." She hugged each of us, and we waited until she entered the clinic.

When I first met Caleb, he'd seemed easygoing.

Today, I'd seen a different side of him, and I didn't like it.

Chapter Fifty-eight

MARC AND I ARRIVED AT STAY AND PLAY with our dogs. It was raining and windy, but there was no thunder or lightning.

We got Sunny and Chubb settled with the other dogs then found Dylan.

"Hey, guys. Griffin's on his way with a couple of the guys. I've been thinking. What if we move this play area to the back corner?" Dylan went into detail of how he pictured the temporary arrangement. He'd become more muscular since the day I first met him. He'd also matured, and I'd grown to care about him like family. "If you like my plan, it'll open up the middle area for the ceremony and reception."

Marc walked around the space. "Yeah, I believe it'll work."

My spirits dropped at the thought of moving everything so we could have our wedding in the barn when it would've been beautiful overlooking the river. I had no control of the weather, but I could control my reaction. I shook off the gloomy thoughts. I was about to marry Marc. It didn't matter where we pledged to spend the rest of our lives together.

Thoughts of Ben and Destiny invaded my mind. Despite different last names, they'd made some kind of pledge to each other and gotten married. How far would either of them go to show love for the other?

Would Destiny resort to murder in order to save her marriage?

My phone vibrated.

Wade had sent a message. *One of the deputies stopped Caleb Fisher. He didn't pass the breathalyzer. He's in jail now. Thanks for the tip.*

"Marc, Caleb was pulled over for driving under the influence."

"Good to know."

Lincoln and Belle arrived, and the star explained his vision for the stage.

Dogs barked more than usual.

I approached Marc. "Between the weather and all the people in the barn, I'm going to try to calm the dogs. Lavender-scented bandanas may help. It's worth a shot anyway." I hurried to the animals. A shiver ran up my spine. Was there more to the dogs' anxiety than the number of people in here?

Chubb lunged for me when I entered the fenced-in area. "Hey, boy." I knelt beside him and rubbed his sides. Despite wearing his storm jacket, he seemed uneasy. "It's going to be okay."

Belle appeared. "Andi Grace, what do you need me to do?"

"Why don't you and Melanie move the small dogs to their kennels for now? Take one at a time and put a lavender-scented bandana on each one."

"I gotcha. They're all out of sorts. Lady whined so much before I left home, I brought her with me. It seemed cruel to leave her in that condition. Dad came with me and can take her home when he leaves." She paused. "He's been acting weird since Zarina's murder. What do you know about it?"

I rubbed on Chubb, and two other dogs joined us. "It could be your imagination."

"Andi Grace, I'm not imagining how often he's come here with me the last few days."

"This is a conversation you should have with your dad. Right now, I need you to take care of the dogs."

"Yes, ma'am. That's what you're paying me for."

"Belle, I'm sorry, but the dogs are worrying me. Another time, I'll be happy to talk to you."

Her laugh surprised me. "Boy oh boy, you probably think I'm a spoiled brat. Sorry. Maybe the dogs are rubbing off on me."

"You're fine. If you see anything unusual, let me know."

Belle picked up a bichon frise. "What kind of unusual?"

The girl was as tenacious as a dog with a bone. "If you see a person that you don't think belongs here, get me. Of find your dad or Marc. Go to someone trustworthy and see if they know the person."

"Stranger danger. Got it." She carried the little white dog to the grooming area where we kept the bandanas.

Sunny nosed her way through the dogs vying for my attention and lay beside me. She knew she was my top dog.

I looked around the space. Had someone snuck in with the intention of harming one of us? I'd keep my eyes open. Nobody else would be harmed on my watch.

Chapter Fifty-nine

BY EARLY THAT EVENING, we had the dogs calmed. Some of the owners had come to pick up their pets. Most knew about the wedding and wanted to lighten my load. Some owners even dropped off wedding gifts.

I sat at my desk, reviewing the dog-walking schedule and the reservations for Stay and Play one last time. Dylan had assured me he could handle it all, and I believed him. Still, I didn't want to set him up for failure.

Marc entered my office and sat across from me. "We've got a plan with Nate and Juliet's blessing, but your bestie is still checking weather reports. She really wants to get married outside."

"Me too, but sometimes I'm more practical than her. Why risk it?"

"Totally agree. Whatcha working on?"

I closed my paper calendar and logged off my scheduling program. "The agenda for the next two weeks. Everything is good. Dylan is in charge, and he'll be fine. I even remembered to officially book Sunny and Chubb to stay while we're in Maine."

"Officially, huh? Sounds good. Are you ready to head back to town?"

I considered his question. "Yeah, I might be able to get a head start on thank-you notes."

"I thought you finished."

"I wrote the ones for the shower gifts, but we're already getting wedding gifts." I pointed to the small stack. "Do you want to help me carry them to the truck?"

"Sure, then we can load the dogs and head home."

The rain had downgraded to a drizzle, and it wasn't hard to get the gifts and animals into Marc's truck.

In addition to Griffin's crew rearranging the barn, there were people unloading chairs and tables for the wedding and reception. Juliet was in her element organizing the transformation from dog barn to wedding venue. Even though our wedding was small, Juliet didn't have enough tablecloths to fit the rental tables. She did have enough mismatched china for the place settings. Good thing mismatched settings were acceptable.

"Let's roll." Marc reached for my hand, and we walked to his truck. He held the door for me before going to the driver's side.

"I never saw your grandparents return. Do they only have one car?"

He slowed near the parking area by the main house. "Yeah. I've only ever seen them drive a Chevy SUV, but I don't see it here."

A black pickup truck pulled out of the parking area, splashing in a puddle before speeding up.

"Marc, that truck looks familiar."

"Yep. Like the one Destiny owns."

"Let's try to follow it."

Marc sped up. "Why?"

"If it's Destiny, why is she here? I don't feel good about this."

"All right. I'll try to catch up with her, if it doesn't put us and the dogs in danger."

It didn't take long before we caught up to the black truck. The moment the driver spotted us was obvious, because the truck pulled away at a crazy speed.

Marc cleared his throat. "It's not worth it."

"You're right. We don't even know who's driving for sure." I couldn't think of a logical reason to call nine-one-one.

Marc slowed, and we rode along in silence. At least we remained quiet until we saw Chris's SUV in a ditch with one tire spinning.

My mouth dried. I called the emergency number while Marc pulled off at a safe spot. He leapt from the truck and ran to his grandparents.

Chubb barked, and Sunny joined him. There were no signs of danger lurking as far as I could tell. "No barking."

Each dog grew quiet and accepted a treat from me.

My attention shifted to the phone call. "Sorry about that. The dogs are upset. I'm upset, too."

"Ma'am, you said you're on River Road?"

"Yes. That's right." I gave the dispatcher our exact location and suggested an ambulance as well as law enforcement. I also asked her to alert the sheriff.

She inquired about the condition of Marc's grandparents.

"Hold on." I opened the door and slid out, only stopping to address Sunny and Chubb. "It's going to be okay. Be good."

Chubb yipped then calmed.

I stepped in a mud puddle and lifted my foot. There was a slight suction, but I broke loose and hurried to the SUV.

"Hello."

"Yes, I'm walking to them now. The vehicle is tilted. The passengers are in their eighties. You'll probably need some kind of tow truck to get their SUV upright so they can both escape."

"All right. I'm adding that to my message. Authorities are en route as we speak."

"Okay."

Marc had pulled the driver's door open and helped Chris get out. The older man seemed dazed, and his airbag had deployed.

I tapped Marc's shoulder. "Let me help Chris. You get Carol."

"Are you sure you've got him?"

"Yeah." I kept my phone on but slid it into my pocket. "Chris, let's get you into the truck. You're pale, and I'd hate for you to pass out."

"I'm fine. Carol's the one who needs help."

A vehicle screeched to a stop.

I froze in place.

It was a dark gray 4Runner.

Footsteps pounded on the ground. "Andi Grace, let me give you a hand."

I met Ike's gaze, and tears sprang to my eyes. We couldn't lose Marc's grandparents after they'd just gotten together. "Ike, I'm so glad you're here."

"Me too, kiddo." He stepped to Chris's other side and wrapped his arm around the older man.

Together we got Chris seated in Marc's truck.

He raised his hands. "I'm fine. Check on Carol."

A siren wailed in the distance.

Ike and I ran to the Chevy.

Marc knelt on the driver's seat and glanced back at us. "Ike, it's good to see you. The seat belt jammed, but I carry a seat belt cutter with me. Always carry one since my parents' accident. So, I cut it off, and I believe I can pull Grandmother out, but I'm afraid of dropping her legs. Can you help me support her as I pull her free?"

I placed my hand on Marc's back. "Would it be better to wait for the tow truck?"

"I don't think so. The vehicle isn't lodged solidly into the ground. I'm afraid it could settle, making it harder to remove her."

Ike said, "It could also cause more harm. You pull. I'll be ready to assist."

I stepped aside, looking for an opportunity to contribute to the rescue.

With the help of her arms, Carol turned her body so her back faced Marc.

He slid his arms under her armpits. "Okay, we're going to take it nice and easy."

"I'm sorry, hon, but I can't seem to make my legs work. I'm just so shaky."

"Don't you worry. Let us do the work."

Ike said, "Would it help if one of us got in the backseat and added support?"

"No. The stability of the vehicle concerns me. I can manage this part." Marc's shirt grew dark with perspiration.

I prayed.

Sirens grew louder.

Marc pulled his grandmother ever so gently toward the exit. Her hip bumped the steering wheel, and the horn honked. "Sorry, did I hurt you?"

"I'm fine." Her shaky voice didn't make me feel confident.

Ike stood at Marc's side. "I'm ready for her hips."

Marc edged his grandmother farther out.

Ike slid his arms under her body. One arm went under her backside, and the other supported her thighs.

I hurried to the opposite side of Ike's body and caught her calves about the time her feet dangled on the car seat.

She was free.

Chris cheered from where he sat.

Marc held his grandmother securely against his body, and she rested her head against his chest. "My grandson, and my hero. Thank you, Marc."

An ambulance stopped in the middle of the two-lane highway near us.

The Chevy SUV groaned and slipped in the mud.

Marc's gaze met mine. "Just in the nick of time."

"Amen."

Chapter Sixty

SUNSHINE PEEPED THROUGH THE BLINDS and woke me up Friday morning.

Today was the rehearsal for my wedding.

Yesterday had contained a few nightmarish hours, but Marc's grandparents were released from the hospital late that night.

It'd been a miracle they left with nothing more than Carol's sprained knee and a few cuts and bruises. Marc had spent the night at Kennady Bed-and-Breakfast to be nearby in case they needed him.

"Good morning, girl! What a glorious day."

My German shepherd barked in agreement, because how could she argue? She was about to get an official brother with Chubb.

"Let's go downstairs and get our day started."

After we went through our morning routine, the sky clouded. Not the fluffy white cumulus clouds. Drat.

My phone rang, and Marc's picture filled the screen. I swiped. "Is everything okay?"

He chuckled. "Yes. Everyone's good. Chris and I are going to look for a new car this morning. It won't make us late for the rehearsal though. If nothing else, we can loan them one of our vehicles."

"Yeah. They could be more comfortable in my Highlander, especially since Carol sprained her knee. Did they tell you how they ran off the road?"

"They won't exactly blame anyone, but they said a black pickup truck was driving toward them at a high rate of speed. It was driving down the center of the highway and didn't swerve back into the other lane soon enough to suit Chris. He slowed and edged over but ran into the mud. I don't know if the results would've been better if we hadn't had so much rain this week or not."

"It sounds like he doesn't want to press charges against the other driver."

"For starters, we don't know who the other driver is. If it'd been in town, security cameras would've picked up the accident."

"Marc, you and I know it had to be the truck we were following."

"Knowing it and proving it are two different things."

I rolled my head back. "Of course, you're right. But if we see a black truck on the farm, we're going to find out who it belongs to."

"I expected no less from you. Just don't tackle it by yourself. Listen, I better run if we're going to find and buy a car before the rehearsal." He paused. "Unless there's something you need me to do."

"No, take care of Chris. We'll talk later. I love you."

"Love you too."

I dressed in shorts and a T-shirt then packed a duffle with toiletries and strappy sandals with heels. In one dress bag I placed my elegant scoop A-line chiffon for the rehearsal. It was a midi dress with cap sleeves. The top was lace, and the skirt twirled nicely. It was sapphire blue and quite lovely.

In the white bridal shop bag, I packed my wedding gown and veil.

With the utmost care, I loaded them into the Highlander. Sunny rode shotgun to Stay and Play, and I moved the clothes to my office before the rain hit.

A group of people were building a stage for Lincoln's band.

Juliet appeared. "Hey, if the florist accidently comes here instead of the house, send her my way. Your hair looks nice."

"Thanks. I hope it holds up to the weather. I'd hate to wear a ponytail to my rehearsal. About the flowers. We don't need them until tomorrow. Won't they look droopy?"

"I forgot to tell you. The florist is bringing small bouquets for tonight. She also has some flower arrangements for tonight's tables."

"Are you sure we'll all fit comfortably in the house?"

"Not a problem. I've got the dining room table, which can extend to seat thirty. It's all under control."

"That's gigantic."

"We'll have the rehearsal in the living room then dinner will be served in the dining room. It won't be as relaxed as if we were outside, but I'm being flexible." She shrugged. "Otherwise, I'll be miserable."

I hugged my friend. "Good for you."

"The bad news is, I need to store some stuff here for better flow."

I didn't want to clutter up the barn after we'd worked so hard to shift the dog areas around. "How much stuff? Should it go in my office so we don't have to move it back to the house before the wedding?"

Juliet looked around. "Yeah, it'll fit in here. I'll have someone bring it over before the rain begins."

"Okay. If I'm working with the dogs, I'll leave the door open."

"Great. And if your hair doesn't last, I'll work on it at the house. You will not wear a ponytail to your wedding rehearsal."

"Thanks." I laughed and sat at my desk. More than likely, nothing would get stolen, but I couldn't take a chance. There were a lot of strangers on the property helping us with wedding preparations. I gathered my laptop and client files and locked them in the file cabinet. The work box with client keys was now in Dylan's possession. I texted him to make sure he'd locked his apartment door. His studio was next to my office, and he probably never locked the thing.

My phone vibrated with a text message from Dylan. *Walking dogs in town. Will you lock it for me? Thanks.*

I smiled at his good manners. *No problem and you're welcome.*

Sunny followed me to Dylan's door. I locked it then found Belle. "How's it going?"

"This is the easiest day I've ever had here. It's almost boring. I can't imagine what John and Vince will do when they arrive."

"Almost boring?"

She held her hand out to Sunny, and my dog went to her, but she didn't elaborate.

"It seems as if I have a little free time. Is there anything I can do?" If felt funny asking my youngest employee what to do, but I'd created the schedule and everyone was performing their duties. "No, but Melanie might need you. She's bathing Pinky and Bo."

I smiled. "I'm surprised Juliet didn't ask her to bathe all of the dogs who will be here tomorrow."

Belle stepped closer. "Shh, don't give her any ideas."

"True. I'll keep it to myself."

"I know we're trying to keep occupancy down the next two days, but the sheriff asked us to watch Duke. Since he's working on a murder investigation, I didn't think I could refuse."

"Right. It's no problem to take care of Duke."

"That's what I thought." I liked her attitude. "John seems to enjoy the animals. We can give each pet some one-on-one time with John."

"What about Vince? It doesn't seem like you need all of us."

"True, but you're experienced. How is John doing?"

"He's a gentle man and the dogs respond to him. I haven't seen anything to worry me if you decide to hire him." She turned her attention to something behind me. "Hey, there are people carrying junk into your office." She squinted. "Wait, let me guess. Juliet is behind whatever is happening."

"Ding, ding, ding. If there'd been a prize for the right answer, you would've won. She's decluttering for the rehearsal, and I asked her to at least put it in my office so we wouldn't need to move it back before the wedding." I watched three men carry miscellaneous items. A standing lamp, a cardboard box with what looked like photo albums, candlesticks, and who knew what all was being dumped into my office. "I better check on Melanie."

"If you don't mind, I'll keep Sunny. Chubb is always happier when she's around."

"Well, they are going to be brother and sister starting tomorrow." I left my dog with her and meandered to the downsized grooming area.

One of the men moving items stopped me in my tracks.

He was on the slender side and not very tall. There was something familiar about his stride. The hairs on my arms jumped up.

Was it possible?

Could Destiny be pretending to be a man and in my barn?

For what purpose?

"Destiny!"

The person's stride broke for only a second. They didn't turn to me, but also didn't run off.

Maybe it was my overactive imagination, but the least I could do was look for the black truck I'd seen at Destiny's farm.

Chapter Sixty-one

I WALKED TOWARD THE PARKING AREA near by the main house, but there was no sign of the black truck I'd hoped to find.

Vince and John arrived driving a conversion van.

Relief eased the tension in my shoulders. I waved at the men then followed them to the barn. "Hi, guys. Did you get new wheels?"

Vince shoved the keys into the pocket of his khakis. "It's a rental. How about a field trip to the beach? For the dogs. Not you."

"It could be fun, but we'll need to contact the owners and get permission. Dylan's walking dogs now and could meet you. I'm sure Belle will be on board. She loves the beach. Let's go check with her." We soon found Belle. "Hey, Vince has a great suggestion to alleviate your boredom."

Her face reddened. "Sorry, I didn't mean—"

I shushed her. "Don't give it a second thought. Vince brought a van big enough for crates and dogs. Would you like to accompany them on a field trip to the beach?"

"Yeah, for sure. After all the rain we've had, the dogs are going to get damp walking around the farm. Why not go to the beach?"

"We can divide the list of owners and make calls. Let's see who gives their permission."

Melanie appeared with hands on hips. "Hold up." Her squeaky voice stopped all of us.

"What's wrong?" I was her boss. She wasn't my boss, but I'd hear her out.

"All the dogs will need baths when you get back. That would be a monumental undertaking on a normal day, but my space is much smaller because of the wedding. There's no way I can give baths to all the animals by myself, especially in the tight area."

"Fair enough." Vince held out his hands. "We'll pitch in and help. Maybe set up an assembly line. One of us will rinse off a dog, bring it to you for the real bath, then another one of us can take the dog and dry it."

Melanie pushed up her glasses. "I guess it could work, but baths only. No extra grooming."

I nodded. "That seems fair. Let's make those calls."

In less than an hour, all the dog owners had agreed, except for Juliet. Melanie was fine with Juliet's decision since she'd just done full grooming on Pinky and Bo.

Melanie said, "I may as well go to the beach with y'all if I'm going to have to clean the dogs."

Her attitude adjustment impressed me. "Agreed. I'll stay here with the two freshly groomed dogs. Dylan will meet you in the pier parking lot."

The others organized transporting the dogs, and I made sure they had enough leashes, treats, and water.

They left, and peace descended on the barn. The stage was ready for the band. Tables were in place, and the dance floor was ready. Pinky and Bo snoozed away, leaving me with more free time.

I stepped into my office to see what Juliet had sent over to be stored. One item was a full-length antique mirror. It was usually propped against a living room wall. Juliet declared it helped make the room brighter by bouncing sunlight around.

I had nothing pressing to do.

Nobody was around to disturb me.

My wedding dress was here, and I hadn't tried it on since I first bought it.

Why not try it on and check it out in the full-length mirror? I wouldn't have this much privacy for a while.

I hung the white garment bag from the bridal shop on the back of my office door, then slipped out of my shorts and T-shirt. The elegant gown with three-quarter sleeves and bateau neckline filled me with happiness.

I slipped it on, and the perfect fit made me smile. Not too tight or too loose. I stepped into white strappy sandals with a three-inch heel. They wouldn't make me eye to eye with Marc, but I'd be closer.

I couldn't wait until tomorrow.

Bo growled.

Pinky yipped.

Thud.

Something in the main area fell.

I hurried to my phone.

The office door swooshed open.

I slid the phone into a hidden pocket on my dress. When I purchased the dress, a pocket seemed silly. Now I was happy to have it.

The person in the doorway glared at me.

Oh, yeah. This wasn't going to be pleasant.

Chapter Sixty-two

BEN LOWE GLARED AT ME. His nostrils flared. Hatred blazed from his eyes. "You couldn't just leave well enough alone. You and Zarina. Two of a kind. Snooping into stuff that's none of your business. You were warned, and so was she."

The dogs kept barking.

I gulped. Zarina was dead. I refused to let him get me too.

Survival instincts kicked in.

"You're right, Ben. I should've listened." But he was on my property. Not the other way around.

"Right. Where are Zarina's photos?"

"I don't have them. The sheriff has been here a lot, and he has the camera case."

"Destiny told me it'd been found. But there are other photos."

I stepped back. No, that was the wrong move. He could trap me in here. My knees shook. "I don't know what you're talking about."

He elbowed me out of his way and looked at the boxes from the main house. "They've got to be here."

I scooted toward the door, keeping my eyes on him.

His attention darted from the boxes to me. "Oh no you don't." His hand darted out and his fingers closed around my wrist, pulling me toward him.

I screamed. I needed help in the worst way. He held the hand that could've reached for my phone to call for help.

"Shut up." He dragged me toward the desk.

I teetered on my sandals.

Ben opened drawers, rooted through them, then slammed them shut.

I toed off my three-inch sandals to increase my stability. "What are you looking for?"

"The pictures, but duct tape would come in handy right about now. I'm not going to tell you again to shut up."

The dogs continued to bark.

A gun had been stuck into the back of Ben's jeans.

If I could only grab it without shooting myself, maybe I'd survive this situation.

"Where are those photos?"

"Ben, I'm getting married tomorrow. If I had whatever pictures you're looking for, I'd give them to you. Why do you think they are here?"

"Destiny believes they were moved from the main house to the barn. She said boxes were moved in here today."

So, she had been here. "I didn't unpack any of the boxes."

Ben frowned. "Okay, then we'll go through them now." He lurched to the first box and dumped the contents onto my desk. The movement forced him to release my wrist.

I stepped back to avoid getting trampled on.

With Ben's attention on the items on my desk, I reached into my pocket and felt for the buttons that would either shut down my phone or allow me to call for help.

My hearing went fuzzy. I was going to pass out. No. I couldn't. I took a deep breath and swiped my finger across the middle of the phone, praying it'd contact the necessary emergency personnel.

"Help me," Ben growled.

"Sure." My voice squeaked. "What exactly am I looking for?"

"Any photographs you see, give to me."

After kicking my shoes out of the way, I walked to a stack of plastic totes. It appeared as if the second one from the top held a pair of scissors. They might come in handy, especially since I lost my opportunity to reach the gun.

I moved the top one to the empty chair for visitors and removed the lid from the second box.

Ben clenched his fists. "What's wrong with that box?"

"Oh, I was just passing it to you. Should I go through it instead?"

He glared at me for long, tense seconds. "You better not be up to something."

"It's no trouble for me to go through that box instead." I reached for the tote in question.

"Never mind. I'll do it."

"Are we looking for pictures that will tie Destiny to Operation Tail-wagger?"

"The less you know, the better."

"Did Destiny kill Zarina? If they got into an argument, law enforcement will understand. It's doubtful she'll have to serve much if any time."

He sighed.

"I can't imagine Destiny planned to murder Zarina ahead of time."

"My wife doesn't have a mean bone in her body. She didn't kill Zarina."

Gulp.

The dogs continued to bark.

"Can't you make them quit barking?"

"No. They sense danger."

He pulled his gun out. "You better figure out a way to shut them up. Or else I will."

My heart leapt, and it became clear Ben had committed the murder. "I'll do it. Give me a minute."

"Don't do anything stupid."

I walked to the dog kennel area. A glance over my shoulder confirmed Ben had remained in the room.

I pulled out my phone.

The operator was speaking, and I had no idea how we hadn't heard her earlier. I pulled it close to my face. "This is Andi Grace Scott. I'm being held hostage at Stay and Play. I can't stay on the phone, but please tell the sheriff." I ended the call.

Bo lunged against the kennel where'd he'd snoozed earlier.

"Hey, boy. It's okay. I wish I could let you out, but Ben might shoot you. Please be quiet." I passed him a treat. "Would you like a healthy dog bone to chew on?"

I moved to the shelf where we usually kept the bones.

"What's taking so long?" Ben's sudden appearance caused me to jump.

"I need to divert their attention from the danger." I pointed to the shelf. "Those bones should do the trick. What do you do when Queenie gets upset?"

"Queenie is Destiny's dog, but yeah. She gives him something like that."

I plucked two bones off the shelf. "Seriously, they will calm down faster without you around."

"I'll keep an eye on you from over there."

Great. Now I couldn't figure out a way to escape with the dogs.

Runaway brides were newsworthy, but they usually ran because they got cold feet. I needed to run away from Ben so I could meet Marc at the altar.

If only I could figure out a way to escape without Ben shooting me.

The sight of him pointing his gun in my direction didn't give me much hope.

Chapter Sixty-three

WALKING INTO MY OFFICE, I glanced around for a weapon.

Bo growled.

Ben yelled, "Quiet."

There. The tripod! We'd been looking everywhere for it, how had it gotten in here? That didn't seem important at the moment.

I snagged it then turned and held it behind my body. For the first time, I was happy to be wearing my wedding dress. If I acted casual, he wouldn't realize it was in my hands.

Ben stormed into the office. Anger rolled off him.

I froze in place.

He glared at me. "Thought you were going through that tote."

"Yes. Right."

He stuffed the gun back into the waistband of his jeans then leaned down and focused on the items he'd dumped onto my desk.

Keeping a tight grip on the tripod, I moved it around and swung, aiming for the back of Ben's head.

"Umph." He staggered but didn't fall.

Still clutching the tripod, I hightailed it out of the office and toward the barn door.

The sheriff's SUV skidded to a stop near the barn.

I waved at him with my free hand. "It's Ben Lowe. He's after me."

"Get somewhere safe, Andi Grace."

Marc's truck flew down the path. He slammed on the brakes and ran to me. "Are you okay?"

"Fine, but Ben's in the barn with a gun."

"Get in the truck."

I hopped in back and lay the tripod beside me then buckled up. Marc slid in the driver's seat. He stepped on the gas and swung the truck around, heading to the front of the main house.

"How'd you know to come?"

"You must have hit the SOS button on your phone. I got a call that you were in danger."

Chris held onto his seat belt. "We ran out of the dealership so fast, it wasn't funny."

More official vehicles from the sheriff's department appeared.

"Can we go into the house and watch what happens?"

Marc nodded. "Sure, but we're walking in the front entrance."

A black pickup truck barreled our way.

"That's got to be Destiny."

Marc jerked the steering wheel, propelling us into the grass.

"Whoa." Chris now held on to his fastened seat belt with one hand and braced his other hand against the dashboard. "Do you kids always have this much excitement?"

"No." I gripped my hands on the back of Marc's seat.

"More often than you'd imagine." Marc eased to a stop in the grass.

Destiny's brake lights popped on. Then she shifted into reverse and backed up toward us.

"Marc, she's coming back."

"Lord, have mercy." The way Chris spoke the words, it was more of a prayer than anything.

Marc mashed the gas again and got out of her way. "She must be on crack. The sheriff's department is here. Why isn't she making a run for it?"

A Charger appeared with lights flashing. Thank goodness for my brother-in-law's appearance. The rest of law enforcement was at the barn, but David could prevent Destiny from escaping.

Destiny stopped her truck and stepped out with her hands in the air. "Don't shoot."

The Charger came to a standstill. With his gun drawn, David approached the woman. "Turn around and put your hands on the truck."

Her head turned from side to side. She stopped when her gaze connected with mine. "It's all my fault. Ben only wanted to protect me."

"Protect you from what?" I exited the truck and held my dress up to avoid the mud.

"I made some bad business decisions."

David glanced at me.

I tapped my chest at about the same spot where his body camera was on him.

He looked down then nodded.

I said, "Destiny, are you responsible for Operation Tail-wagger?"

"Yes, I was trying to help dogs in need."

"Maybe, but you were also taking money from donors, weren't you?"

"The farm was a money pit and I didn't know what else to do. And it was so easy. The dog lovers were easy targets."

"You used their love of dogs against them. Was Ben part of the plan?"

"No." Her voice dropped.

"How about Caleb Fisher?"

Her face reddened. "Caleb kind of fell into my lap. I met him at his school when I was researching dog breeding, and we got to talking, and the next thing I knew he was more than ready to go along with my plan. He said he needed the money and that the vet he was working for, Doc Hewitt, was a total softie and it would be easy to take advantage of him. How'd you know?"

"It wasn't that hard to put together." In fact, it'd taken more than a bit of digging to find their connection. "How did it get to this point? Why was Ben threatening me? What photos is he looking for?"

Her shoulders drooped. "Zarina had pictures of me in disguises promoting the operation."

Marc said, "Was she blackmailing you?"

"No. She was quite decent, in fact. She showed the pictures to me and told me to quit hustling people, or else she'd report me to Sheriff Stone. I should've quit and gone back to dog breeding, but it's a long process."

"And the puppies annoyed your husband."

"Yeah. When I told Ben about Zarina and Operation Tail-wagger, he blew a gasket. Don't you see? It's all my fault. I'm a terrible businesswoman. I took advantage of people's kindness." She held her hands out to David. "Cuff me. I'm the one you want."

This wasn't right. "Destiny, did you murder Zarina?"

"It's my fault she's dead."

"But Ben killed her, right?"

"Yes, but it's because of me. I'm the one who needs to go to prison." She shook her fists at David.

He motioned for Destiny to turn, then he cuffed her and read her rights.

"One last thing, Andi Grace. Will you go to the farm and take care of Queenie?"

No way I'd let her corgi suffer for Destiny and Ben's actions. "Yes. I'll bring her here until you get out."

In the distance, Deputy Harris put Ben in the back of her vehicle.

David walked over and hugged me. "I'm glad you're safe."

"You're on vacation. How'd you know to come?"

"Lacey Jane and I got a message saying you'd contacted emergency services, and they gave us your location."

"Good thing you insisted we all have each other's information when Lacey Jane was pregnant."

"Yeah, so I geared up and immediately came over. It didn't take a rocket scientist to know you were involved in solving Zarina's murder."

Juliet ran out of the house with her hair wrapped in a green towel. "Andi Grace, Nate called and said you were in trouble. And why are you wearing your wedding dress? You're going to get it all dirty. It took too long to find one you liked to risk ruining it."

We all laughed at her.

It was such a relief to have Zarina's killer in custody.

Juliet reached for my hand. "Come on inside. You can catch me up."

I turned back to Marc. "My other clothes are in my office, including my dress for tonight. Would you ask Wade to please let me have them even though—"

"Don't worry. I'm sure it won't be a problem."

Chapter Sixty-four

THE WEDDING REHEARSAL the night before had gone smoothly. More rain in the evening confirmed we'd made the right decision to move all festivities inside.

I was moments away from having Ike escort me down a small aisle to marry Marc. Griffin was prepared to escort Juliet, and I'd heard the grooms were waiting at the altar with Pastor Mays.

Skylar entered my office. "I've already taken a lot of pictures, but did you remember to bring Zarina's tripod? I don't want to risk shaky hands when you walk down the aisle."

I moved to my desk chair and picked it up. "Here you go. It's nice to have a part of Zarina here for the wedding."

Skylar shook her finger at me. "No crying."

Ike looked at both of us. "There will be no crying before the wedding. If you need to shed happy tears later, that's another thing."

I elbowed him. "Let's get our picture taken together."

"Yeah. I'll get official pictures of you after the ceremony, but relaxed shots are fun too." She set up the tripod, and it rocked.

"Let me see. Those little clasps make the legs longer and shorter."

"I'm taller than Zarina was."

"Yeah, but she had it collapsed when I found it." I tried to lengthen one leg, but something was still wonky. "Maybe I messed it up when I used it to hit Ben."

Ike held out his hands. "Don't take a chance on getting your dress dirty. Let me try."

I laughed. If only he'd seen me wearing it around the farm yesterday with a killer.

Skylar looked at me. "Wade said that Ben confessed to murdering Zarina. It wasn't premeditated. He wanted the evidence Zarina had on Destiny, but she refused to give it to him. He just kinda went ballistic and killed her."

"Love of dogs drove Operation Tail-wagger, but Destiny stole no telling how much money from her victims. Then love for his wife caused Ben to kill Zarina."

Ike huffed. "That's a warped kind of love."

"Yeah." I'd do a lot for Marc, but I wouldn't murder somebody because of crimes he'd committed. "Do you suppose something is stuck in that leg?"

Ike shook it.

Then I remembered J.T. said there was a secret compartment. "Guys, in all the stress of the last few days, I forgot. There's a hiding place in the tripod."

"Now you tell us." Ike ran his hands over it.

My heart skipped a beat. "The reason Ben showed up yesterday was to find some photos that would increase the chance of Destiny getting arrested. I bet she hid them in there."

Skylar opened her phone and began filming as Ike twisted the leg off. "Here we go."

Four-by-six photos slid onto the floor.

"What do you know?" Ike grabbed a tissue, then bent down and retrieved them.

"Zarina had a good eye for detail. Those look like the same person."

With care, Ike lay them on my desk. "Sometimes Destiny has the same dog but she's wearing different disguises."

"But there are different dogs too." Skylar pointed to the photos.

"She helped so many dogs, but she took advantage of a lot of people in the process. We need to report this to Wade."

Griffin and Juliet entered the room. "The music started."

Skylar said, "I'll text Wade, but I'll also ask him to wait until after the ceremony to collect the evidence we found."

Juliet groaned. "Please tell me you didn't find something that will ruin our wedding."

I stood next to Ike and placed my hand in the crook of his elbow. "Let's hope not."

Skylar opened the door. "I'll just hold the camera to avoid contaminating the tripod."

The music shifted to the wedding march.

Griffin patted his sister's hand. "It's time."

Ike and I followed Griffin and Juliet down the aisle. It was a small event, but every single person was important to me.

At the front were my brother and sister. Nate took his eyes from Juliet to smile at me. Instead of a corsage, Lacey Jane held baby Lizzy, and David stood beside Nate.

The guests were my people. Doc and Gloria held hands and smiled at me. Dylan sat beside Melanie, but I knew they were only friends. Belle sat beside her dad. Lincoln wore his cowboy best. Tony was beside his new girlfriend, Floriana. No doubt they'd put the rest of us to shame on the dance floor. My older adult friends, Leroy, Frank and Jeremiah, sat close to Wade, who gave me a wink. Rylee sat next to Vince and John. While I hadn't known the men long, our love of dogs had formed a lasting friendship. Chris and Carol held a place of honor in the front row, and Ike would join them soon.

Sunny, Chubb, Bo, and Pinky all stood in the corner. We'd practiced with them the night before and they all behaved. They'd get lots of treats soon.

My gaze met Marc's. He looked so handsome in his black tux. He'd gotten his hair trimmed, but summer blonde highlights remained. His gray eyes sparkled, and I couldn't wait to be Mrs. Marc Williams.

"You're beautiful," he whispered.

"Thanks. You look more handsome than ever."

The pastor cleared his throat.

The ceremony was short but sweet, and soon I was dancing with my husband to a song he'd written. Lincoln crooned the romantic tune.

Marc held me close. "I mean every word he's singing."

"I've never been so happy."

"Me either." He twirled me out and I spun back to him. "Looks like the dance lessons are paying off."

"We need to dance while we're in Maine."

"True, but brace yourself. I like holding you in my arms. We may have to dance every night."

"I love the sound of that."

The song ended, and we danced with Chris and Carol and other family members, including Ike.

Rain pattered on the barn's roof, but we were dry and happy.

A few hours later, we waved to our friends, and Lincoln drove us to the airport. The honeymoon would be the beginning of our new life together. I didn't know what the future held for us, but as long as we were together, we could face anything.

About the Author

Former Kentuckian Jackie Layton loves her new life in the Low Country. She enjoys time on the beach, despite one vacation that ended with cracked ribs from riding her boogie board with the kids and another trip that ended with a fish hook in her foot and a trip to the emergency room. There's nothing like time at the beach, although she tends to be a bit more cautious these days. Jackie is the author of six Low Country Dog Walker Mysteries.